A Hint of Scandal

Rhonda Woodward

A SIGNET BOOK

SIGNET
Published by New American Library, a division of
Penguin Putnam Inc., 375 Hudson Street,
New York, New York 10014, U.S.A.
Penguin Books Ltd, 80 Strand,
London WC2R 0RL, England
Penguin Books Australia Ltd, 250 Camberwell Road,
Camberwell, Victoria 3124, Australia
Penguin Books Canada Ltd, 10 Alcorn Avenue,
Toronto, Ontario, Canada M4V 3B2
Penguin Books (N.Z.) Ltd, Cnr Rosedale and Airborne Roads,
Albany, Auckland 1310, New Zealand

Penguin Books Ltd, Registered Offices:
Harmondsworth, Middlesex, England

First published by Signet, an imprint of New American Library,
a division of Penguin Putnam Inc.

First Printing, May 2003
10 9 8 7 6 5 4 3 2 1

 REGISTERED TRADEMARK—MARCA REGISTRADA

Printed in the United States of America

PUBLISHER'S NOTE
This is a work of fiction. Names, characters, places, and incidents either are the
product of the author's imagination or are used fictitiously, and any resemblance
to actual persons, living or dead, business establishments, events, or locales is
entirely coincidental.

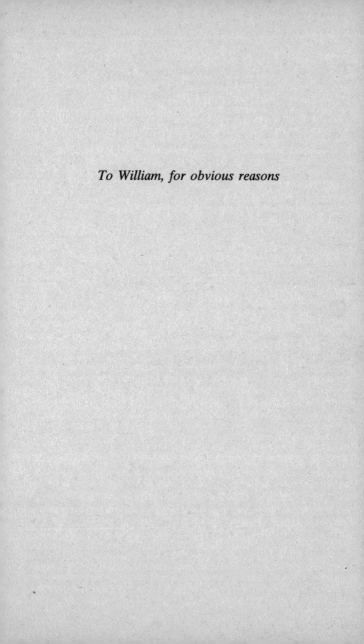

To William, for obvious reasons

Chapter One

1818

Seated in a threadbare chair near the fireplace, the tall man pulled a gold timepiece from his pocket for the third time in the last twenty minutes.

It was well past two o'clock in the morning, he noted, his jaw tightening with worry and irritation. Replacing the watch, he turned to look over his shoulder, almost willing there to be a sign of Johnny, his groom. Again, he was disappointed.

He continued to scan the public room of the shabby little posting inn where he'd been cooling his spurs for several hours. Though he was impatient to leave this dank place, he and Johnny had felt themselves lucky to happen upon it earlier that evening. The Blue Boar, despite its shabbiness, had at least been shelter from the raging storm that still whirled outside.

The tall man's piercing gray eyes went to the proprietor, the common room's only other occupant. As if he had been waiting for some sign from his guest, the rotund little man hurried over, hastily wiping his hands on the grimy apron wrapped around his waist.

"Yes, guv'nor? What else can I be doing for ye?" the innkeeper asked in his most solicitous tone. And it was no wonder, for he was still reeling from the coin he'd already received from the imposing man.

"Yes, good man, locate my groom and send him to me."

Bobbing his head, the innkeeper turned to do his guest's bidding just as the thick wooden door opened and a slim young man entered, rain dripping from his tricornered hat.

"Ah, there you are, Johnny," said the man, rising to his full height as his drenched young groom approached. "I trust the horses are ready. We must be off." His tone brooked no tolerance for any more delays.

With impressive agility for one so round, the inn's proprietor darted to the coatrack and quickly brought over the imposing man's belongings. Without acknowledging the others in his presence, the man pulled on his black beaver hat, split-tail coat, and calfskin gloves with spare, graceful movements.

"Yes, your grace. I'm sorry for the delay," the young groom said quickly, wiping his wet face with a red handkerchief. "Zeus was none too pleased to be reshod. This weather has him a bit spooked."

Nodding his response, the impatient traveler quickly strode past the two others, tossing a gold coin on the counter with one fluid motion before exiting the posting house with long strides.

He stopped a moment on the stoop to allow his eyes to adjust to the darkness that suddenly engulfed him. He was keenly aware of a growing sense of anxiousness to reach his destination.

The innkeeper, his eyes bulging at the weight of the gold coin in his hand, turned to the tall man's groom. "Who be your master, boy?"

Heading toward the door, Johnny turned and looked over his shoulder. With a grin and an obvious note of pride in his voice, he said, "His grace, Alexander Arthur Henry George, Duke of Westlake." Johnny shut the door behind him, leaving the proprietor with his mouth agape.

Johnny followed his master into the courtyard and trotted over to where the horses stood tethered to the hitching post. "At least the rain has slowed a bit, your grace," Johnny said, squinting up at the night sky. He hoped he did not sound as if he were complaining, for indeed, he felt it was a great honor and privilege to accompany his master anywhere.

"Yes, the rain has almost stopped and the full moon is out. We shall now be able to find our way with more ease," the duke said with satisfaction as he walked over to his horse.

Johnny saw the quick flash of the duke's smile as he helped his master mount the large black stallion.

Once Johnny was on his horse, the two men left The Blue Boar's courtyard and led their horses through the darkness onto the High Road, which went north.

"We are less than two hours from Tilbourne, possibly closer to an hour now that the weather has cleared and the horses are rested," the duke said to Johnny as the younger man's horse trotted next to Zeus.

"You are brave to come with me on such a night." The duke's tone held obvious praise for his young groom.

Johnny shifted shyly in his saddle. "We would not want your grace to travel such a long way alone."

The duke spurred Zeus into a light canter and allowed a gently amused smile to touch his lips at Johnny's use of the royal *we*.

Soon the smile faded as they trotted along the deserted country road, with only the sound of the horses' hooves clopping on the road in the moon-drenched darkness. The duke thanked providence, something he rarely did, for the meager brightness of the moon. Without it they would be completely unable to avoid the ruts and puddles that riddled the road. As things stood, he assessed that they should be able to make up some lost time.

Westlake allowed his thoughts to return to earlier that day, and the events that had brought him to this lonely road.

The party taking place at Autley had been merry, despite the harshness of the late-February weather. His guests were an assemblage of society's most toplofty members. They included his mother, the Dowager Duchess of Westlake, and his two younger sisters, Alice, Lady Edgeton, and Louisa, who was engaged to the young Duke of Malverton. There were also various other family friends and a number of what the *ton* called the "Westlake Set."

Cards, conversation, and reading had been the preferred pursuits during the last few days. The duke rather enjoyed playing host, especially since his friends, the Duke and Duchess of Severly and Major Rotham and his wife, the Duchess of Harbrooke, had accepted his invitation.

But this particular evening a few of the ladies, led by the high-spirited Louisa, had decided that nothing would do but dancing.

So after charging the servants to roll up the carpets in the main salon, the dowager and Alice had been cajoled into playing the piano. There was much laughter and teasing amongst the group as Louisa tried to teach them all the steps of a new country reel.

While the younger people danced, Westlake had been standing in front of the massive fireplace with a few of his friends, wagering on which of the royal dukes would be the first to beget an heir to the throne. Since the sudden death of Princess Charlotte some months ago, and since the regent would not, in all likelihood, father another child, it was left to the regent's brothers to provide an heir.

"I think it is dashed ironic that among the Dukes of Kent, Clarence, and Cambridge there are likely two dozen by-blows and not one of them a legitimate candidate for the throne," Sir Edward Field had laughingly stated to the other gentlemen, who agreed with him.

After catching a significant look from his mother, Westlake recalled his duties and excused himself from his friends to circulate among his other guests.

He made his way over to where Lady Caroline Netherby stood with the Duke and Duchess of Cragmoore.

"Oh, Westlake, I believe you are clairvoyant," Lady Caroline said to him with an impish smile that had made her the rage of the Season for several years running.

"How so?" he asked, giving his former mistress a rare smile.

He could not help noticing that Lady Caroline was in great looks tonight. She had been the wealthy widow of a lord when their very discreet affair had started. It had ended amiably some months later when she had informed Westlake of her plans to marry Lord Netherby. That had been more than a year ago.

"I was just thinking how, of all things, I love to dance, and suddenly you were at my elbow."

The duke and duchess laughed at the boldness of her hint as Westlake gave a graceful bow and led her to the converted dance floor.

"Alex, the feeling between us is still strong," the lady had said to him with an intimate whisper after a few moments of dancing. "You know Cecil retires early. I would find it delightful to meet you in your charming atrium later this evening."

It was more like Cecil would pass out early, Westlake had thought cynically, knowing why Cecil retired so soon after dinner. The duke had contempt for any man who could not hold his liquor.

As he continued to lead the duchess around the impromptu dance floor, Westlake struggled to find a gentlemanly way of declining her offer. For in the pocket of his waistcoat were notes from Lady Helen Bingley, his latest conquest, and Lady Bolton, who had been making it quite plain that she was eager to replace Lady Helen in his affections. Each was beseeching him, one unbeknownst to the other, to meet her in the atrium at about the same time Lady Caroline was planning to sneak out of her bedchamber.

As if Hollings, his very astute butler, had surmised the duke's need of a diversion, the solemn servant suddenly approached his master bearing a letter upon a salver.

At first Westlake had wondered, somewhat wryly, if it were yet another female trying to arrange a tryst with him.

Instead, to his dismay, it was a letter from the vicar of Tilbourne informing him that a serious accident had befallen Henry, his nephew and heir.

Westlake had read the cryptic and disturbing missive quickly, with growing concern. He had then excused himself from the party, had a private word with his sister, Alice, to play hostess in his absence, and reread the note as he took the great staircase two steps at a time, calling for his valet on the way to his bedchamber.

He barked orders at his servants, not taking the time to change fully out of his evening clothes, but deciding to discard just his evening coat and knee breeches for buckskin trousers, Hessian boots, and a heavy woolen overcoat.

Moments later Westlake descended the great staircase,

giving last-minute orders for a carriage with supplies and extra clothing to follow him to Tilbourne in the morning. His mother had followed him to the door, concern etched deeply into her beautiful aristocratic features.

"Alex, does the letter give any indication of how bad Henry is?" she questioned, placing her hand on his arm to stay his progress for a moment.

"You know how Margaret is prone to exaggeration, Mama," he said. "I will send word back to you tomorrow." He did not want his mother to worry unduly, for he knew she had never gotten over the death of her youngest son, James, Henry's father. Kissing her cheek again quickly, he left her standing in the foyer as he quit the warmth of his home and entered the brewing storm.

Now he could easily recall the words of the note informing him of the terrible accident that had befallen his ten-year-old nephew, Henry. The note had gone on to say that a doctor had already been sent for, but that the boy hung close to death. Margaret, Henry's mother and the widow of the duke's only brother, was hysterical and requested the duke's presence as quickly as he was able to reach Tilbourne.

How like Margaret to become hysterical when she was needed most, he thought disdainfully, for he had never understood his younger brother's attraction to the bird-witted young woman.

It usually took three and a half hours to reach Tilbourne, but the journey had been plagued by setbacks almost from the moment they left the beautiful gates of Autley.

Within an hour a torrential rainstorm had forced them to take shelter at a farm on the outskirts of his estate. The farmer's shy wife had offered the duke and his groom fresh warm bread and cider. The duke's dashing smile had caused the farmer's wife to almost drop the mugs, she later told her husband. What a true gentleman his grace was, she had continued, for he had not even blinked at her clumsiness and had told her she must be the best baker in the county.

They had been on the road again for no more than three-quarters of an hour, covering very few miles, when Zeus had thrown a shoe, the duke recalled, hoping his string of bad luck was now over.

The duke had dismounted the beast, walking the rest of

the way to The Blue Boar as the storm whipped around them. It had taken the innkeeper an inordinate amount of time, and a large sum of the duke's blunt, to find a smith to attend to the temperamental steed in the middle of the night.

But now that they were finally on their way again, the duke breathed in the cold night air with relief. He had never been good at waiting, and with Henry's life so gravely in danger, he was even less patient now.

The rain had now completely stopped, but had left the road an inch deep in mud. The air was clear and cold; every night sound was carrying to the horses' sensitive ears.

Bending forward in his saddle, the duke spoke softly to Zeus and patted his neck reassuringly, trying to calm the animal's growing restiveness.

Suddenly, with the sound of rustling branches and the flapping of large wings, an owl swooped down in front of Zeus, causing the startled animal to rear up, almost throwing his rider.

Johnny watched in silent shock as the duke struggled to keep control of the large horse.

With a half-smothered curse, the split tail of his riding coat flying behind him like giant raven's wings, the duke kept his seat as the horse reared again, his hooves flailing the air.

Tightening his grip on the reins, the duke gritted his teeth with his efforts to manage Zeus. To his left he saw Johnny's horse prancing and snorting, upset by the stallion's behavior.

"Keep her back!" he shouted, fearful that Zeus would hoof the filly if Johnny allowed her to sidle too close.

An odd sound reached the duke's ears amidst this sudden noise and confusion. Glancing swiftly in the direction from which the owl had flown from its perch, the duke caught sight of two shadowy figures emerging from the dense, dark foliage.

For a split second the duke was only peripherally aware that these figures were approaching; his attention was still focused on trying to calm his bolting animal.

Abruptly Zeus reared again, steam coming from his flaring nostrils.

A second later a sharp report rang out in the dead night air, and a searing pain burned through the duke's left shoulder.

"Highwaymen!"

The duke heard Johnny's breathless shout. Somehow, from pure instinct, Westlake did not release the reins, but whipped his head around to see where the shot had come from.

On the dark country road, not forty strides from them, were two men on horseback, dressed in dark clothes with dark kerchiefs covering their faces. The one nearest the duke held a pistol; the smoke coming from the barrel wafted blue in the milky moonlight. Westlake could smell gunpowder in the cold night air.

The other man was raising his pistol toward Johnny.

With a mighty effort the duke pulled Zeus down and around, blocking the filly as best he could. It seemed to him as if all the movements taking place had slowed down, so that he could anticipate several moves ahead.

The duke cast a swift look toward Johnny. The young man appeared ghostlike with his mouth wide open in a silent scream. His filly rose on her hind legs and whinnied her distress.

With no waste of movement, the duke reached his right hand into his coat and pulled a pistol from his leather belt.

Cocking the weapon before it cleared his coat, Westlake shouted as he took aim: "Johnny! Into the woods! Now!"

The brigand aiming his pistol at Johnny now swung the weapon toward Westlake.

After squeezing the trigger, the duke saw the man drop from his horse a second later.

Seeing Johnny fast disappearing into the dense forest, Westlake risked a quick glance down at his left shoulder. He saw a dark hole in the heavy material of his coat.

"Damn it," he said through gritted teeth, for he suddenly became aware that his left hand was involuntarily losing its grip on the reins.

"Damn it," he said again, quickly looking up to see the remaining highwayman reaching into his coat.

Dropping the now useless pistol, the duke took both

reins into his right hand and spurred Zeus as he had never spurred the animal before.

With the horse's massive muscles straining to do his master's bidding, they were instantly crashing through the shrub border of the road into the forest beyond. The duke gave the horse his head and lowered his own against the branches that tore at his face and body.

He had no notion where he was going, only that with his arm soon useless, and the scoundrel behind him almost rearmed, he would be a sitting duck if he did not get far away very quickly.

Zeus's hooves made little noise as he galloped over the thick underbrush, but the duke heard his own heart pounding so loudly he thought anyone within fifty yards would hear it.

What a fool he'd been, he told himself harshly as he hazarded a look at his shoulder again. Though he had not heard of this part of the country having a particular problem with highwaymen, it had been foolish to travel virtually unprotected on such a lonely road. He knew as well as anyone of the growing problem with thieves since the war had ended.

The thoroughbred continued to move swiftly, weaving in and out of the trees, not showing any sign of tiring.

The duke reset his grip on the reins as they continued to gallop through the night. He did not bother to look at his shoulder again, for the moonlight barely reached him under the canopy of trees, but he could feel the blood flowing from the wound beneath his coat. It felt warm next to his skin.

Almost dispassionately, he realized he would not survive this night; he was losing his blood too quickly. He did not think that the ball had shattered the bone, but that was of no import now. He had seen too many men die of blood loss on the battlefield from wounds that could have been treated had there only been time.

On the horse galloped through the eerie, muffled quiet of the forest. After a time the duke noticed he was becoming dizzy. With his last ounce of strength he pulled back the reins, knowing that if Zeus continued at this pace, it would be impossible to stay in the saddle once he lost consciousness.

He slowed the horse to almost a walk. With a great effort he turned to look back. Wincing from the searing pain in his shoulder, the duke did not see or sense anyone behind him. He looked down and saw that he had dropped the reins. It was as if he were seeing his own hand from a great distance.

In his mind's eye, he saw his mother and two younger sisters, Alice and Louisa. They would miss him. Louisa would be terribly disappointed that he would not be able to walk her down the aisle this coming spring.

He saw young Henry, his dead brother's son and his own heir. At ten, the dark-haired boy was already showing the Westlake penchant for height.

Henry would now be the Duke of Westlake. He felt sorry for the burden his death would put on the boy. He sent up a brief prayer that the boy would recover from whatever accident had befallen him.

The duke's last conscious thought was for Johnny. He hoped his groom would make it back safely to Autley. Johnny was the only one who could tell his family how he had died.

Chapter Two

"Bella! Wake up, Bella!"

Feeling something shaking her shoulder, Arabella slowly opened her eyes. The room was dimly aglow with early dawn light as Arabella groggily pushed herself up onto her elbows. She looked around to see her younger brother, Tommy, kneeling next to her bed.

"Why on earth are you bothering me at this ungodly hour?" she questioned through a yawn.

"I have found a gentleman. You must come now. I think he is almost dead." Tommy's tone was urgent as he began to pull her arm again.

"You found a what?" Arabella's eyes flew wide open as she tried to comprehend what Tommy was saying to her.

"A half-dead gentleman. You must hurry," he urged, pulling harder on her arm as she resisted.

"Tommy, wait. Stop pulling my arm and allow me to put on my robe." She sat up and waved him away.

Standing with his back to her in the doorway, Tommy explained: "Something woke me up. I thought it was the storm again, but I kept hearing what sounded like snorting and whinnying outside my window. I got up and went outside and around to the back garden. There stood a huge black horse with a man slumped over the saddle. I led the horse around to the front and tied it to the post. I cannot get the man off by myself. I don't think he's dead yet."

"Good heavens!" Bella was fully awake now, as she

quickly followed Tommy out of her room, down the stairs, and to the front door.

Holding high a hastily lit lantern, Bella stepped out of the house into the freezing wet dawn. To her complete astonishment, there indeed stood a huge horse with a dark mass draped over its back.

"Good heavens!" She stepped closer to the horse, her slippered feet sinking into the mud. In the yellow light of her lantern, she could see that the animal was lathered with sweat.

"Would you stop saying 'Good heavens' and help me figure out how to get him off this horse?"

Bella set the lantern on the front steps, deciding not to chastise the twelve-year-old for his disrespectful manner. Quickly assessing the situation, Bella said to her dark-haired brother, "It's too bad this storm has prevented Papa from returning from the Park tonight. I just hope we are strong enough to get him down by ourselves. He seems awfully large."

"The man or the horse?" Tommy asked.

"Both," she said, moving close to the big animal. Bella gathered her resolve and assessed the situation. "Let's remove his feet from the stirrups first. Then you take one arm and I the other and we'll ease him off. I hope this beast stays still."

The black horse did stand docile, out of exhaustion or trust, Bella could not tell. It was no easy feat to hold the man steady as they pulled him sideways off the horse, especially since it was difficult to keep their footing on the rain-soaked ground.

Once they got the unconscious man down, Bella knelt next to him and felt his neck for a pulse. Though it was weak, he was definitely alive. Sighing with relief, Bella struggled against her wet bedclothes to rise from the sodden earth. It had begun to rain again.

"Whatever is wrong with him will not be helped by being out in this weather," Bella told her equally soaked brother.

Tommy nodded. "How are we going to get him inside, Bella?" he asked, wiping rain from his face.

"We certainly can't carry him in." After thinking a moment, she said, "We must roll him onto a blanket and drag

him into the house. Tommy, go get the blanket from my
bed."

Tommy nodded and went quickly into the house to do
her bidding.

"I wonder what in the world happened to him," Tommy
questioned aloud upon returning to the drive with the
blanket.

"God only knows," his sister replied, as they began to
roll the man carefully onto the blanket.

Several hours later, Arabella placed her hands flat on the
narrow bed and pushed herself wearily to her feet. A worried frown creased her brow as she gazed down at the pale,
prone man.

Blessedly, the bleeding from the ugly wound marring his
left shoulder had almost stopped. Very gently she reached
down and placed her hand on the bandage she had created
out of an old but still perfectly usable nightgown.

Still frowning, Arabella pulled a sputtering candle stub
closer to the unconscious man. She wanted to make sure
that there was no blood seeping from beneath the torn
strips of cloth.

Sighing with tired relief, Arabella lifted the heavy braid
off of her shoulder and watched the large man's chest rise
and fall in a shallow rhythm. Somewhere in the back of her
mind it registered that the rain had stopped beating against
the house, and the quiet lay heavy on the morning.

Arabella's eyes traveled from the man's chest to his face.
Though she had worked frantically for hours on this most
unlikely patient, she had, as yet, not really looked at his
face.

Padding softly to the corner of the room in her stock-
inged feet, she took hold of a small rocking chair and
dragged it next to the bed. Pulling her shawl closer around
her neck, she seated herself, rocked forward, and looked
for the first time at this mysterious stranger who was still
so close to death.

His hair was dark, she noted, very glossy with a hint of
a wave. Her weary eyes traveled to his brows, which were
also dark and slightly arched over closed lids with long
curling lashes. Beatrice, her cousin and best friend, would

be green with envy over such lashes, she thought, as she continued her perusal of his features.

Tilting her head, she continued to examine his face. She decided she liked the shape of his aquiline nose, and wondered if his square jaw indicated a stubborn nature, as some people claimed.

Who was he? she wondered for the hundredth time this morning. Reaching down next to her chair, Arabella gathered up the pile of clothing she and Tommy had removed from the man earlier.

Hesitating, she made no other move for a few moments. She knew she was being much too particular under the circumstances, but she felt as if she would be grossly invading his privacy to go through his clothing.

Shaking off such nonsense, she examined the white shirt with the bloodstained hole. Her fingers caressed the soft material. Never had she felt such exquisite fabric. Stitches in the seams were so tiny and perfectly even. Arabella, not being much of a seamstress, was impressed with the expert workmanship.

A faint, woodsy, spicy scent reached her nose. She lifted the shirt to her face and inhaled. An unidentifiable, yet somehow intoxicating smell filled her senses.

She refused to allow her thoughts to dwell on the horrible possibility that this nameless man could die any moment in her bed.

When she had watched the man long enough to assure herself that he was not immediately going to expire, Arabella resumed her inspection of his clothing.

His leather breeches revealed nothing. Setting those aside, she pulled his heavy jacket onto her lap. It was dark green and made of the finest wool she had ever seen. Even her uncle David wore nothing so exquisite, she mused, and he was an earl. Again that indefinable, spicy, smoky scent permeated the material.

Her slender fingers went over the jacket swiftly, stopping as they encountered something solid in the inside pocket.

Pulling a leather pouch from the jacket, Arabella placed the envelope-shaped case on her lap. She could see that the butter-soft leather was expertly tooled, and she noted that it bulged slightly. Picking the pouch up, Arabella turned it over and saw that something was embossed on the flap.

Lifting the pouch closer to the dripping nub of the candle, she saw that there was some sort of crest tooled in gold on the soft leather. Casting a curious frown at the unconscious man, Arabella examined the pouch closer.

She saw that it was a coat of arms. There was an embossed shield in the middle flanked by a mythical beast on one side and a falcon on the other. Entwined with the animals and shield was a depiction of ivy and ribbon intricately tooled with the words *Virtute et Armis.*

Bella was able to translate the motto easily: *By Valor and Arms.*

Taking a deep breath, Arabella lifted the flap and emptied the contents of the pouch onto her lap. The candlelit silence of the room was shattered by Arabella's shocked gasp. Glistening in her lap was a pile of coins and notes.

Arabella stared at the treasure for a stunned moment. In her estimation she held a small fortune. Shaking her head in bemusement, she put the money back into the pouch and returned it to the jacket pocket.

The waistcoat was next. She was about to set it on the jacket when something crunched under her fingers. She pulled two pieces of paper from the small front pocket.

Ah! These might reveal the identity of her mystery man. A small anticipatory smile touched her tired features.

Unfolding the first note, she saw it was written in a small, delicate hand on fine vellum.

I can no longer deny my feelings! I am yours!
I will be in the atrium at midnight! Come to me, my love!

That was all. Arabella glanced again to the prone man, raising one delicately arched brow in surprise. "What an indiscriminate use of exclamation points," she said aloud before turning to the next note.

My love, what was once between us can never be buried.
You are the only man who has ever claimed my heart.

*Can you ever forget the nights I have spent in your
arms? I will be waiting for you at half past midnight in
the atrium.*

"Good Lord." Arabella felt her cheeks growing warm
from a blush. What a sticky situation that could be, she
thought looking askance at the prone Lothario in her bed.
The handwriting in this missive was definitely not the same
as that in the first letter.

But again, this letter was as little help as the first in
identifying the mystery man. Hesitantly she refolded the
letters, still blushing at what she had read. Shaking her
head at the continuing mystery, Bella put the notes back
in the pocket.

Holding his clothing close to her breast, she stood up
and moved to the small chest at the foot of the bed. Kneeling with her bundle, she carefully folded each item and
placed it inside.

Closing the lid, she turned to the large, heavy coat with
its six layers of capes at the shoulders. Surely this article
of clothing had helped save the man's life, she deduced. It
was so dense that it must have slowed the lead ball's force.

Her hands shook now at the horrible memory of the
previous few hours. She had never faced so perilous a task
as to remove a slug from someone's flesh. Yet she had
known that it would be much better for the man if the
piece of lead could be removed quickly.

Arabella had always been one to do what needed to be
done. Ever since her mother's death, she had had to be the
practical one in her family.

So, with a fervent prayer and items from her sewing bag,
Arabella had set out to carefully remove the lead ball from
the gaping wound in the unconscious man's shoulder. She
had instructed Tommy to hold the stranger's arm securely,
and she'd been thankful the prone man had only flinched
reflexively once or twice at her probing. Arabella had held
her breath, the large darning needle poised above his
bloody shoulder as he moved restlessly. Arabella knew that
it would have been difficult for Tommy to have tried to
restrain him if he had suddenly regained his senses or
begun to thrash about.

But luckily he had remained unaware, and the slug had been fairly easy to dislodge, to Arabella's weak-kneed relief.

"Good show, Bella," Tommy had said as she placed the piece of lead in an old chipped cup.

The wound had still been bleeding steadily even after she had cleaned it and carefully sewn it up, so she had spent a considerable time pressing a pad of cloth against it, hoping to stem the flow of blood.

The bleeding had stopped long enough for her to make a bandage from her old gown. She had almost cried in exhausted frustration when the bleeding started again as she attempted to bandage his wound. She was neither weak nor petite, but it had been an exhausting struggle to lift the stranger's large body enough to wrap the strips of muslin around his shoulder and across his chest to keep the arm from moving. If only her papa had not been detained overnight at Penninghurst Park because of the dreadful storm, they would have fared much better, she had thought.

Now she stood looking down at the very pale stranger, holding his heavy coat with the many capes, and hoping as she had never hoped for anything that she had done enough to save him.

The damp, early-morning chill seemed to permeate the room. Arabella hugged the coat closer and suddenly felt something hard amongst its folds. Looking down, she fumbled with the coat until she found a pocket. Her fingers pulled something cold, small, and hard from an interior pocket of the garment.

It was a gold watch. Sitting down again, she examined the watch closely, turning it repeatedly in her hands until it was warm, looking for anything that would give another clue to the stranger's identity. In exquisite detail, the same coat of arms that was on the leather pouch was engraved on the back of the timepiece. Her thumb found the catch, and she opened the front piece. It was almost nine o'clock, she noted. On the inside of the front piece, intertwined in beautiful scrollwork, were the initials A.W.

A. She mused over the letter as, again, she looked at the aristocratic features of the very still man in her bed. Allen? Adam? Albert? She hoped he would soon be able to assuage her curiosity about his name. And about many other things too, she thought as she closed the watch and put it back in the coat pocket. Such as, What in the world was a man like him doing in Mabry Green in the middle of the night with a lead ball in his shoulder?

Chapter Three

Bella was relieved beyond measure when she looked out her window and saw Mrs. Ash coming up the path. Mrs. Ash was a large, good-natured woman who spent three days a week at the manor helping Bella with the housework. Normally she was quite unflappable.

Today proved the exception.

Upon entering the house from the back door, as was her habit, she went from the mudroom to the kitchen and into the front room and let out a shrill scream.

Bella jumped at the unearthly sound and rushed out of her bedroom to where Mrs. Ash stood screaming about bloody murder in the front room.

"Mrs. Ash!" Bella shouted, raising her hands in a calming motion to the extremely distressed woman. "We are all fine, Mrs. Ash. Please calm yourself," Bella said with weary firmness.

"Where did all this blood come from? Did Tommy hurt himself again? I vow that boy gets into more scrapes—"

"No, no," Bella uncharacteristically interrupted the older woman. "Tommy is perfectly well. But he did find a half-dead gentleman early this morning. Tommy and I brought him in and I removed a ball from his shoulder. He is unconscious in my bed right now. I have sent Tommy for the doctor. Papa never came home from the Park last night, due to the storm, no doubt."

Mrs. Ash stood with her mouth agape at this rather disjointed speech, shock plainly visible in her pale blue eyes.

"A half-dead gentleman? Whatever are you saying, Miss Bella?"

"Come, I'll show you. I don't think he should be left alone." Bella led the older woman up the staircase to her room.

The man was exactly as she had left him moments ago. Mrs. Ash walked to the foot of the bed as Arabella went to the window and pushed the drapery aside to allow the feeble late-winter sun help brighten the room.

"Well, bless me, it really is a gentleman," Mrs. Ash said with some surprise as she looked from the prone man to Bella.

"Of course it is. Did you think my attic was to let?" Bella asked as she moved to stand next to Mrs. Ash. She looked down at her patient with a frown.

"It's just so unexpected. How does he happen to be here?"

Bella explained in greater detail the events of the early morning as Mrs. Ash set about tidying the room. She tut-tutted and made properly shocked sounds as Bella described the horrific task of removing the lead ball from the man's shoulder.

"Oh, Miss Bella! What a tale. You certainly did the right thing. The poor man would surely be dead if you and Tommy had not been able to help him." She nodded her head for emphasis before continuing, "Goodness, Mabry Green has not seen this much excitement in years. Wait until I tell Mr. Ash. He'll want to take a look at him too."

"Heavens, Mrs. Ash, he is not an exhibit in a museum," Bella said with a little laugh. But she understood what Mrs. Ash meant. Not a lot went on in the tiny village of Mabry Green.

Despite her exhaustion, Bella helped Mrs. Ash clean the sitting room floor before going off to take her bath, leaving Mrs. Ash to keep an eye on the patient.

A little while later, as she coiled her hair into a neat bun at the back of her head, Bella fretted over why it was taking Tommy so long to bring the doctor. He'd been gone for hours; she frowned as she put the last pin in her hair.

After making sure her appearance was tidy, Bella returned to her room to join Mrs. Ash.

"Now, you just sit yourself in this comfortable rocking chair while I set up some lunch. I'm sure you've eaten nothing all day."

Bella accepted the kind woman's offer and sank gratefully into the rocking chair. Leaning her head back, she watched the stranger for some moments. Was his breathing less shallow? She fervently hoped so.

Mrs. Ash bustled in at that moment, with a tray bearing a bowl of savory winter stew.

"You just tuck into that and you'll feel much better. 'Tis a good thing I started the stew yesterday, Miss Bella. Less work today," she said, setting the tray on Bella's lap. "I'll be attending to the mess in the front room if you need me."

Bella thanked Mrs. Ash while hiding a yawn behind her hand.

The appetizing aroma of the stew made Bella suddenly realize how hungry she was. She ate slowly while she continued to watch her patient for any sign of improvement.

After finishing her lunch, Bella placed the tray on the floor next to her chair. Leaning her head back, she closed her eyes to rest for a few moments.

How long she slept she wasn't sure. It wasn't until she was awakened by a gentle touch upon her shoulder that she realized she had been asleep.

"Miss Bella, Lord Penninghurst's coach is turning up the drive."

Blinking sleep away, Bella thanked Mrs. Ash for giving her the news. Her uncle must have sent her papa home in his coach because of the inclement weather.

Bella left her room and went to stand on the front doorstep as the coach trundled to a stop on the muddy drive. The coachman jumped down and placed wooden steps in front of the coach doors. Bella smiled as her father stepped from the coach and waved at her, his balding head quite bare to the winter chill. *He's probably left his best hat at the Park,* she thought with fond impatience over father's chronic forgetfulness.

To her surprise, Dr. Pearce followed her papa out of the coach.

"I thought you said you sent Tommy for the doctor," Mrs. Ash declared as she came to stand next to Bella in the open doorway.

"I did," Bella replied, a confused frown settling on her brow.

To Bella's further surprise, her cousin, Lady Beatrice Tichley, also exited the carriage, followed by the young lady's parents, the Earl and Countess of Penninghurst. Finally Tommy jumped out of the conveyance, disregarding the steps.

"Heavens, my entire family has descended upon us, Mrs. Ash," Bella said to the good woman with some chagrin.

"Humph." Mrs. Ash snorted with the familiarity of long acquaintance. "Beggin' your pardon, miss, I don't envy you having to manage this lot a bit. They are too high-strung and difficult if you ask me—always making a Cheltenham tragedy out of every little thing. This mystery man will probably give them all the vapors."

Though fiercely loyal and protective of her family, Bella had to choke back laughter at Mrs. Ash's accurate assessment of them. Stepping down from the stoop, she moved to the gravel drive to greet her guests.

"I'll show the doctor to your room, miss, and then put a pot of tea on the stove," Mrs. Ash offered.

Bella looked back at Mrs. Ash and nodded gratefully, then turned to Dr. Pearce, who barely addressed her as he handed her his hat and overcoat before he went off with Mrs. Ash.

Bella put the doctor's things on the entryway chair just as Tommy came running past the rest of them up to the front steps. Before he could enter, Bella put up a censorious hand to halt his progress.

"Take those muddy shoes off before you come in this house, young man. And never say you wasted all this time going all the way to Penninghurst Park when you should have been fetching the doctor posthaste."

"Don't be a clunch, Bella." Her brother scowled at her with dark blue eyes the color of hers before bending over to remove his boots. "I ran the whole way to the doctor's house, only to have Mrs. Pearce tell me that he was all the way over in Hareton, tending a sick old man. So I went on to the Park and told Papa what had happened. Uncle summoned the coach and we all went over to Hareton, located the doctor, then came straight here."

Lady Beatrice came up the steps at that moment. "This is terribly exciting, Bella!" she called. "We all want to see your injured gentleman."

Bella turned to her petite blond cousin. "He is not *my* gentleman, Triss. And I do not think it is at all the thing to be so excited. After all, he could die at any moment," she finished with some asperity.

"Oh, there you go, being the correct Miss Tichley," Triss said, using the label that some of the villagers teasingly used to describe Bella. Lady Beatrice made a face at her cousin, her ebullient mood now deflated. "I still want to have a look at him," she stated as she went past Bella into the sitting room.

Rolling her eyes, Bella then turned her attention to her aunt and uncle. Giving them a quick curtsy as they entered the house, Bella could not help but notice how beautiful her aunt looked in a wool coat of sapphire blue with a matching muff lined in ermine.

Aunt Elizabeth kissed Bella's cheek before commenting on how tired the girl looked.

Uncle David, a larger, gruffer version of Papa, also stepped forward to kiss his niece. "Thought we had better see what all the fuss-up is about. When Tommy said he'd found a man with a slug in him, wasn't sure if he wasn't bamming us at first," the earl said in his gruff voice.

"We have another carriage coming, Bella," put in Lady Penninghurst as she removed her bonnet. "It has a hamper of food, extra blankets, bandages, and such."

Bella thanked her aunt as she set about making her unexpected guests comfortable.

"Triss, would you please see how the tea is coming while I see if the doctor needs any assistance?" Bella said to her cousin, who instead was heading toward the staircase.

The younger girl stopped and turned with a flounce. "Oh, this is not any fun."

"Triss!" Bella's laughter was more shocked than amused at her cousin's incorrigibility. "A man has been shot."

"I know. Isn't it bloodcurdling?" Beatrice said with an impish grin. "Do you think he's a highwayman?"

"Enough, you goose! Go help Mrs. Ash with the tea." Bella gave Triss a little shove toward the kitchen.

With a feeling of dread, Bella left her relatives and returned to her room. She hoped the doctor would not fault her for anything she had done to the man.

Standing in the doorway, Bella watched the doctor as he cut away the bandages she had so carefully made and began to probe the torn flesh she had sewn together.

"Did you do this?" the doctor questioned without looking up from the man's shoulder. Bella could not tell by his tone whether he approved or not.

"If you are referring to the needlework, yes, I did that," she said quietly.

The white-haired man did not immediately respond, but continued to examine the unconscious man. Gently he lifted the stranger's closed lids and looked at his eyes for some moments.

"His pulse is weak, but there seem to be no other injuries beyond the hole in his shoulder. If he survives the loss of blood, he may have a chance." Finally the doctor turned to look at Bella and saw the look of relief enter her eyes.

"Do you believe you removed the entire slug?" he questioned sharply.

Bella moved swiftly to the nightstand and picked up the old chipped cup. "I kept it. It seems intact. I . . . I tried to be very careful." Exhaustion and fear were evident in her voice.

The doctor sat back and watched her keenly for a moment. "You look as tired as I feel," he told her, his gruff tone softening. "I was called away late last night to attend a dying man in Hareton. Then Lord Penninghurst and the rest of the lot descended upon me and brought me here." He continued as he began to put his medical tools back in his black bag, "You have done a good job of it. If he can avoid fever and infection, he may survive. Help me rebandage him."

The task was much easier with the doctor's help.

"He's a big bloke, isn't he?" The doctor grunted as he lifted the man so that Bella could slip the bandages underneath him and around his shoulder.

"There," Bella said with relief as she tied the last strip of bandage around the patient's shoulder.

Rising from the edge of the bed, the doctor gave her a stern look. "If he awakens, give him water, a little broth. No food. I will leave you some laudanum. Give him a few drops if he becomes too restless. Tearing that wound open again could be fatal. He mustn't be moved."

Bella nodded her understanding of his instructions.

The doctor moved to the doorway, then turned back to give her a look of sympathy. "After spending more than an hour in the coach with your family, it is clear to me that you will not have much help nursing this man. Do you have any idea who he is?"

Bella glanced down at the stranger. How odd that his long lashes now seemed so familiar.

"No, I have no idea," she said as she followed the doctor down to the sitting room, where the rest of the family, save for Tommy, was having tea and biscuits.

Bella offered the gruff doctor a cup of tea. He drank it quickly, and as soon as he was finished, he stood up, saying that it was time he returned home.

Papa and the earl escorted the doctor out to the waiting carriage. Bella heard Uncle David's rather booming voice instruct the coachman to return to the house after taking the doctor home.

Bella groaned inwardly. As much as she loved her family, she was not looking forward to spending the rest of the afternoon with them.

Setting her cup down on the tray, Beatrice looked over to Bella eagerly. "May we look at him now?" she asked.

With another inward groan Bella acknowledged defeat. For she knew full well when Triss decided to do something there was little, except the rarely expressed wrath of her cousin's father that would stop her from doing what she desired.

Despite her tiredness and worry, Bella could not help finding her cousin's avid curiosity about the stranger amusing.

Beatrice was a year and a half younger than Bella, and very pretty. Golden-haired and slender, she had an ethereal quality that belied a hoydenish streak that caught those who did not know her well off guard.

At three and twenty, the biggest disappointment in Lady Beatrice's life was that she had not yet made her curtsy at court. Every year since she'd reached the age of eighteen, something had occurred to prevent her from having her London Season.

The first year had been the sad death of Bella's mama. Beatrice would not have considered leaving her cousin in mourning to run off to London.

The next year had been the death of their grandfather, the third Earl of Penninghurst. Though again disappointed that she would miss the Season, Beatrice had been mollified by the notion that it would be much better to be presented as "Lady Beatrice" instead of just "Honorable."

The year after that had been the death of her mother's father, Lord Marlowe. Beatrice had been bitterly disappointed to miss yet another Season, and had made her pique clear to the entire family, but Lady Penninghurst had been adamant about observing the proper duration of mourning. "After all, Triss, dear," she had told her daughter at the time, "it would not be at all the thing to go gallivanting off to London, considering how much money your grandpapa left us."

Her luck had not improved since. And so another Season was missed. Even though Triss lamented that she would be well on the shelf before she ever made her come-out, in truth, she had only grown prettier.

Lady Beatrice had had another scare when it had been announced in church last fall that young Princess Charlotte had died. Beatrice had been practically overcome with the vapors lest the regent do something as improbable as cancel the upcoming Season. To her immense relief, no such announcement had been made. Soon the fashion magazines directed that half-mourning would be the appropriate mode for the Season. Beatrice was vastly relieved and even more excited, if that were possible, for she felt the particular shades of half-mourning suited her well.

Now, though it was only February, Beatrice was in an ecstasy of planning every detail of her impending come-out in the spring. She spent a fortune on magazines, and she and Bella spent hours poring over the latest fashions, agonizing over what styles and colors would show her to the best advantage.

The only thing that dampened her rhapsody over her upcoming London Season was the fact that Bella would not be joining her. Bella's papa could not afford the expense involved. In Triss's opinion, her uncle Alfred's pride was a ridiculous reason not to let his older brother pay for Bella's Season. Beatrice had told Bella repeatedly, and with great vehemence, of her annoyance with Uncle Alfred's stubbornness.

"After all, Father would be perfectly happy to pay for your come-out. Father actually thinks you are a good influence on me, so you would be doing him a favor by coming to London with us. I cannot see why your papa is being so odious. And I can't understand why Father won't just override Uncle Alfred's silly notion of pride," she had said to Bella with a note of petulance.

"Give over, Triss," Bella had responded with characteristic pragmatism. "You are giving everyone, including me, a headache. You know as well as I that Papa will not entertain the notion."

"Well, it's not fair," Beatrice had pouted. Suddenly her face had cleared and a sly look entered her sparkling blue eyes. "Bella, I have just had a capital idea! This will solve everything! I shall marry a duke or maybe even a prince. Then I shall give you the best ball London has ever seen, and there will be nothing Uncle Alfred can do about it."

Bella laughed outright at her cousin's flight of fancy. "What makes you so sure your husband will be so willing to pay for my Season?" she had goaded her cousin.

"Because he shall be so in love with me, he will do anything to ensure my happiness."

"A London Season is very expensive. He would have to be completely besotted," Bella pointed out.

"I would not have it any other way," Beatrice had said with supreme confidence, her pert nose going up in the air.

Unlike her cousin, who found life in the country a dead bore, Bella had no real desire for a London Season, save to please Triss. She recalled going to London with her parents as a child, and she had found it a dirty, noisy place.

No, Bella much preferred the peace of her childhood home and could not imagine living anywhere else. To her mind there was nothing lovelier than the quaint, cobbled streets of the tiny village. Bella loved her picturesque home, her garden, and the pretty little Norman church at the end of the lane. She found it comforting to know everyone in Mabry Green, and to know that everyone knew her. It pleased her to be recognized as a very good housekeeper, and her singing voice was much admired, too. She put it to good use in church, and her uncle often prevailed upon her to sing after dinner at Penninghurst Park.

But the main reason Bella cared little for a London Season was because of Robert Fortiscue. He was a gentleman farmer who owned several hundred acres and a lovely Tudor manor.

Robert Fortiscue was considered a keen goer when it came to the hunt, and was also the handsomest man in the county. He was from a very good family, his mother being a relation of Robert Stewart, the current Viscount Castlereagh.

And he was smitten with one Miss Arabella Tichley.

If it had not been for Papa's unexplainable dislike of Robert, Bella now mused, they would have been married last fall.

But Bella felt that a marriage to Robert Fortiscue would be ideal, for Oakdale was close by, and she did not want to be far from Papa and Tommy. So, while Triss planned her come-out in London, Bella planned the changes she would make at Oakdale, Robert's home, hopefully soon to be hers as well.

Triss brought Bella back to the present with yet another demand to see the mystery man.

"All right then," Bella started, throwing up her hands. "I know you shall give us no peace until you have stared your fill at him."

To Bella's surprise, Aunt Elizabeth rose also.

At Bella's expression, the older lady said somewhat defensively, "I might as well have a look at the poor man, too."

The three of them crowded into Bella's bedchamber, and

were silent for some moments as they looked down at the invalid's still features.

"Oh, my, he's quite a large man, isn't he?" commented Aunt Elizabeth.

"Good Lord! Look at those lashes; must be half an inch long. What a waste on a man," Beatrice lamented.

"Indeed," Bella agreed.

Hearing her father call her name, Bella led Aunt Elizabeth and Triss back to the sitting room.

"Your uncle and I were just discussing what to do about our unexpected guest," Bella's father informed them.

"Good," Aunt Elizabeth said as the ladies reseated themselves in the comfortably worn chairs. "Everything must be done to discover his identity. I'm sure his family is already frantically searching for him."

"Agreed," stated Uncle David. "I shall send men to the neighboring villages to make inquiries."

Bella was only half listening to what the others were saying. She was preoccupied with worry over her patient.

Seeing her niece's tired features, Aunt Elizabeth took the situation in hand. "I can see that the other carriage has arrived," she stated after looking out the front window. "We shall have the servants bring the hampers in, and see what Cook has prepared for us."

Bella met her aunt's kind gaze with gratitude.

At that moment Tommy came bounding into the house, disheveled and muddy.

"Oh, what next?" Bella said, fed up at the sight of Tommy tracking mud onto her freshly scrubbed floors.

"Where have you been, young man?" Papa had grabbed Tommy before he could go any farther.

"I have been seeing to the man's horse," Tommy told them. "I took him over to the stables at the Park. He's a prime piece of blood. The man must be as rich as a lord."

This last comment jogged Bella's memory, causing her to jump to her feet quickly. "Oh, I am tired. I forgot the watch," she said, and swiftly left the room, causing the others to look after her in confusion.

Bella went back up to the room. Going to the foot of the bed, she lifted the beautiful, heavy woolen coat from the chest. Fumbling a moment, she pulled the watch from the pocket and returned to the sitting room.

Handing the gold timepiece to her aunt, Bella said, "There is a crest on his watch, Aunt Elizabeth. Maybe you can recognize it."

Her aunt, with the rest them looking on curiously, took the watch and walked over to the window. She studied it closely for a few moments, before shaking her head and handing the object back to Bella.

"I've rusticated too long to recognize a crest by sight. Certainly, though, this watch belongs to a nobleman."

"Oh, famous!" Beatrice said, "I *do* hope he lives. Your patient is either a nobleman or he stole that watch from one."

"And you, goose, think one scenario is as good as the other," Bella said.

"Absolutely," Beatrice replied shamelessly.

Chapter Four

During the days that followed, the normal routine of Bella's well-ordered life ceased. The stranger's care took all of her time. After only a day or so Bella began to find it curious that his presence, though he was barely conscious most of the time, filled the house.

Bella pondered how best to care for the man, knowing she could not take on such a responsibility alone. But because of her father's rather thrifty ways, he had never seen the need to have any live-in servants. So Bella approached Mrs. Ash about staying at the manor to help take care of the stranger. The good woman had shaken her head and pursed her lips. "I am sorry, Miss Bella, but Mr. Ash don't like me gone from home at night. But I will come every day as long as you need me," she offered.

Mrs. Ash did come daily, partly to help look after the wounded man and give Bella a chance to rest, and partly to make tea for all the unexpected guests that suddenly started to appear on their doorstep.

To Bella's annoyance, the Tichleys were suddenly the most popular family in the village.

Tommy and Papa speculated endlessly on the identity of the gentleman. There was much discussion at supper on how he came to be in Mabry Green and, most important, how he had gotten himself shot.

The local constable came knocking on the front door bright and early the next morning. Bella had politely shown the constable to her room, where he took a good, long look at the prone man. He harrumphed to himself and asked a few questions before he took himself off, muttering about how much bother this situation would be causing him.

After the constable, the vicar and his wife knocked on the front door. They gave the excuse that it had been much too long since they had called. Bella was too polite to point out that the good vicar and his wife had not called upon the Tichley household since Mama had died years ago.

Bella served them tea in the sitting room, and no matter how they hinted at their desire to look at the man, Bella politely kept them at bay.

Keeping a smile fixed to her lips, Bella showed them to the door when they had finally, yet reluctantly, taken their leave. Upon closing the door, Bella paused to examine the new emotions she was experiencing. To her surprise she found that she felt quite protective of her patient and did not want the entire village to come gawk at him as if he were a five-legged calf.

Some of the local ladies even went so far as to bring savory dishes to the house, hoping their gifts would gain them entrance into Bella's room to have a look at the mystery man. Though Papa and Tommy were no end pleased with the offerings, Bella was steadfast in her polite but firm refusal to allow anyone admittance.

Periodically, to Bella's immense relief, the patient would occasionally awaken. When he did he seemed unaware of his surroundings, but Bella was able to get him to drink a little broth. He then would fall back into what Bella hoped was a healing sleep.

The hours would pass, and Bella found she was catching up on her darning and sewing as she kept vigil next to the bed. She sometimes stopped to sponge the man's chest and lean, angular face with cool water, hoping to prevent fever from taking hold of him. He looked so helpless and vulnerable with his long dark lashes lying so boyishly against his cheeks. She prayed constantly that he would recover quickly.

Occasionally she was forced to leave his side, as was the case on the third day. Because the afternoon promised to be unexpectedly fine, she and Mrs. Ash decided to wash all the bedclothes and hang them out on a line in the side garden that faced south. After a little while, as they set about their chores in companionable silence, Bella found it good to be outside on such a clear, crisp day. She was not one to like staying indoors for too long.

The two women had almost finished the arduous task when Bella heard a noise and turned to see her uncle riding up the path on his dappled gray mare. Straightening up from the laundry basket, Bella waved to him before wiping her chore-reddened hands on her apron.

After dismounting, Uncle David tethered his mount to a snarled old oak tree and stepped through the garden gate to greet his niece.

"Any news?" she questioned as he drew near. They both knew to what she was referring.

Pressing his lips together, the earl shook his head. "Nothing from Mabry Green or Hareton. I have just instructed my men to go farther afield. It's dammed odd, Bella; it's as if the bloke dropped here from the moon."

Bella smiled at her uncle's imaginative description as she helped Mrs. Ash peg a pillow cover to the line.

"I'm sure it's only a matter of time before we find out who he is, Uncle. Surely somebody is looking for him."

"Let me finish the wash, Miss Bella. You and Lord Penninghurst go in and have a spot of tea," Mrs. Ash offered, making shooing motions toward the house.

Bella smiled gratefully to the older woman and led her uncle to the side door, through the kitchen, and into the sitting room.

"How is our mysterious stranger?" the earl asked as he followed her into the house.

"He is about the same. I am grateful he is not worse," Bella replied, her concern for the man evident in her dark blue eyes.

"Yes, indeed," her uncle agreed. "And where might my brother be today?" Uncle David questioned as he settled himself comfortably in the chair by the window.

"Papa rose very early today," she began as she gathered the tea things from the large mahogany sideboard by the dining table, "and rode all the way to Horely. He heard a rumor that someone dug up a Roman coin in their garden."

"That's enough to make my brother's scholarly heart sing," the earl observed with a chuckle. "Though from everything I've ever read, Horely would be too far south for any Roman archeology."

"One would think so, but Papa believes the Romans occupied a larger portion of England than previously believed. You know he loves nothing more than getting his papers on the subject printed in those academic publications he is always reading. His research keeps him happy and busy," Bella explained.

"Yes, yes," her uncle said. "And he is becoming quite respected in those circles."

Bella excused herself to go prepare the tea, leaving her uncle to peruse a sporting magazine for a few moments.

She returned shortly with a tray bearing tea and biscuits. After seating herself across from her uncle, Bella poured him a cup of steaming tea, thinking how nice it was to relax for a few moments.

"Where is that young scoundrel Tommy?" Lord Penninghurst asked, after accepting a cup of tea and a warm biscuit from his niece.

"Tending our patient's horse at your stables, Uncle," Bella responded after taking a sip of the fragrant brew. "He is constantly with that brute of an animal. He thinks the stables at Penninghurst Park are more worthy of such a horse. I'm sure he'd sleep in the stable if he thought you would permit it."

Uncle David smiled and said, "The boy is horse-mad. But I own that I have never seen such a prime bit of horseflesh."

Bella nodded her agreement and they enjoyed their tea in silence for a few moments before she asked after her aunt and cousin.

"My good wife and daughter are in the village spending my blunt. They heard tell that the mantuamaker has just got in some outrageously expensive material."

"Triss is determined to cast every other young lady in the shade this Season." Bella smiled at her uncle's disgruntled demeanor, knowing from experience to what lengths Triss would go to be the most fashionable lady in the county.

"Once we get this business with your injured man dealt

with, I plan to approach my brother again with the subject of your coming to London with us."

Sighing, Bella replaced her cup in her saucer and looked at her uncle's heavy, yet still handsome features.

"Uncle David, you are very generous, but you know Papa will never allow you to pay for my Season." The family had visited this topic many times, and Bella saw no point in going over it again.

"My brother is being unreasonable," the earl stated, irritation evident in his tone. "There is no reason why you should not accompany us. Besides the fact that Tommy is my heir, you have always been a good example of proper behavior and decorum. Truth be told, Triss can be a complete hoyden. Elizabeth and I would feel more at ease if you were on hand to keep an eye on her. She certainly pays more attention to you than she has ever paid to us. I am highly annoyed that Alfred is being so difficult." He finished his speech and reached for another biscuit.

Bella looked at her uncle with understanding.

Even though Uncle David and Papa looked alike, Bella knew how dissimilar in character they were. Papa was studious and sensitive, and cared little for anything else but his old books and researching the countryside for signs of the ancient Roman occupation of England. Bella thought it sad that since Mama's death, Papa seemed to resent any attempt to divert him from his particular pursuits.

Uncle David, on the other hand, was much more jovial and interested in the goings-on of his family. He loved to hunt and entertain, and despite his sometimes gruff manner, he could not deny his wife, daughter, or niece anything they requested of him.

Bella knew that since Tommy was the heir to the earldom, her uncle took an even more particular interest in his brother's family. This was just one more reason for Papa to resent what he considered his brother's meddling in his affairs. Papa was also sensitive over the fact that his father, the fifth Earl of Penninghurst, had not been overly generous to his second son in his will.

Because of this occasional friction, Bella was often the buffer between her father and uncle.

"Enough of London." The earl waved away the tired

subject. "I was hoping that when you had a little time, you might come over to the Park and have a word with Michaels. He has gone off again with some strange plan for the gardens. Elizabeth and I don't like it, but you know he pays us no mind."

Bella smiled with exasperated indulgence at her uncle. Her aunt and uncle seemed to find it almost impossible to gainsay their own servants. It was often left to Bella to coax and cajole, or outright demand, that a defiant servant do his masters' bidding.

Before she could respond, their conversation was interrupted by a knock on the front door. "Probably another neighbor trying to gawk at my patient," Bella predicted.

To her surprise, Robert Fortiscue stood on the doorstep. Bella's blue eyes went wide and she felt a flush coming to her cheeks. She said nothing for a moment as he doffed his hat and greeted her.

Bella looked at his very pale, very romantic features with pleasure. His blond hair was slightly tousled and his eyes a lighter blue than her own. He was an inch or so taller than she, and she often described his delicate-looking hands as "artistic."

"Mr. Fortiscue!" she finally said. "Won't you come in? My uncle and I were just having our tea." Bella smiled her pleasure at his arrival and stood back to let him enter.

"How kind of you, Miss Tichley," he said with a flourishing bow before turning to her uncle.

"Lord Penninghurst! How good to see you! How well you look." Robert's tone was almost lilting.

"How do you do, Fortiscue," the earl said in a measured tone before rising and shaking the younger gentleman's hand. He had the feeling that he might break Robert's fingers if he gripped them too hard. The earl cast a quizzical glance toward his niece, who was gazing at Fortiscue with unabashed admiration. The earl did not understand it; his niece usually showed such superior judgment in all things.

That was, until Robert Fortiscue began to exhibit a particular interest in her.

At first the family had thought Bella's usual good sense would surface and she would dismiss the young man. But, to everyone's surprise, she seemed to enjoy his attentions.

The one thing he and his younger brother agreed upon, the earl thought with some asperity, was that Robert Fortiscue was full of fustian and flummery.

Still, it was very unlike his levelheaded niece to be taken in by such a sapskull, the earl thought as he watched Bella practically hang on every gesture Fortiscue made.

He had discussed Bella's uncharacteristic behavior with his wife and daughter recently, and they seemed to find it more understandable than he did. Triss believed she knew why Bella was partial to Fortiscue.

"She likes him because he is so undemanding and easy to please," she had explained one morning over breakfast.

"What does that have to do with anything?" the earl had questioned through a mouthful of toast and jam.

"Well, you have to admit, my dear," his wife had interjected, "we are always relying on Bella to smooth everything over. She not only runs her father's household, but she helps us with ours also."

"How do you mean?" the earl asked, rather dumbfounded by his wife's comment.

"For instance, last month when you insulted Cook and he had given notice, whom did you call upon to fix it all?"

"Bella," the earl stated, beginning to understand where his wife was leading.

"Yes, Bella," she continued. "We are always making demands on her. Why, I cannot plan a house party without Bella. Triss would have scandalized the countryside long ago if Bella had not extricated her from one scrape after another."

"Oh, Mother," Triss had protested in a petulant tone.

"You know it's true," Lady Penninghurst had told her daughter in a scolding tone. "No wonder she is partial to that bland, unexciting blunderbuss."

Watching his niece now, the earl believed his wife and daughter were correct in their assessment of the situation.

After they reseated themselves, Bella looked again at Robert with a serene smile gracing her lovely features. She had not seen him for several weeks and had missed his good-natured visits.

He was dressed in a very tightfitting coat of blue wool and dark brown trousers. Bella admired the shine of his boots as he accepted a cup of tea from her.

Casting a harried glance at her uncle, Bella hoped he would not be sandoffish to Robert. She was very aware that Uncle David seemed to have the same erroneous opinion of Robert as her papa did.

Even though she fully intended to marry Robert Fortiscue, Bella had to own to herself that she did not find him perfect. Indeed, the way he held his pinky finger up in the air while he sipped his tea was rather irritating. Feeling rather petty for her observation, Bella dismissed from her mind this critique of her intended. After all, no one was perfect.

But still, it was very strange to Bella that her family could not see Robert's finer qualities. Could they not see how convenient and practical it would be for her to reside at Oakdale? Sometimes Bella thought her family displayed a severe lack of common sense.

Robert cleared his throat and asked after everyone at Penninghurst Park before turning to Bella and asking after her father and brother. When he had dispensed with these formalities, he turned his questioning to the mysterious stranger.

"What is this about young Tommy finding a half-dead chap in your garden? The whole village can speak of nothing else."

Bella explained to him the events that had brought the man to the house.

"The doctor is due back this afternoon," she said as she finished the tale. "The stranger does not seem to be any worse, thank goodness, but I cannot tell if he is improving."

"Heavens! Miss Tichley, what a nine days' wonder! Have you no clue as to his identity?" he questioned as he nibbled delicately on a biscuit.

"Not a notion. My uncle thinks the gentleman may have dropped from the moon." Bella smiled at her uncle, who was scowling at Robert's raised pinky finger.

"What is being done to find out who the man is?" Robert turned his questioning pale blue eyes to the earl.

"I have several men scouring the countryside as we speak. That's what's being done," the earl blustered at Fortiscue, taking umbrage to the implied criticism in the younger man's tone.

Robert blinked several times at the earl and seemed to shrink back into his chair.

Groaning inwardly at her uncle's defensiveness, Bella said soothingly, "Yes, Uncle, we know that everything that is humanly possible is being done to discover who the man is."

"Well, as I have traveled extensively through the country, and since you say the man appears to be a gentleman, mayhap I should have a look at him. It is possible that I might recognize him."

Bella hesitated a moment before casting aside her previous resistance to visitors. After all, there really was no harm in letting Robert see the man. And, though improbable, it would be very good luck if Robert did happen to recognize the stranger, she concluded.

Rising from her chair, Bella nodded to Robert. "Please come this way."

Uncle David followed, and the three of them proceeded to Bella's bedchamber.

Bella watched Robert's face for any signs of recognition as the blond man looked down at the invalid. She saw Robert's pale brows go up.

"Yes?" Bella questioned. "Do you know him?"

"Er . . . no. I am just surprised at what a ruffian he looks. He's quite a big chap, isn't he?"

Bella felt that Robert's tone was disapproving, and she wondered at it.

"Well, certainly he has grown a bit of a beard, but I would not say that he looks like a ruffian." She ended this statement on a softer tone when she realized she was responding a little defensively.

Robert looked back down at the patient and sniffed. "I must say, Miss Tichley, does he have to remain here? You know nothing about this man. He could be a highwayman."

Bella looked at Robert in surprise. "No, he cannot be moved, Mr. Fortiscue. He is not yet out of danger. Besides, I believe him to be a gentleman."

Mr. Fortiscue sniffed again.

With that, the three of them returned to the front room. Uncle David did not sit down, but turned to his niece.

"I thank you for your hospitality, niece, but I must return to the Park."

Bella thought her uncle spoke a little too loudly as he cast Robert a significant look.

"Oh, yes, I must take my leave also," Robert said quickly as he took the earl's meaning.

Smiling to herself, Bella retrieved the gentlemen's things. Her uncle was correct in his subtle hint that it would be improper for Robert to remain alone with Bella.

But she was very pleased that Robert had come, and she said good-bye to him as warmly as she could.

He kissed her fingers delicately. "I shall call upon you soon, if I may."

"You may," Bella said, smiling into his pale blue eyes.

It was well past midnight when Tommy rose from his pallet at the foot of the stranger's bed. He had been roused by the sounds of the stranger's low moaning and tossing about as if he were trying to get out of the bed.

"Hold still, sir," Tommy said before padding out of the room. Bella was using a spare room while the invalid occupied hers.

"Bella," he whispered to the shapeless form under the mound of blankets.

Instantly she sat up, pushing her dark braid off her shoulder.

"Tommy? Is he worse?" Bella was already pushing aside the heavy blankets and reaching for her woolen robe.

"Yes. He's making noises and trying to get up again," Tommy informed her with a half-stifled yawn as he followed his sister back into the bedroom.

To her deep concern, Bella saw that the stranger was half out of the bed, his broad, deeply muscled chest gleaming in the firelight.

Bella did not bother to stifle her gasp of distress at the red stains of fresh blood evident on the bandages on the stranger's left shoulder.

"Tommy, get my things and the clean bandages. Hurry," she urged as she rushed over to the big man who was still struggling to rise.

"You mustn't! Please, sir, you will damage your wound

further." She tried to keep her voice calm but firm as she put her hands on his chest and gently pushed him down. His skin felt hot to her touch, she noted with dismay. She might as well have been pushing against the oak tree in the front drive for all the effect her efforts had on him. How could he still be so strong when he was so ill? She shook her head in wonder at his strength.

"Leave off," he said in a growl, trying to push her aside. "I am a sitting duck here. I won't have a chance against the bastards."

Bella frowned again. He had said much the same on the previous night. But before, his ranting had not been this intelligible. Bella glanced to the door, wishing Tommy would hurry. She knew she could not handle the stranger by herself.

She decided to try reasoning with him, since he seemed a little more lucid, despite his raging fever. Bracing herself, she took advantage of his trembling legs and pushed with all her might. He fell back into a sitting position on the bed. He continued to struggle with her, trying to push her from him. Shoving his hands away as best she could, Bella grabbed his face between her hands and forced him to look up at her.

His dark gray eyes glittered up at her feverishly, angrily.

"Sir, you are safe here. You must lie down now, or you will tear your wound open further." Gently she pushed the silky strands of his thick black hair away from his damp, hot forehead. "You have been here for three days. No one has come for you. You have eluded your attackers. We will not let anyone harm you. You are safe here."

He had ceased his struggles, but did not lie back on the bed.

Her voice penetrated his fever-fogged brain. Her voice: low and clear and melodious, with a slight huskiness that was very memorable. Blinking, he glanced around the little room. A vague memory of the last few days began to come back to him.

He remembered this girl with the beautiful voice and gentle hands. Her hands still held his face, and he looked up at her, trying to make out her features in the firelit shadows. He now recalled that this girl and her family had taken him in and nursed him. Without a doubt, he knew he would be dead in the shrubbery if not for her.

At this moment he was not sure what shrubbery or exactly why he would be dead, but he knew this girl was important.

"Please, sir, lie back now. I am not strong enough to constrain you in your delirium."

He felt the pressure of her hands upon his chest and looked down to see her slender fingers splayed against him. Distantly he wondered how many times he had seen a woman's hand upon him like this. But never under these circumstances, he mused in fevered distraction.

"What is your name?" He wanted a name to put with the voice that spoke so soothingly to him in his fever.

"Arabella, sir, and yours?" she said softly, well pleased that he no longer seemed delirious.

He allowed her to push him back against the pillows and place the blankets over him.

To her relief, Tommy had finally returned with the things from her sewing kit and the strips of torn-up nightgown.

As gently as she could, she began to cut through the bloody bandages.

"West . . ." he forced out through clenched teeth as pain stabbed through his body and he slipped again into unconsciousness.

Chapter Five

Despite occasional moments of lucidness, the stranger—or Mr. West, as she now thought of him—still had a raging fever the next morning.

Bella fretted over him, a frown of concern often between her brows as she sponged cool water over his flushed, hot skin.

Dr. Pearce arrived early, more out of curiosity than to actually do anything, Bella suspected. He offered little help.

"I don't think cupping him would help. He's lost enough blood as it is. The fever will either break or not." The doctor shrugged. "Give him a few more drops of laudanum when he wakes."

"But the longer the fever lasts, the weaker he becomes," she had protested to the doctor. "Surely there is something we can do."

"Only time will tell if he can survive this," the doctor stated flatly before taking his leave.

Bella continued to care for the man as best she could. Sometimes he was delirious and hard for her to handle. During these times she would speak to him softly. Bella had noticed on previous nights that her voice seemed to calm him.

Papa and Tommy did their best to be helpful, though it did little good. The man only fussed when anyone but Bella tried to tend to him.

Uncle David and Aunt Elizabeth called, but they brought no news of the man's identity.

"No one in three villages is aware of a missing Mr. West," her uncle had lamented.

It was not surprising to Bella that after the first few days, Triss found the house a dead bore, as she had put it, and had not visited since.

So the hours blended and Bella continued to pray that the man would soon be better.

Later that night, during the wee hours, when he was quiet, Bella retrieved the letters from the pocket of his greatcoat. Unfolding the vellum, Bella reread the tryst notes and wondered which lady he had chosen to meet.

"I hope you did not choose the one who uses too many exclamation points," she said to her patient, smiling a little at her own absurdity in the quiet room.

For some reason that she could not identify, Bella had not shown anyone else the notes.

Refolding the notes and placing them back in the pocket, Bella looked at her patient closely, almost willing him to heal. Her gaze traveled over his angular features, down his aquiline nose to his square jaw.

"My, you are growing quite a beard," she observed.

He did not move, and she continued to scan his features.

His lips were perfectly sculpted. It was a mouth that revealed sensitivity and kindness, she mused.

She moved down to his broad chest and felt an irrepressible blush coming to her cheeks. Bella had never come into such intimate contact with a man close to her own age. She found it rather disconcerting. There in the shadowy dimness of her room, Bella found herself thinking that her patient looked like one of the heroes in the storybooks she loved to read. *Did he look more like Sir Galahad or Apollo?* she wondered, tilting her head to the side so that she could examine him more closely.

She wondered if he liked poetry. Or history?

His hands looked strong and capable. The fingers, splayed on top of the blanket above his waist, were long and bore no calluses. She decided they were handsome hands. *Certainly not artistic like Robert's,* she thought quickly in defense of her intended, *but still handsome.* Bella made a face, recalling that Papa had once said Robert's hands looked weak.

As she grew sleepy, her thoughts drifted to Robert. She wondered when he would officially propose to her. Though there had been definite discussions regarding a future together, Robert had not approached Papa yet to ask for her hand. Bella suspected Robert knew that Papa and her uncle did not hold him in high regard.

Leaning back in the rocking chair, Bella gave in to her favorite pleasure of mentally redecorating Robert's home. Oakdale was a large, well-appointed house that boasted not less than eight bedchambers.

Unfortunately Oakdale was sadly out of style. And no wonder, since it had not been redecorated for more than thirty years. Robert's mother had been a new bride when she had arrived at Oakdale. Robert's father had died shortly after Robert's birth, and Mrs. Fortiscue had not wanted to change anything about the place. The gardens were beautiful, though, if overgrown. And the stables had been recently refurbished.

Bella thought it would be lovely to be mistress of her own home. "After all," she said aloud to her patient, "I am almost five and twenty. It is time that I have a home of my own."

Westlake showed no sign of hearing her.

She also wanted a family. It was her opinion that Robert, with his good-natured gentleness, would make a very fine father.

It pleased her that she and Robert were so well suited. But what she liked best about him was that he did not mind that she enjoyed reading so much.

Over the years, a number of young men whose families were well known to hers had paid court to her. But she had ultimately declined them all because they had thought her love of learning was something to be discouraged.

Triss had often told her that gentlemen had an aversion to bluestockings. "No matter how pretty you are, Bella, no man wants a wife who is smarter than he is. You are in danger of remaining on the shelf," Triss had warned. But Bella had paid her cousin no mind.

Robert was different. He seemed to like the fact that

Bella was intelligent and sensible. He had often paid her this compliment during their walks to church.

It pleased Bella that she and Robert had practically grown up together. It was important to her that she wed someone from Mabry Green. She loved the tiny village, and felt a certain satisfaction, and even a little pride, in the fact that she was invited to all social functions, and that her opinions on any number of subjects were well respected.

Being the only practical one in her family had caused Bella to appreciate peace and normalcy, and Robert had often stated that he desired those qualities also. So it seemed to Bella that Mr. Fortiscue was the wisest choice she could make. It would have been even better to actually be in love with Robert Fortiscue, but one could not have everything, she mused philosophically.

Looking back down at her patient, Bella wondered if he was married. If he was, she certainly pitied his wife. How horrible it would be to have no trust in one's husband, to always worry about him disappearing to meet ladies in atriums.

No, thank you, she thought as her lids grew heavy. *I will take trustworthy Robert over a philanderer any day.*

Sometime later Bella jerked awake, almost falling off the chair as it rocked forward.

The candle had burned itself out, and the fire in the grate was now only glowing embers.

Bella held still for a moment, listening intently for an indication of what had awakened her.

"Johnny, into the woods." The man's voice was a harsh rasp. "I must reach Henry."

Bella instinctively reached out to him in the dark. Her hand touched his upper arm as he was trying to push the blanket aside. His skin felt hot to her touch.

As quickly as she could, Bella reached over, fumbling to find the nightstand. When she did, she located the matches and lit the lantern. "Oh, sir, your fever is raging," she said in exhausted dismay.

If anyone else had been in the room with her, they would have heard the fear in her voice. In the dim lamplight she saw beads of moisture on his forehead and upper lip. His cheeks were flushed and his legs moved restlessly under the covers.

Pouring a cup of water from the pitcher on the nightstand, Bella moved to sit on the bed next to him. As gently as she could, she slipped an arm under his shoulder and lifted him so that she could put the cup to his lips.

"You must drink. It will help your fever," she whispered urgently, knowing that it would be extremely dangerous if his fever lasted too long.

An appetizing aroma wafted up to the bedroom, rousing Westlake from his near-unconscious slumber. Shifting his head slightly on the soft pillow, he allowed his heavy lids to open slightly.

His sluggish thoughts drifted aimlessly, as his gaze took in the unfamiliar room. It was odd, but he did not care a whit that he had no idea where he was.

How long he lay there, in a state of half wakefulness, he did not know.

The appetizing aroma again reached his senses. His thoughts began to clear when he realized he was ravenously hungry.

Stretching like a big cat, he rolled onto to his side, until a searing pain in his shoulder halted his movement. He looked down at his left shoulder and frowned curiously at the bandages he saw.

Looking around the room, Westlake was suddenly and inexplicably disappointed to see that the low rocking chair near the bed was empty.

Tentatively he sat up, swung his legs around, and placed his feet on the floor. Immediately a wave of dizziness engulfed him. Feeling as if he were about to faint, Westlake wonder if he had drunk too much whiskey the night before.

No, that was not right, he thought as his brain cleared a little.

Slowly the events of that wild night, the night he had received the note about Henry's accident, came back to him.

He recalled the two horses emerging from the forest, and the smoking pistol.

Gritting his teeth against the pain and dizziness, Westlake rose unsteadily, but with determination, to his feet. He needed to find out where he was. He needed to find out about Henry.

Standing next to the bed, swaying slightly, he looked again at the rocking chair. The image of a pair of darkly fringed blue eyes and a long dark braid came to mind.

His nurse. The young woman who put cool compresses on his forehead and fed him broth. The images flashed through his mind. She had spoken to him in a soothing, melodious, unforgettable voice.

"Damn," he said to himself, breathing as hard as if he had just finished a fencing lesson. He took a couple of wobbly steps toward a stand that held a pitcher of water and a basin.

He put his hand on the bureau next to the stand as his knees threatened to give way. He looked around the room for his boots and clothes and caught sight of them on the chest at the foot of the bed. After a moment he attempted to wash his face with his right hand. Though it was difficult to perform his ablutions with only his right hand, the cold water helped clear his head. There was no mirror in the small room, but by running his hand over his jaw he could tell he was badly in need of a shave.

A wave of sickening dizziness swept over him again and he moved back to sit down on the unmade bed. Breathing as slowly as he could, he waited for the dizziness to recede before picking up a freshly laundered white shirt and his breeches from the end of the bed. After wrestling with the breeches for some time, he finally got them on over his small clothes. He rested for a few moments before slipping his left arm into the sleeve of the lawn shirt. Taking a very deep breath, Westlake decided not to even attempt tying his neckcloth. Picking up one of his Hessian boots, he tried, one-handed, to pull the boot onto his left foot. After only a few moments exertion, Westlake's hand shook with exhaustion, and he still had not managed to pull the boot on.

A self-disgusted scowl formed a crease on his brow. He let another moment pass before he held his breath and redoubled his efforts to pull the boot on. Grimacing, he continued to hold the boot in his right hand while trying to push his foot in.

"You vexing man!"

The boot went flying across the room at the sound of the startled, angry voice.

Westlake snapped his head up to see a dark-haired, blue-eyed young woman standing in the doorway. Even with her angry tone, Westlake recognized her voice: She was the one who had nursed him.

He did not move and did not try to retrieve his boot. He just looked at her.

She was disarmingly lovely. He could not recall when he had last seen such an exquisite creature. The deep garnet of her simple gown flattered the flawless ivory of her complexion. Her dark hair, almost black, was pulled back in a simple twist. The style showed her fine, deep blue eyes to great advantage—beautiful, revealing eyes that were now gazing at him with a touch of anger and a great deal of concern.

A surge of gratitude swelled in his heart. This beautiful young woman had nursed him, had in all likelihood saved his life. He had so many questions he wanted to ask her, but first he needed to thank her. Paying no heed to the pain and dizziness, he rose as steadily as he could to his feet.

"Oh, sir, please do not get up!" Bella moved swiftly toward him, appalled at seeing him almost dressed and trying to stand.

"I do not have the words to express my gratitude—"

"Never mind that." Bella so forgot her usual manners in her distress that she uncharacteristically interrupted him. "Please sit down before you fall down. And please tell me who you are and where we can reach your people. I am sure they are worried sick."

Westlake remained standing. It went against his innate good manners to sit down while a lady remained standing.

"Yes, I am sure you are correct. I am Westlake. My home is Autley. I left there when I received word that my nephew, who lives in Tilbourne, was injured. Two black-guards set upon my groom and me. I was shot, but I trust my groom got away safely and returned to Autley," he explained, growing almost breathless by the end of his explanation.

"Westlake!" Bella exclaimed. "But I thought your name

was Mr. West." Bella put a hand to her head and laughed, the days of pent-up tension finally finding a release.

"Mr. West." She laughed again, shaking her head. "Westlake. And you live at Autley. . . ." The smile on her lips faded as the words sank in. "Autley." Though she had never had the pleasure of visiting the place, Bella was familiar with the vast estate of the Duke of Westlake. Everyone in Kent was familiar with Autley, for it was considered one of the finest estates in all of Britain.

The Duke of Westlake.

"Good heavens!" Bella looked up at him in complete surprise. It was not until she saw him sway slightly that Bella caught hold of herself.

"Forgive me, your grace. But you must sit down. My name is Arabella Tichley, and you have been at our house for four days. My uncle, Lord Penninghurst, has men out looking for anyone who might have missed you. We shall send word immediately to your people at Autley."

"Thank you, Miss Tichley," he said, finally complying with her request to be seated. In truth, he did not think he could remain standing for much longer. "And I would also like to send a note to my sister-in-law, if I may. I need to know how my nephew fares."

"Of course, your grace. I shall return momentarily with quill and ink. Please stay still," she cautioned as she left the room.

He looked paler, if that was possible, when she returned moments later with the writing implements. Placing the paper, quill, and inkpot on the tiny desk by the window, Bella cast a quick look at the pallid man seated on her bed. *Good Lord,* she thought, *he is a duke!* She had been caring for the Duke of Westlake all this time.

He rose slowly and took a few steps toward the desk. Bella moved to his side to help steady him. She became suddenly aware that he was quite tall.

Without speaking, for he was feeling thoroughly ill, Westlake wrote two short missives: one to his mother and one to Margaret, his sister-in-law. He then wrote the directions on each note before sanding and folding them.

Bella stepped forward, silently offering to help him back to the bed. Even though it was only a few steps it took some moments for them to traverse the distance. Bella stayed quiet. It was obvious that the duke was an exceedingly proud man, demonstrated by his attempt to get up and dress himself. Bella, though wanting to help, did not want to cause him further embarrassment by calling attention to the fact that he needed assistance.

Once he was seated, Bella hesitated before him. Now that he was fully conscious, the matter of his care was a different proposition.

Coming to a decision, Bella took the matter in hand. "You must rest, your grace. I will send my younger brother, Tommy, to help you undress. Please lie back. I will have your letters sent immediately," she said softly yet firmly before turning to the desk to pick up his letters.

When she turned back, she found him lying against the pillows, already slipping once more into sleep.

After quietly closing the door on the exhausted duke, Bella moved quickly to the front room, where Papa and Tommy were reading.

"Tommy! You must go to the Park at once and have one of our uncle's men deliver these letters immediately," she directed, deciding that she could send Tommy to attend the duke when he returned.

"Yes, Bella, I will depart at once," Tommy told his sister, jumping up from his chair.

"How may I help, my dear?" her papa questioned, setting aside his paper.

"Would you mind riding over to Dr. Pearce's home and asking him to come this afternoon or first thing in the morning?"

"Not in the least," he replied, rising from his comfortable chair. "Have you finally discovered the identity of our unknown guest?"

"Yes!" Bella practically burst out. "He is the Duke of Westlake!"

"The Duke of Westlake!" Papa and Tommy exclaimed in unison, looking at each other in great surprise.

"No wonder he has such a remarkable horse," Tommy remarked.

"The Duke of Westlake," her papa said again. "I would certainly like to have a look at his library."

Bella laughed at that. "Off with you both while I prepare lunch."

It was several hours later when Bella entered her room with a neatly arranged tray and smiled at her patient. It was odd, but now that he was awake he seemed much too large for her bed. She took note that his skin was very pale and his eyes still had that slightly glassy, feverish look. Upon closer inspection, she noticed green flecks in the gray irises around his pupils. She found his eyes quite striking.

But his jaw was now clean-shaven and his hair neatly combed. She thought he looked much more comfortable in one of her papa's soft lawn nightshirts.

"I must say that your little brother makes a very good valet," the duke stated with a grin, running his hand over his smooth jaw.

"I am certainly glad that you did not nick yourself." She smiled and set the tray next to the bed. "Do you think you could eat a little something, your grace?"

That voice. Velvet music to my ears, he thought.

He did feel like eating, but refused to let her feed him. He found it annoying that so simple a task could prove so arduous. But the thick vegetable stew was satisfying and he ate slowly.

"Tommy has informed me that our uncle has dispatched two messengers with your notes," Bella told him after seating herself in the rocking chair. "My uncle is also sending for the constable so that you may describe your attackers. It is no wonder we could not locate anyone who was looking for you, for Tilbourne is miles and miles away. Your people were probably checking all the villages between Autley and Tilbourne for you. Your horse carried you a great distance away from your original destination," she observed.

"Yes, he did, to my very good luck," the duke told her quietly.

After having heard the whole story earlier from Tommy—of how they had found him and dragged him indoors, and how Bella had removed the ball from his shoulder—Westlake was at even more of a loss as to how to express his appreciation. And he found it humbling that the Tichley family had no desire for his gratitude.

"You have a very good cook," he complimented, instead of trying to thank her again, and placed the bowl back on the tray.

Bella laughed in surprise. "I am the cook, sir, and thank you," she said as she began to tidy the room.

Glancing up at her in surprise, Alex felt unexpectedly ashamed of himself. What a bufflehead he was, he thought self-deprecatingly. His innate good manners caused him guilt because of the extra work he knew he was causing her. As he continued to watch her activities, Alex wondered how he would ever begin to repay her and her family for their kindness to him.

"There," Bella said, patting the neatly folded blanket at the foot of his bed. "Is there anything else I can get for you at the moment, sir?"

"No. You do too much, Miss Tichley."

Bella decided to ignore his remark and came around the bed to feel his forehead for fever. Westlake had the sudden desire to take her cool, slim hand and hold it against his cheek.

"You are a little warm. Will you rest now, sir?"

Though it was only early afternoon, he felt it had already been a long day. "Yes," he said, leaning back against the pillows.

At the door, she turned and looked at him. He was a surprisingly handsome man, she thought for the first time. His features now seemed completely different than they had while he had been unconscious. She saw that his gray-green eyes were almost silver in the firelight. There was also a new, lordly air about him. This was emphasized by the slight rogue's smile he wore as he lounged back on her bed.

"Dignitate cum laudanum," she whispered, and then realizing she had said the words aloud, she quickly left the room.

Westlake stared at the closed door. *"Dignitate cum laudanum,"* he repeated the words to himself. Latin had not been his favorite subject at school, and it took him some minutes to work it out.

Dignity and . . . peace? No. Dignity with . . . ? Suddenly he smiled. So that was her image of him: *Leisure with dignity*. It was a surprise to find his beautiful nurse was also a scholar.

Chapter Six

It was very early the next morning when Dr. Pearce drove up to the house in a small gig.

"I hear from your father that the crisis has passed with our patient," he said as soon as Bella opened the door to him.

"Yes, his grace's fever broke last night. He has eaten a little and seems vastly improved," she responded as the doctor moved past her to stand in the middle of the room.

"Does he? We shall see," he stated cryptically.

Bella followed the doctor up to her room, where they found the duke already sitting up in bed.

"Your grace, may I present Dr. Pearce?"

"How do you do, Dr. Pearce? Shall I live?" the duke questioned with cheerful irreverence.

A little nonplussed at the duke's attitude, Dr. Pearce stuttered for a moment, casting a quizzical glance to Bella.

Bella shrugged slightly, and smiled. Since the duke had come out of his fever, she, too, was finding him a surprise.

"Well, we shall see, your grace. Let's have a look at you."

Dr. Pearce helped Westlake remove his nightshirt. He then retrieved a pair of scissors from his black bag and proceeded to cut away the bandages wrapping the duke's shoulder.

Bella stood back and watched with her hands clasped

tightly together, wincing as the doctor probed the ugly, swollen wound with none-too-gentle fingers.

"Humph," the doctor grunted, continuing his examination.

Bella could not help but marvel at the duke's tolerance for pain, for she recoiled at the doctor's attentions more than he did.

Just when she was about to lose control and shout out to the physician to be careful, he finally sat back and gave the duke an assessing look.

"Well, it certainly could be worse, but I have seen a lot better," he said. "I don't like the amount of swelling, and by the looks of the bandages, the wound has been seeping. But there does not seem to be any obvious infection."

The duke nodded his understanding to what the doctor was saying. Looking past Dr. Pearce, Westlake was struck by Bella's concerned expression. Most of the ladies of his acquaintance would be reaching for the hartshorn by now, he thought, unaccountably touched by her gentle and unexpected kindness.

"You must have complete rest for another full week, at least. You are still feverish, which may be due to being out in the storm. I'd be happier if you rested a fortnight, but I have the feeling that you are an impatient young man," the physician declared.

The duke had no response and allowed the doctor to rebandage his shoulder in silence.

Bella was enormously relieved when she saw the doctor to the door. He was right: It certainly could have been worse.

Bella went back to her room to see how the duke was faring after the doctor's rough treatment of him. She found him still sitting up, but his eyes were closed. Hesitantly, she decided to leave him to rest. Turning, she walked softly to the door.

"Won't you please stay a moment, Miss Tichley?"

His deep voice stopped her movement. "Of course, your grace." She walked back and seated herself in the rocking chair. Silently, she watched him for a few moments. Her concern for him grew as she noticed a muscle jumping in his jaw.

"The pain must be very bad." She almost whispered the words.

He turned his head toward her slightly and opened his eyes. He met her beautiful gaze, and again saw the concern and compassion there.

A wry little smile touched his lips. "It could be worse," he said, repeating the doctor's succinct words. He closed his eyes again.

Trying to find some way to ease his pain, Bella suddenly recalled the small vial of laudanum the doctor had left days ago. She had given him very little of it, so she knew there was some left.

"Your grace, will you take a few drops of laudanum? It will help with the pain."

He opened his eyes and looked at her with his startling gray gaze. "No, Miss Tichley, no laudanum." He shook his head emphatically.

Seeing the question in her eyes, he continued: "I have seen too many men, brave soldiers, reduced to bland, needy simpletons because they were given too much laudanum after being injured on the battlefield."

An expression of surprised curiosity spread across Bella's features.

"Were you in the war, your grace?"

"Yes," the duke replied. He really had very little desire to speak, but he wanted her to stay and talk with him, so he went on: "I was in for four years. Was sent home when my father died, as I was the oldest son, but not before we trounced the frogs at Salamanca."

"Never say you were at Salamanca!" Bella gasped. "I have read many accounts of this great battle. Two French eagles were captured!"

He again looked at Bella in surprise, impressed with her knowledge. *What an unusual girl,* he mused as he watched the genuine interest on her face.

"It was a glorious victory and will, no doubt, be considered one of the most important battles of the entire war."

"And you were a part of it," Bella said, her tone filled with awe.

Feeling a little embarrassed, for he never spoke of the war, the duke changed the subject.

"And what of you, Miss Tichley? How comes a young lady to speak Latin and have knowledge of military history?"

Bella's eyes dropped shyly before his. "I enjoy learning, your grace," she stated simply.

After that, they were quiet for some moments. But Bella felt it was an easy, natural silence.

"I have been reading a very interesting book, *The Life of Nelson,* by Robert Southey. If you would like, I will read a few pages aloud to you," Bella offered after a little while, thinking that this might help divert him from the pain.

"I would like that very much, Miss Tichley," the duke said quietly. He did not even consider telling her that he had already read the book.

Later that day, while Bella still sat with her patient, Tommy came bounding through the open bedroom door. "Bella, come quick!" he urged excitedly. Setting her sewing aside, Bella rose from her chair.

"It's the largest coach I have ever seen. Four matched grays and four outriders! They are coming up our lane," he told them before rushing out of the room.

Bella turned to look down at Westlake and saw a smile starting at the corners of his mouth. Her brow raised in question at his expression.

"I believe my family has arrived," he stated.

"Yes. It must be them. They have made very good time," Bella exclaimed before abruptly rushing from the room.

She hurried into the little dressing closet next to her room to tidy her hair and remove her apron.

Good heavens, why am I in such a pet? she wondered to herself. *Because his mother is a duchess,* came the immediate thought.

Bella was normally not one to be intimidated, but this was certainly a daunting situation. She checked her appearance in the looking glass one last time and saw the worry in her darkly fringed blue eyes.

With an effort, she forced her expression to some semblance of serenity before going into the front room.

Tommy was standing at the window. "They are getting closer," he reported.

"Come, Tommy, let us go out and greet our guests."
Bella was pleased that her voice sounded calmer than she
really felt.

She opened the front door and they walked out to the
cobbled front drive. Bella quickly tried to smooth Tommy's
unruly dark hair.

"Let's make a good show of ourselves, young man," she
said to her little brother as the coach rounded the curve of
the drive.

When it stopped, the coachman and groom jumped down
from the box and placed a wooden stoop in front of the
coach door, which was emblazoned with the Westlake ducal
crest. A moment later a tall woman emerged, wearing the
most beautiful carriage coat Bella had ever seen. It was
made of emerald velvet overlapping in the front and falling
to the lady's ankles in deep scallops. The high standing
collar, cuffs, and hem were trimmed in a rich dark fur. Her
bonnet was small with a high crown and also trimmed in
emerald velvet. Beneath the bonnet was a profusion of light
brown curls framing a striking, dignified countenance.

Sucking in her breath for courage, Bella stepped forward
and curtsied deeply.

Tommy was so dazzled by the carriage, the matched
grays, and the liveried outriders that he forgot to bow until
he felt his sister tug on his arm.

"Miss Tichley?" the stately woman questioned imperiously.

"Yes, your grace," Bella said as she rose from her curtsy.

"My son is really here?"

"Oh, yes, your grace. Your son has just finished lunch
and is now waiting for you." Bella had heard the anxiety
beneath the lady's peremptory tone and immediately felt
compassion for the dowager duchess. What agonies she
must have gone through these last few days. Bella was very
glad that the duke was now so much improved.

The elegant lady closed her eyes for a moment.

"Thank our Lord," she whispered before opening her
eyes and straightening her already erect posture.

"I have brought Dr. Kensington with me." She gestured
toward the carriage behind her, where a heavyset man was
laboriously exiting the conveyance. "But before we let the

doctor have a look, I want to spend a moment with my son," she said.

"Of course, your grace. Please come in." She led the lady into the house.

As the dowager moved past Tommy, she turned and gave the boy an assessing gaze. "Who might you be, young man?"

"I—I am Thomas Tichley, your grace," Tommy replied, bowing again.

"Ah. Then you are the young man who found my son."

"Er . . . you see, your grace, it was his horse who alerted me," Tommy said modestly.

"I shall want to hear every detail after I have seen my son," she informed him, then followed Bella into the sitting room.

Bella smiled to herself when she saw that Papa was already bowing when they entered the room.

"Your grace, may I introduce my father, Alfred Tichley?"

"It is a pleasure, sir, to make your acquaintance. In fact, it is my deepest pleasure to meet your entire family. I have just come from Penninghurst Park, where your good brother and his wife have assured me that my son has been in your very excellent care. I have not the words to express my gratitude to you."

Bella's father blinked several times. He was not sure how to respond to this grand lady after such a gracious speech.

"You are very welcome, your grace. We are very glad to be able to report that your son is much improved and is, I'm sure, as anxious to see you as you are to see him."

Bella looked at her father with pride. Normally he was a man of very few words, and those words were usually blunt.

"If you will come this way, your grace." Bella gestured toward the staircase and led the lady to her room.

Before she entered, the dowager stopped and looked at Bella keenly. "I hope my son has not been difficult, Miss Tichley," she asked, thinking how pretty Bella was.

"Oh, no, your grace, your son has been a model patient," Bella assured her.

"Really?" The dowager raised a brow. "Who would have guessed?"

The duchess then entered the room, and Bella closed the door quietly behind her just as she heard the tall lady exclaim, "Oh, Alex!"

Alex was indeed very glad to see his mother, and smiled his pleasure as she rushed to his side and sat on the bed next to him.

"Oh, my dear son, you have no idea the agonies we have suffered since you left Autley," she told him, her eyes drinking in every feature of his gaunt face. "You have no idea what we feared."

"I can well imagine, *ma mère*," he said, taking her hand and raising it to his lips.

"Alex, you look dreadful. I will call Dr. Kensington in immediately. We will speak after he has assured me of your health."

"If you insist. But first, do you have news of Henry?"

He saw anger replace the worry on his mother's face.

"That is the worst part of this whole nightmare! When Johnny returned with the horrid news that you had been set upon by highwaymen, we were frenzied with worry. I sent a dozen men to look for you and went to Tilbourne myself. I stopped at every village along the way. No one had news of you. It was as if you had vanished! Who would have guessed that your horse would have brought you to the other side of Ashdown forest? When I arrived at Margaret's house, there was Henry, playing King Arthur in the nursery. It was a mere scratch on his leg," she said in a tone of great disgust.

Alex looked at his mother sharply.

"Are you sure, *ma mère?* The note specifically said that they feared for the boy's life. I cannot imagine that even Margaret would be such a hen-wit as to exaggerate a scratch out of all proportion."

"But she did, Alex. There was truly nothing wrong with Henry. I do not mind telling you that I rang such a peal over her head that she cried during the whole of my visit."

Westlake was silent for a few moments, a fierce frown between his brows as he contemplated his mother's words.

The dowager said nothing. She recognized the look on his face—it was the same look his father used to have when he was trying to solve a puzzle.

"You did not bring Alice or Louisa with you?" he asked, bringing his eyes back to her face.

"No, I had no idea what condition you would be in, and you know they are little help during a crisis. But of course they send their love."

"I am glad they did not come," the duke said with a lopsided smile. "I assume you brought an entourage?"

"Yes," she replied, wondering what he was getting at.

"Is Johnny among them?"

"Yes. Though I did try to dissuade him from coming. He has driven himself to exhaustion searching for you. I have also brought your valet and two menservants to attend you until the doctor says it is safe for you to be moved," she explained.

The duke came to a decision.

"*Ma mère,* you must listen to me very carefully," he said to her in a very serious tone.

"Of course, my love, what is it?"

"Before you send the doctor in, send Johnny to me first. I have need to speak to him. Then—and I know this will be difficult for you—you must leave at once for Tilbourne. Also, send the rest of the servants and Dr. Kensington back home."

"Leave you now? But why, Alex?"

"You must go to Margaret's, get Henry, and take him back to Autley with you. Tell Margaret anything you like, but you must take Henry to Autley. Do you understand?" he asked in a tone that men, without hesitation, had obeyed on the battlefield.

After searching his features with deeply concerned eyes, she nodded. "Of course, Alex, but please tell me what is wrong."

The duke's lips pressed together in a grim line. "Maybe nothing, my dear, but it is extremely important that you take Henry to Autley and keep him there until I am well enough to return home. I also intend to start my own investigation into these highwaymen—I mean to find the man who shot me."

His mother could not mistake the grave seriousness she saw in his eyes.

"Yes, my love. I will go at once. Dr. Kensington can

return home in the second coach. The rest will come with me to Tilbourne. You do not even want your valet?" she asked, rising from the edge of the bed.

"Send everyone else home, *ma mère*," Westlake repeated. "I will also need you to deliver one or two letters for me."

The duchess shook her head, mystified at her son's instructions, but did not question him further. "I will be honest, Alex: It pains me to leave you so suddenly."

"I know, but you must trust me on this."

"Of course I trust you," she replied, leaning down to kiss his lean cheek. "But I do hope you will soon explain this mysterious request to me."

"It is probably nothing. Send Johnny to me now. And do not worry. I shall be back at Autley very soon," he said with a reassuring smile.

"I am counting on it," the dowager duchess said firmly before slipping from the room.

Chapter Seven

"I knew I'd be seeing you soon, once you knew the duke was awake," Bella accused her cousin.

Lady Beatrice Tichley was standing in the sitting room, garbed in a cranberry-colored riding habit with flashing jet beads buttoning the front from collar to hem.

"Well, you couldn't expect me to visit when his grace was so ill," she stated, seating herself in the chair by the window, across from Bella. "Now that he is feeling a little more the thing, I'm sure he would enjoy some company to break up the monotony of his convalescence."

"How generous of you," Bella said in a tone of mild sarcasm. "Seriously, Triss, he is still very weak, and he has already had a busy day. You must not tire him further," she said after looking up to the heavens for patience.

"I shall be gentle and soothing," Triss said breezily. "Imagine, Bella! The Duke of Westlake! We shall have entrée into the most exclusive salons in London this Season."

"You are not going to use the fact that he happens to be here because of a near tragedy to gain entrance into Society," Bella stated.

"Why ever not? He will probably be happy to make a few introductions for us. I have read all about the Duke of Westlake over the years. You know Father always takes the London papers. The duke is considered the most dashing, most sought after nonpareil in the country. He is so unique, so original that he cannot be defined. Is he a Corinthian? Is he a dandy? He is a formidable fencer, yet the prince regent himself often consults Westlake on matters of wardrobe. It is too delicious that we have him here, Bella."

"Be that as it may, Triss, you are not to bother him about London." Bella was a little surprised to hear Triss's description of the Duke of Westlake. It bore little resemblance to the courteous, gentle man she was coming to know.

"Again, why ever not? After all, it's the least he can do for us."

"You astonish me!" Bella looked askance at her cousin. "He does not owe *us* a thing! Even if he did, I am not going to London with you this spring. Really, Triss, you are much too coming."

Triss pouted at her cousin. Bella knew her well enough to know that this meant she was just changing tactics.

"You have always been too much of a high stickler, Bella. I was not going to be so bold as to come right out and ask him to take us up in London; I was going to let him think the idea was his. Besides, Father says that he is going to insist that Uncle Alfred let you come to London with us. May I see the duke now?"

"No, he is still asleep. And I am not going to London with you. I have no desire to follow you around while you hunt for a husband," Bella said.

"Don't you want a husband too, Bella?" Triss questioned, her eyes wide with sham innocence.

"I have told you a hundred times that I intend to marry Robert Fortiscue," Bella said as patiently as she could.

"Oh, him. If you were not in such a bad humor, I would ask you again to tell me why you want to marry that puddinghead."

"If I am in a bad humor it is only because you are being so vexing," Bella replied, refusing to rise to her cousin's bait.

"Am I really being so vexing?"

"Yes. Anyone listening to us right now would think that we don't really like each other," Bella said wryly.

"Then it's very good that *we* know we like each other," Triss said with a grin. "All right, then, enough of Mr. Fortissue and enough of the duke. What of his mother? I vow I have never seen such an exquisitely dressed lady. When Father sent the messenger to Autley with the duke's note, he thought it best to add one of his own, directing the dowager to come to the Park first, as it is difficult to find your home. I am so glad he did. Otherwise I would not have been able to have a look at her. Why do you think she departed so quickly?"

Bella gave a little shrug. "The duke explained that his mother needed to go to Tilbourne and see to his nephew, who I understand is his heir. The boy is the reason the duke was on the road so late the night he was shot," Bella explained.

"Do you not think it odd that there aren't at least ten servants attending him, now that his people know that he is here? I thought a duke never went anywhere without a small army of servants to do his bidding."

"Well, Dr. Pearce and Dr. Kensington have said that he is still to rest as much as possible, and that it would be dangerous for him to be moved before the week is out. There probably seemed no point to the duke to have any servants hanging about." Bella had wondered about this too, and this was the only explanation she had come up with.

"That makes sense," Triss replied. "What is he like, Bella?"

"I've hardly had time to form an opinion of him. He is a very good patient; he never complains. He is very brave and has a good sense of humor. And his manners are exquisite," she finished.

Triss looked at Bella with new interest.

"Goodness! I can't wait to hear what you have to say when you *have* had time to form an opinion," Triss responded with a little chuckle. "How long do you think he will sleep this afternoon?"

With a resigned sigh, Bella realized that Triss was going to stay put until she had seen the duke.

"I will go and see if he is awake. But you must not stay long, Triss," Bella told her cousin firmly.

"I promise," Triss called merrily as Bella left the room.

Poking her head through the partially open bedroom door, Bella found that the duke was awake and sitting up in bed.

Hearing a slight noise, the duke looked up and smiled when he saw Bella.

"Come in, Miss Tichley."

"I do not wish to disturb you, your grace." She hesitated.

"You can't," he replied, putting aside the book.

She stepped farther into the room. "Did you have a nice rest?"

"Yes, but I grow weary of lying about," he replied.

"You must be patient, your grace. It has been only a few days. It takes time to heal."

The duke gave her an amused, yet searching look.

"Are you always patient, Miss Tichley?" he questioned.

"I try to be."

"I have never liked having to wait for something I want."

Something in his tone and the look in his eyes made the breath catch in Bella's throat. He was so confusing, she thought, standing before him uncertainly. One moment he was almost formal in his politeness, and the next he easily made her blush.

She decided to change the subject as quickly as she could.

"Your grace, do you feel well enough to have some company for a few minutes?"

The duke's eyes gleamed, and she had the feeling that he found her attempt to divert him amusing.

Pushing himself further up on the pillows, he said, "Of course, who is it?"

"My cousin, Lady Beatrice Tichley, wishes to be made known to you," she informed him.

"By all means. I would be delighted."

Biting her lip, Bella hesitated before going to get Triss.

"What is it?" Westlake asked, seeing her pause.

"I think I should warn your grace that my cousin can be disarmingly outspoken on occasion," she explained.

"Then I would be even more delighted to make her acquaintance." The duke grinned.

Bella met his smile with her own before leaving the room. "Do not say I did not warn you," she tossed over her shoulder, and heard his deep laugh in response.

"He will meet you," Bella said to Triss upon returning to the front room.

Jumping up from her chair, Triss looked nervously at Bella.

"Oh, dear! I rather expected you to say no. I hope I don't make a cake of myself by giggling," she said with chagrin.

"You wanted to meet him; now come." Bella laughed lightly at her flighty cousin and led her up to her bedroom.

As the two ladies entered the room, the duke looked at Lady Beatrice with interest. He saw some family resemblance between the two young women, mostly in the shape of their eyes and the height of their cheekbones.

That was where the resemblance ended, he noted. Lady Beatrice was several inches shorter than Bella and had golden blond hair instead of dark. Her features were delicate and elegant, but he definitely detected an impish light in her vivid blue eyes.

Lady Beatrice suddenly sank into a full court curtsy beside the bed.

Taken aback, the duke looked over the lady's collapsed figure to Bella. After rolling her eyes heavenward, Bella stepped forward.

"Your grace, may I present Lady Beatrice Tichley?"

"I am pleased to meet you, Lady Beatrice," the duke said in mock formality. "Won't you both please be seated?"

Wobbling a little on her way back up, Triss gave the duke her most dazzling smile. Triss proceeded to seat herself in the rocking chair nearest the duke, while Bella pulled out the chair that belonged to the little desk.

"Your grace, we are so glad that you are so much improved. You had us all quite worried."

"Did I?" He looked at the petite blonde with undisguised amusement. "But I have had such a good nurse that it is no wonder I am improving so quickly."

"Oh, indeed, our dear Arabella is one of the most capable young ladies of my acquaintance," Triss replied.

"But she does expect me to take too many naps." The duke looked past Triss to give Bella a mischievous grin.

"I own that my cousin can be a bit bossy at times." Triss leaned forward and said this in a conspiratorial whisper.

"So it's not just a penchant she directs toward me, then?"

"Oh, no! Bella has always been that way. She is a most curious creature. The rest of the Tichleys have always been an easygoing lot—but Bella likes to manage everyone. She must have a plan for everything, while the rest of the family enjoys spontaneity. In the village she is known as 'the correct Miss Tichley,'" she explained to the avidly listening duke.

"All the Tichleys can't be loons, Triss," Bella said sweetly to her cousin, suppressing a laugh at the duke's expression.

"Oh, fiddle-faddle, Bella," Triss said with a touch of petulance, for she so wanted to appear sophisticated in front of the duke.

"I shall be making my curtsy this spring, your grace." Triss turned back to the duke. "I am sure you will be able to direct me to the most fashionable modiste in London?"

Bella gave an inward groan at Triss's obvious attempt to receive some sort of invitation from the duke.

"I shall give you the direction of my sister, Lady Edgeton. She is all the kick and thinks of little else but clothes and bonnets and such," the duke offered generously.

"How kind!" Triss clapped her hands together in her excitement.

"And what of you, Miss Tichley?" The duke directed his gaze to Bella. "Will you be going to town for the Season?"

"Bella loathes the idea of a Season," Triss piped in before Bella had a chance to respond to the duke's query. "She has *plans* here in Mabry Green." Triss giggled at her own play on words.

"Do you not wish to enjoy the delights of London, Miss Tichley?" The duke pursued his line of questioning because he had never met a young lady who did not wish to make her come-out.

"I own that the idea of the theater and museums is sometimes tempting, your grace, but other than that, London holds little appeal for me," she explained.

The duke held his gaze on the serene beauty of Bella's face, thinking again that she was an extremely unusual young woman.

"Your grace, you must endeavor to feel better very

quickly," Triss said, calling his attention back to her, "for my mother wishes to invite you to dine with us at Penninghurst Park."

"I shall be delighted anytime," the duke replied.

"Capital! I shall inform my mother," Triss said.

"Not until Dr. Pearce gives his consent," cautioned Bella.

"See what I mean?" Triss beamed at the duke, quite pleased with herself. "The correct Miss Tichley."

Again the duke looked past Lady Beatrice to Bella's composed expression and wondered how accurate the title really was.

Chapter Eight

A day later, Bella took pity on her pale patient and offered to help him out to a low chair in the garden. "There is not much to look at," she apologized. "Spring has not yet arrived, but the day is not too chilly and we will wrap you in blankets."

She had said this to him as if she were offering a treat to a child.

The duke said nothing for a moment. He looked up at her as she stood in the doorway. She was quite lovely, he thought. With her dark hair and stormy blue eyes, she had a sultry, haunting beauty that was most appealing. He was almost tempted to start a flirtation with her.

Two things stopped him. For one, despite her beauty and obvious intelligence, it was quite apparent that she was a simple country lass and would probably mistake his attentions. The second reason was that she would probably laugh at him outright.

Besides, it was dashed difficult to flirt when he could barely stand by himself, he thought with growing impatience at his own weakness.

"Thank you. It would be pleasant to be out-of-doors for a while."

The gentle smile on Bella's face stilled at the formality of his tone. Frowning slightly, she moved across the room to help him as he struggled to his feet.

"Take your time. Remember what the doctor said. You

mustn't overexert yourself," she cautioned as she stood close enough so that he could lean on her with his right arm.

Very slowly they made their way out of the bedchamber. The duke did his best not to lean too heavily on Bella. It was humiliating enough for a man renowned for his physical prowess to have to depend on a slip of a girl to help him out of a chair, much less to walk across a room.

The duke was determined, despite his fatigue, to be as active as he could. He needed to get his strength back, he thought with grim resolution.

Bella said nothing as they slowly made their way.

Again Bella was surprised by the duke's height. She had grown used to his being prone. It was a bit startling to find that he was nearly a foot taller than she was.

By the time they reached the low wooden chair in the winter-barren garden, the duke was leaning heavily on Bella, despite his resolve. She could perceive that his breathing had grown labored during their walk.

As gently as she could, Bella helped steady him as he lowered himself into the chair. Her concern for him grew when she noticed how pale he had become.

"I won't be a moment, your grace. Enjoy the sunlight while I fetch some blankets for you."

Not trusting his voice to sound firm at that moment, the duke said nothing and only nodded as Bella turned swiftly and reentered the house. Again he cursed his weakness and tried to ignore the piercing throb in his shoulder and the light-headedness that seemed to increase every time he moved.

In spite of his discomfort, Westlake was glad to be out-of-doors. Shifting his weight in the chair, he looked around the garden with its dormant flower beds and leafless trees. He thought the gardens were well designed, and that the manor was decorated in refined taste, but was rather small. He estimated that the entire manor, kitchen and all, would fit into the great hall at Autley, with room to spare. No wonder he was beginning to feel claustrophobic, he thought.

But in spite of the close quarters, the Tichley family was

obviously happy, the duke concluded. Bella and Tommy laughed a lot and teased each other. Mr. Tichley played chess with both Bella and Tommy, and was obviously proud of his children. The duke very much admired the closeness they all displayed.

Bella interrupted these musings when she appeared next to him, arms laden with blankets.

"Here we are. You shall be more comfortable momentarily," Bella said brightly as she approached him.

As she knelt to tuck the blankets around his shoulders and legs, she thought again how romantic he looked, like a wounded lion.

"There. You can now enjoy the afternoon while I prepare our tea." She rose from her kneeling position and smiled at him.

The duke nodded and watched her return to the house. A moment later, he espied Tommy at the far end of the garden, near what he assumed was a chicken coop.

"Greetings, young Thomas. How fare you today?" he called to the boy.

Tommy smiled and approached the duke shyly. "I am well, thank you. I hope you are feeling better, your grace."

The duke looked at the solemn youngster for a moment, thinking how much he looked like his sister.

"Much better. How is Zeus? Your uncle tells me that you have taken on the responsibility of tending him. I warn you, he can be difficult."

"Oh, no, sir! He is a bit particular, but as long as he has had a good gallop in the morning, he is no trouble."

"Gallop? Do you mean to say that beast lets you ride him?" the duke questioned in a tone of mild surprise.

Tommy hesitated and tugged on his brown woolen coat nervously. Suddenly he worried that maybe he should not have taken the liberty of exercising the duke's horse.

"I apologize, your grace. I should have asked permission first," Tommy said, biting his lip.

"That would have been difficult, as I have been indisposed for a few days," the duke said with a deep chuckle. "I appreciate your care of Zeus. I am just surprised, and impressed, that he behaves with you. My best groom has a hard time handling a high-spirited blood like Zeus. Treat him as yours," he finished, leaning his head back on the wooden chair and pulling the blanket closer around him.

A relieved smile spread across Tommy's face. "Thank you very much, your grace."

Behind Tommy, in the distance, coming across a low hill, the duke noticed a horse and rider approaching.

Tommy looked over his shoulder to see what the duke was looking at.

"That is Robert Fortiscue, Bella's beau," Tommy informed him.

The duke straightened his shoulders.

Bella stepped out of the house bearing a tea tray and also took note of the rider approaching.

"Tommy, would you please bring us another teacup? We may have another guest." Bella set the tray on a low stone table before seating herself in the chair next to the duke's. "You are not feeling at all chilly, are you, your grace?" Bella asked her patient with concern.

"I am perfectly comfortable. Thank you, Miss Tichley," he said as firmly as he could. He did not say that his shoulder felt as if someone were taking a pickax to it every minute or so.

The rider had reached the garden, dismounted, and stepped through the gate, waving a greeting to them.

The Duke of Westlake, whose only rival in sartorial elegance had been Beau Brummell, immediately noticed the multitude of capes gracing the visitor's greatcoat. The sheer weight of the garment seemed to engulf the man, who, in the duke's opinion, obviously had not the height, nor the breadth of shoulder, to carry off such a fashion.

"I wonder that he doesn't topple over." The duke drawled this aside to Tommy, who had seated himself on a stool next to the duke.

Tommy hid his snigger behind his hand as Bella made the introductions.

"Forgive me if I don't get up, Mr. Fortiscue," the duke said to the newcomer.

"Not at all! Not at all, your grace." Mr. Fortiscue bowed deeply. "May I say that it is very good to see your grace up and about, so to speak."

"Thank you." Westlake briefly inclined his head as Mr. Fortiscue seated himself on a bench across from the duke and Bella.

"I am off to London next week," Mr. Fortiscue told them, without preamble. "I have business to attend to and I must also see my tailor." Robert gave the duke a familiar, conspiratorial grin. "We men of fashion must be slaves to our tailors on occasion. Eh, your grace?"

The duke looked at Mr. Fortiscue for a moment before responding. If he had encountered such a toad-eating parvenu at one of his clubs in London, he would have given him a very direct set-down. As it was, he would be nothing but gracious to anyone Miss Tichley welcomed to her home.

"Yes. Tailors can be as temperamental as artists," he finally responded.

"I have very definite opinions on fashion, which I am sure your grace will agree with," Robert stated as he accepted a cup of tea from Bella.

For her part, Bella was looking at Robert with some surprise. She had never seen this side of him before. He was being much too familiar with the duke, she thought, throwing a glance at the duke to see if he was offended. Bella was not much relieved to notice that the duke's expression was completely closed.

"I believe fashion," Robert continued, waving his hand in a flamboyant gesture, "is the main difference that separates humans from animals."

The duke raised one eyebrow at this statement.

"Egad. And here I always thought it had something to do with the size of our brains and the ever useful opposable thumb," Westlake said dryly.

Bella had to bite her lip to keep from laughing out loud. But Robert was not at all deterred from his dissertation.

"Fashion is a unique expression of human individuality. I am sure you agree."

"To be sure," the duke said obligingly.

"Especially for gentlemen," Robert continued. "I believe there is nothing more civilized than a gentleman of fashion."

"Especially for gentlemen? What about ladies of fashion?" Bella asked, thinking that this whole topic bordered on the absurd.

Robert sighed patiently. "I stand by my opinion, Miss Tichley. I believe there is nothing more civilized than gentlemen of fashion, such as the duke and me. And I will confess that I find ladies of fashion unnatural and annoying. That is why I have long admired your simple taste in dress, Miss Tichley."

"Really, Mr. Fortiscue. How can anyone find a lady of fashion annoying or unnatural?" Bella was becoming annoyed herself.

"I am very interested in Mr. Fortiscue's opinions," the duke stated, wondering what else Mr. Fortiscue would say to make himself ridiculous. "Please go on."

Mr. Fortiscue preened a little at the duke's approval.

"I believe it is unnatural for ladies to garb themselves in bright colors, as so-called ladies of fashion often do," he stated baldly, raising his cup to his lips with his pinky raised high. "I will use the animal world as an example. It is always the male of the species who is more beautiful. Take birds, for instance: the male always has the more elaborate, brightly colored plumage. So ladies of fashion, truth be told, are going against nature. I should never tolerate a wife of mine wearing colors more vibrant than my own."

"What a unique perspective you have, Mr. Fortiscue," the duke opined.

"I believe a lady should wear whatever color she deems flattering," Bella said firmly. She looked at Robert with a frown between her blue eyes. She had known him for most of her life and had had no notion that he subscribed to such fustian. She found this new side to him quite disturbing.

Having finally exhausted the subject of fashion, Mr. Fortiscue turned once again to the duke.

"Your grace, I have had the pleasure of touring the grounds of your magnificent estate some years ago. I am curious as to how it came to be named Autley?"

The duke shrugged. "I really have no notion; it has been called Autley for close to six hundred years." He had the casual self-assuredness of someone who could trace his ancestry back to William the Conqueror.

"Er . . . quite so," Mr. Fortiscue fumbled.

The conversation then turned to such mundane topics as the weather and farming, and soon Bella decided it was time to get her charge indoors.

"You must excuse us, Mr. Fortiscue. It is time for his grace to rest."

"Certainly, Miss Tichley. Your grace, I have enjoyed our visit and look forward to continuing our conversation when you are feeling better." Mr. Fortiscue executed a flourishing bow to the duke.

"I, too, look forward to our next conversation, Mr. Fortiscue," the duke replied with a slight smile.

After Mr. Fortiscue took his leave, Tommy announced he was going to Penninghurst Park to visit Zeus. Bella nodded and helped the duke back into the house. When they reached her room, the duke sat on the bed and Bella knelt to help him take off his boots.

Glancing up, Bella was slightly taken aback by a new, indefinable expression in the duke's eyes as he looked down at her. Dropping her gaze from his, she felt unaccountably disturbed.

"So, Miss Tichley, I am quite interested in your Mr. Fortiscue. Have you been acquainted long?"

"Yes, for many years," she replied as one boot came off.

"Oh? What an interesting fellow he is."

Bella looked up, suspecting she heard a hint of mockery in his tone.

"Mr. Fortiscue and I have an understanding, your grace," she said a little stiffly as the other boot came off. Despite Robert's rather foolish behavior earlier, Bella was still loyal to him.

Westlake looked down at the closed features of his lovely young nurse and felt something close to astonishment. It seemed incomprehensible to him that someone as obviously intelligent and sensitive as Arabella would be partial to an overweening coxcomb like Robert Fortiscue.

He continued to watch her for some moments as she placed his boots at the end of the bed.

"I confess I'm incredulous, Miss Tichley. You cannot possibly believe yourself in love with that . . . Mr. Fortiscue," he said with a disbelieving laugh.

As she straightened, it was Bella's turn to look at the duke with surprise.

"In love?" she repeated. "Of course I am not in love, your grace. Why do you say so?"

The duke looked at Bella with one arched brow raised. "I find you a most unusual young lady, Miss Tichley. It is my understanding from having two younger sisters that young ladies wish to be in love with the men they are going to marry."

Frowning at her patient, Bella wondered at the hint of censure she saw in his piercing eyes. She suddenly felt ill at ease discussing this topic with him. Seating herself in the rocking chair so he would not have to strain his neck to look at her, Bella took her time responding to him.

"In matters of marriage, I believe it is more important to be well suited than to be in love," she began as he continued to watch her closely. "I think it is more beneficial to the long-term harmony of the married couple if they determine to make themselves agreeable and treat each other with respect. If they have common interests, so much the better. These ingredients constitute a successful marriage, in my opinion," she finished.

"You astound me, Miss Tichley. I would say that what you just described would be an ideal relationship with one's solicitor or secretary, but not one's spouse."

Rocking slightly, Bella digested his words. "But surely, your grace, you would agree that in most cases the first flush of romantic love always fades? Wouldn't it be better to have started the marriage on a much sturdier foundation?"

Suddenly she recalled the tryst notes secreted in the pocket of his waistcoat and wondered at his talk of love in marriage.

"I agree that it would be unwise to marry in haste because of mere infatuation," he replied. "I know this from the unfortunate situation of my brother, James, who came to regret marrying his hen-witted, troublesome wife, Margaret, before his untimely death."

Bella was a little surprised, but touched, that he would share something so personal with her.

Seeing her expression, the duke smiled slightly. "Surely, Miss Tichley, it is obvious to me that your uncle and aunt love each other, so by what example do you form your opinions?" He returned to his first line of questioning.

"My uncle and aunt are an exception, as were my parents. But I, too, have seen any number of young couples over the years who have grown to keenly dislike each other's company after seeming so in love at first. Marriage should be entered into with the most sober and serious consideration, especially for a woman, whose very existence will be dependent upon her husband."

"And you believe you are considering your future with Mr. Fortiscue in a sober and serious light?"

"Very much so."

"I see. What in particular do you find appealing in Mr. Fortiscue?"

Bella looked down to examine her fingernails for a moment. "I am the only practical one in a family of mild eccentrics. I am sure you have noticed that my father lives in ancient Rome, and Tommy lives in the stable. My dearest friend and cousin, Triss, thinks of nothing else but making her come-out. My aunt and uncle Penninghurst, whom I adore, are afraid of their servants."

The duke's laugh was gentle with understanding.

"So," she continued, "a life with Mr. Fortiscue, here in Mabry Green, seems very peaceful to me."

She saw the amusement fade from his eyes.

"I see. When may I send you a wedding gift?"

Bella's gaze dropped before his.

"I am not quite sure. You see, Papa has not exactly given his consent."

Mr. Tichley's good sense went up in Westlake's esteem. The duke watched the soft flush rise to her cheeks and decided not to pursue the subject further.

"Forgive my intrusion into so personal a matter, Miss Tichley. You see, I look upon you and your entire family as new but dear friends—and am only concerned with your future happiness."

Bella was well aware of his gratitude for her care of him, but she also felt that during the last few days a friendship had been growing between them. So she was not offended by these personal questions.

"Thank you, Your Grace," Bella said, wondering why she was not more pleased at his declaration of friendship. "Was James your only brother?" she questioned gently.

"Yes. We were very close, as he was only two years younger than me," he explained as he readjusted his sling to a more comfortable position. "But he was always a wild one when it came to the horses. One night he rode out too late after too much port. I am the one who found him the next day."

Despite the neutral tone in his voice, Bella could sense that this was still a memory that pained him.

"But his son, Henry, and I are close. He grows more like his father every time I see him. I would like for Tommy and Henry to meet."

"I am sure that Tommy would enjoy meeting your nephew," Bella told him.

"My youngest sister, Louisa, is engaged to the Duke of Malverton. I am sure she, in particular, is happy that I am alive so that I may escort her up the aisle," he continued with dry humor.

Bella laughed and settled a little more comfortably in her chair. "Do you have any other siblings, your grace?"

"Yes, my sister Alice, Lady Edgeton. She has three little girls, Edwina, Diana, and Caroline. They are all charming and terribly spoiled."

"I am certain that their uncle has nothing to do with their being spoiled," she teased.

"Me? I would never dream of indulging my nieces and nephew," he replied with a smile.

Despite his being a peer of the realm, and a rather formidable one at that, Bella found that she quite liked what she was learning of the duke.

Chapter Nine

"Today is going to be a very long day for you, your grace. So I hope you will rest for the remainder of the afternoon until it is time to depart for Penninghurst Park."

Bella saw the duke's jaw tighten stubbornly at her request, and her heart sank. Although Dr. Pearce had approved this outing, he had also cautioned the duke about doing too much.

Westlake's wound was healing, he had pointed out, but the lead ball had caused deep damage, and there was still the risk of infection.

Bella had not been in favor of accepting the invitation for dinner when the footman had arrived with the note from her aunt. But the duke had insisted that he was feeling well enough for the short trip, which was less than two miles, to the Park.

Bella did not acquiesce until the doctor had arrived, examined the duke, and grudgingly given his consent to the outing.

"Miss Tichley, I am feeling quite fit and am in no need of a nap." The duke's slight smile softened the authoritative tone in his voice.

Bella had given up with a shrug, and smiled to herself at the change that was coming over the duke. He was starting to sound more and more regal, though it was still difficult for her to see him as anything other than her patient.

Later in the day, as she was drying her hair by the fire

after her bath, it suddenly occurred to her that very soon the duke would be well enough for the journey back to his home.

An inexplicable sadness touched Bella at this thought, for she knew that they would probably never meet again.

She was thoroughly enjoying his company, she mused as she combed her still-damp tresses. The duke was very well-read and very knowledgeable on any number of subjects. She felt he enjoyed their debates on current political issues, and she found that gratifying. The duke was also very witty.

But it was apparent that he was growing increasingly impatient with his convalescence, and must be anxious to return to his life. It was also time for her to resume the normal routine of her days. Yes, she would miss him, she decided, as she began to twist her hair into its usual coil on the back of her head.

As she was deciding what gown to wear for the evening, Bella recalled Robert's objection to ladies wearing vibrant colors. Making a face, she resolutely put the simple gown she had chosen back, and pulled a different gown from the wardrobe.

This choice was also a simply made gown, though the neckline was a little lower than she normally wore. Triss had insisted that it was quite the latest fashion when she had had it made several months ago. The dress was made of sapphire blue *berege,* and Bella thought the color flattered her eyes.

As she finished dressing, her thoughts again went to Robert. There really was no way of avoiding the truth, she admitted to herself. She did not feel the same about him.

It was very odd that something as simple as a discussion about fashion could cause so material a change in her opinion that she could no longer consider a future with him. She also considered the duke's words about a marriage needing more than respect and common interests to be a success.

Bella pulled a string of pearls that had belonged to her mother from a silk bag and fastened them around her neck. What was even stranger about this momentous decision was that she was not in the least upset about her change of plans where Robert was concerned.

Maybe she was a little disappointed, she thought. After all, she had spent a number of years planning a future with Robert Fortiscue. But no longer. At least nothing as formal as an engagement had been announced, Bella mused with relief.

Papa will certainly be happy, she thought a little wryly.

After tying the ribbons to her black chamois slippers, Bella looked at her reflection one more time and was satisfied that she was presentable. She left the small dressing room after collecting her black satin cape, sure that her uncle's coach was waiting to take them to Penninghurst Park.

Upon entering the sitting room, she found Papa and Tommy waiting. They were dressed in their best clothes; Tommy had even combed his hair, she noticed with approval.

"Where is the duke?" Bella asked after glancing around the room.

"He will be joining us momentarily," Tommy answered. "He certainly is particular about his clothes," he added.

Bella nodded. She was very curious to see what the duke would be wearing this evening.

It had caused quite a stir in her household when a coach had arrived that morning. Two footmen had brought in a trunk of clothes and other items the Dowager Duchess of Westlake had deemed necessary for her son's comfort. Tommy had been charged to perform valet duties.

"He had me help him tie his neckcloth three times. I still don't think he is satisfied," Tommy informed them in a loud whisper.

"Humph. Even my brother does not spend that much time on his appearance," Bella's father commented.

Looking at her father now, Bella was glad to see that he was wearing his neckcloth. One never knew what he might forget, she thought with some chagrin.

"The duke says a gentleman is known by how he ties his cravat," Tommy continued.

At a noise Bella turned, and the smile on her face froze at the sight of the duke as he entered the sitting room.

He looked magnificent. In spite of the weight he had lost and the sling on his left arm, his evening clothes fit him to near perfection. His black tailcoat was made of some exquisite material, and his double-breasted waistcoat was snowy white. His neckcloth, she noted, was indeed a work of art, with its precise and intricate folds.

Her eyes traveled back up to his face. The slightly mocking amusement she was coming to know was evident in his eyes as he met her gaze.

He, in turn, swept her with his intense gaze from head to toe. Bella felt herself blushing at the boldness of his perusal. He suddenly seemed a complete stranger, she thought in confusion. She felt she hardly knew him, and avoided looking in his direction as they all went out to the carriage.

Papa and Tommy had already entered the vehicle when Bella looked back at the duke in the light of the coach lantern. Again she saw the intimate boldness of his gaze lingering upon her. Her blush intensified, and she did not know where to look or how to respond to the unfamiliar feelings his gaze aroused in her.

Now he was standing very close to her in the cool evening air, and her senses were assailed by the subtle smoky, woodsy fragrance she associated with him. She kept her eyes fixed on his cravat as she tried to calm the sudden quick beating of her heart, and yet she did not move away from him.

Then indignation came to her rescue as she recalled the two tryst notes she had found in his pocket.

"I wish you would not do that, your grace," she blurted before she thought better.

"Do what, Miss Tichley?" His husky voice was almost a whisper above her ear.

"Flirt with me," she said flatly. "I understand the practice is very fashionable, and in the circles you frequent such behavior is meaningless, but I am unused to it and it makes me uncomfortable."

"Meaningless flirtation?" he responded, giving her a look of amused indulgence. "And what would the correct Miss Tichley know of flirtation, meaningless or otherwise?"

"I have no personal experience, but I am aware of your penchant for meeting ladies in *atriums,*" she said archly, turning to walk the last few steps to the coach. "I know you are bored, your grace, but surely you can find another way to amuse yourself?"

To her great ire, she heard his deep laugh behind her.

"Atriums?" he said with another chuckle.

Bella stopped and turned to look back at him with annoyance.

"I wondered if you had happened upon those notes," he continued with amusement warming his cool eyes. "Oh, Arabella, you really are an innocent if you think assignations in atriums have any importance."

Afraid that he thought her a naïve fool, Bella lifted her chin to a haughty angle. "I have no desire to discuss such things with you, your grace," she said in what she hoped was a dismissive tone, and turned back to the carriage.

"Miss Tichley, I do believe I have never been less bored in my life," he said just as she stepped into the coach.

Bella settled herself next to her father as the duke pulled himself into the conveyance and sat next to Tommy. Trying her best to avoid looking at the duke, she fussed with the drawstring of her reticule. She decided the best course she could take was to completely discard the exchange that had just taken place between them. After all, it was only meaningless flirting, she reminded herself harshly.

Yet as much as she tried to ignore him, she found his amused gaze directed upon her unaccountably disturbing.

Her uncle's coach was relatively new and well sprung, but the ride to Penninghurst Park proved more arduous than anyone expected, due to the deep ruts in the road caused by the recent rains.

As they traveled the few miles to the Park, Bella was growing deeply concerned for the duke, and was having second thoughts about this outing. She now could not help noticing how he had begun to wince as the coach jolted side to side. At one point Tommy was thrown against the duke, and they all heard his sharp intake of breath.

"Not to worry." He had dismissed the boy's profuse apologies. "I am quite well."

Bella knew they all released a collective sigh of relief when the coach pulled up to the large half-timbered Tudor mansion.

Goodson, the family's ancient butler, opened the door

and led the little group across the immense foyer to the drawing room, where Lord and Lady Penninghurst, Lady Beatrice, and their other guests, Lord and Lady Crayton, were enjoying an aperitif before dinner. Lord and Lady Penninghurst immediately set out to make the new arrivals welcome.

Bella hid a smile when her father presented the duke to her aunt, for it was apparent by the lady's somewhat flummoxed expression that she was quite bowled over by their imposing guest. He had much the same effect on plump Lady Crayton, who stared at the duke the way some people looked at museum exhibits.

The sight of Triss, standing behind Uncle David winking, and making head gestures to Bella as her father introduced Lord Crayton to the duke, caught her attention. When the gentlemen, including the duke, moved to stand before the fireplace, Triss came over, grabbed Bella's arm, and practically dragged her to the other side of the room.

"What is wrong with you? Why have you suddenly developed this tic?" Bella questioned her cousin, who was looking particularly angelic in an evening gown of pink satin.

"I must speak to you in private before we go in to dinner," Triss answered, looking around to make sure no one was close enough to listen. "What a day we have had here! Mother is about to have the vapors over the question of protocol. Here she is a countess and she has no notion of what to do with the duke," Triss said disgustedly.

Bella laughed at this, not in the least surprised. Her aunt and uncle had entertained the same group of people for the last thirty years, with little attention given to formalities. Any deviation from her normal mode would always throw her aunt into a fit of the worries.

"But what I really want to speak to you about," Triss continued, "is that Mother thinks that now that the duke is feeling a little better he should come here for the rest of his convalescence."

"I have never considered the idea," Bella replied in a surprised tone. "But would you not prefer him to be here? It would be much easier for you to practice your skills of flirtation on him this way."

Triss did not catch the tease in Bella's tone and shook

her golden curls vehemently. "I would much rather visit him at your home—Mother would constantly be shooing me from him if he were here," she explained.

Bella smiled wryly at Triss's logic and turned her head slightly to look at the duke across the room. Again it struck her how handsome he looked in his elegant evening attire.

At that moment the duke turned his head and met her gaze. Their eyes held for a moment, and Bella was not aware that she had been holding her breath until a slow, perceptive smile spread across his lips.

"I told Mother that it would be as if she were questioning your care of the duke if she invited him to stay here now. But she is afraid he will be insulted if she does not—so she doesn't know what to do," Triss continued.

Pulling her attention back to her cousin, Bella took a deep breath to stop her heart from beating so quickly. "Aunt Elizabeth will have to do what she deems best. I shall defer to her wishes in this matter."

Triss looked at her cousin and then quickly turned to look at the duke. A speculative gleam entered her pretty blue eyes.

"And another thing, Bella: Mother was all set to invite Mr. Fortiscue to join us this evening. But Father and I put our foot down, or is that feet? Anyway, we refused to have the duke's first outing ruined by having to endure Mr. Fortiscue."

Bella smiled at her cousin. "I have some news that will make you happy, Triss, dear. I have decided this very day that Mr. Fortiscue and I will not suit after all."

Triss gasped, looking at her cousin with undisguised pleasure. "Bella, you are not hoaxing, are you?"

"No, of course not," she said with a little spurt of laughter. "I have recently discovered that Mr. Fortiscue has some odd notions that I cannot abide."

"Heavens! You must tell me every detail of what has finally brought you to your senses where that sapskull is concerned."

"No, no. I shall save it for another time. We are being terribly rude, standing here in the corner whispering. Let us join the others."

Arm in arm, the two young ladies returned to the group,

where Triss proceeded to monopolize the conversation by regaling everyone with descriptions about her excitement over her impending come-out.

Bella caught the duke looking at her with an amused expression over his glass of champagne. She had the sudden feeling that they were sharing a private joke, and a warm feeling spread its way through her veins.

They were all saved from hearing a detailed description of Triss's court gown when Goodson opened the wide double doors that led to the dining room and announced that dinner was served.

Aunt Elizabeth froze in front of them all, momentarily at a loss as to the correct way to proceed at this point.

Very smoothly, the duke stepped froward and offered Lady Penninghurst his arm, while keeping up a light discussion on the excellent vintages of Lord Penninghurst's cellar.

Aunt Elizabeth smiled her relief as she and the duke led the little procession into the dining room, followed by Lord Penninghurst, Lord and Lady Crayton, Triss, Tommy, and, lastly, Bella on her papa's arm.

It was agreed that Lady Penninghurst had outdone herself in her preparations for dinner. The long dining table held a profusion of delicacies displayed as artistically as the servants could turn out. A pig had been roasted. Two pheasants had been killed and prepared for this occasion, and a multitude of side dishes were constantly being presented at each remove.

Bella was a little concerned at how little the duke was eating, but he did seem to be enjoying the evening.

No matter how the duke tried to turn the conversation from himself, the rest of his dinner companions always returned it to him. Especially Triss, who was asking many questions about London.

"Do you often go to the theater when you are in town, your grace?" she questioned.

"I do enjoy the theater, Lady Triss, and you may make use of my box whenever you wish when you are in town," he offered generously to the delighted young lady.

Bella smiled at his indulgence of her cousin. Though Bella was much farther down the table from the duke, she was becoming aware of how his eyes searched for hers over the candles. Again it seemed to her that they communicated a shared amusement over the behavior of the others.

Halfway through the meal, while Lord Crayton was retelling a favorite old chestnut about a past foxhunting experience, Bella could not help noticing how the duke was losing what little color he had. By the fourth course his cheeks had grown positively ashen, and she saw to her growing alarm that his hand shook slightly as he set his crystal wineglass back in its place with a definite clink.

Bella did not know what to do. She looked over to Triss to see if she had taken notice of the duke's distress. Their eyes met, and Triss briefly frowned her understanding of the situation.

The duke gave no other indication that he was not feeling well, and steadfastly tried to continue participating in the general conversation.

As soon as the meal was over, Bella gave her cousin a significant look. Triss, never one to be shy, jumped up before her mother could suggest that the ladies leave the gentlemen to their port.

"Why don't we all repair to the drawing room? It would be ever so much cozier, and we ladies would miss your masculine company too dreadfully if you stayed." She cast irresistible, beseeching blue eyes to her father and Lord Crayton, who both instantly agreed with her plan.

As they all rose and began migrating to the drawing room, Bella lagged back with the duke, allowing the others to move well ahead of them.

"Your grace, I fear this evening is proving too arduous for you," she told him gently.

The duke looked down into Bella's anxious eyes. In truth, he felt as if he were about to humiliate himself by fainting.

"Dash it, Bella, I hate being a bother, but I would like to return to the manor."

"Of course, your grace," Bella said quickly as Triss approached.

As if from a distance Westlake heard Lady Beatrice say, "Leave everything to me, Bella. Bring his grace into the antechamber across the hall to rest while I have the coach brought around."

Placing her arm around the duke's waist, thereby forcing him to lean upon her, Bella led Westlake into the antechamber. Soon he found himself lying on a soft leather couch in a room with burgundy velvet drapery.

"Please make my apologies to Lord and Lady Penninghurst."

Bella looked down at the duke's waxen features as his words faded away.

"He has fainted," Bella said worriedly to Triss. "I had a very bad feeling about this evening. It was much too soon for him to be out like this. It has only been a week since he was shot. And for the first few days he was barely conscious."

"As usual, you are right, Bella," Triss replied, chewing her bottom lip. "I still think it best that you return to the manor. It is obviously what he wants, and this way he will not be waking up in a strange place."

"You are right," Bella agreed, too distracted by her worry for the duke to catch the mischievous gleam in her cousin's eye.

"I will make your apologies to everyone, so do not worry."

"Thank you, Triss." Bella seated herself on the couch next to the duke's hip.

Triss stood by the door, watching the deep worry on her cousin's face, and a look of determination settled on her own features as she quietly slipped from the room.

Bella put her hand gently to the duke's forehead to check for fever, and was dismayed to feel how warm he was. His eyelids fluttered open and her gaze met the full intensity of his.

"I am sorry to be such a damned bother, Bella," he said, attempting a small grin.

"Hush," Bella said softly. "You are no bother. You are very brave. It was just too soon for you to attempt something this strenuous. You must listen to me and not be so stubborn in the future."

"I should like to listen to you in all things, Arabella," the duke said solemnly after a pause.

Inexplicably, Bella's heart seemed to skip a beat. After

a moment she found she could not pull her eyes from the intense beauty of his gray-green gaze.

Bella stayed very still for a very long moment. Suddenly she was keenly aware of every little thing about him. The clean angles of his handsome, chiseled features. The impossible length of his dark lashes. The heat of his hip pressed against hers.

His lips parted as if he were about to say something when a gentle knock intruded on the moment.

He watched with a feeling of satisfaction as a flush crept up the ivory of her cheeks while she breathlessly bade whomever was at the door to enter.

A footman opened the door and bowed quickly. "Lady Beatrice said I was to help his grace to the coach, miss."

"Thank you," Bella said as she rose from the couch. "We shall be home soon, your grace," she told the duke as she helped him to a sitting position.

The footman was young and strong and had no trouble helping the large yet weakened man from the house and into the waiting coach. As Bella and the duke settled in, Triss appeared at the open coach door.

"I will send Uncle Alfred and Tommy home later. Do not worry about anything," she said, and stepped back before nodding to the coachman to close the door.

As she watched the coach leave the drive, Lady Beatrice finally allowed the satisfied smile she had been keeping in check to escape.

Picking up the skirt of her beautiful pink evening gown, she skipped up the steps back into the house and to the salon, where her papa was watching Uncle Alfred and Lord Crayton play chess by the fireplace. Her mama and Lady Crayton were seated at the card table, playing piquet.

She did not concern herself with Tommy; he had disappeared a while ago, and she assumed he was in the stable, as usual.

"Mother, dear," she said, "his grace has asked me to extend his apologies, but as he is feeling quite fatigued you will have to continue to enjoy your evening without him."

"Oh? Oh!" Lady Penninghurst said, startled by this turn of events, and not sure how to proceed.

"Not to worry, Mother," Triss continued. "I have taken care of everything. The duke is safely tucked away in the blue guest chamber upstairs," she lied cheerfully.

"Oh," Lady Penninghurst said again, and laid her cards down on the table. "Shall I go to him?" She hesitated.

"No need," Triss said, seating herself on a small settee near the card table. "He said he did not wish to disturb your evening, as the night is still young. He shall ring if he needs anything. I have sent Mrs. Harris to him with a hot brick. You and Lady Crayton continue your game. His grace would be embarrassed if he thought he was causing a disturbance."

Biting her lip, Lady Penninghurst looked over to her husband, still not sure of how to proceed when hosting a duke.

"He did look peaked at dinner, my dear. Let him rest," Lord Penninghurst said, and turned his attention back to the game.

"I agree, Elizabeth," Lady Crayton said. "Besides, it's your turn," she said pointedly, for she was keen on cards.

Lady Penninghurst smiled her relief and picked up her hand of cards. "Thank you, Beatrice, for seeing to the duke's comfort."

"You are welcome, Mother." Triss smiled sweetly at her mother and Lady Crayton.

"I must say, the duke is certainly not what I expected," Lady Crayton said after making another discard.

"How so?" Triss asked with keen interest.

"Lord Crayton and I were in London several Seasons ago, and the town was full of gossip about the dukes of Westlake and Severly. They are purported to be the best of chums, you know. Anyway, Lord Crayton and I do not move in the same circles as the duke, but the tales were very clear that the duke had a shocking reputation as a highflier and a rogue. Am I not correct, Crayton?" she called across the room to her husband.

"What? Oh, yes, m'dear," Lord Crayton said, glancing up briefly from the chessboard. "Veritable rakehell was the consensus."

"That so?" Alfred Tichley asked. "Well, he certainly has been a complete gentleman since we have known him."

The conversation ceased while the chess game continued

and the ladies became involved in their card game. Triss remained silent.

"Beatrice, where is my daughter?" Uncle Alfred called a little while later, pausing before making his next move.

"Bella?" Triss said with supreme innocence. "She decided to return to the manor. She's been very tired of late, what with taking care of the duke and all."

"She did not wish to say good-bye?" Lady Penninghurst frowned at her daughter over her cards, for she found this lack of attention to manners very unlike Arabella.

Squelching her growing nervousness, Triss turned her clear blue eyes to her mother. "I told her I would say her good-byes. She did not want Uncle Alfred to feel he had to return home early also, so she just decided to slip out. You know Uncle rarely has the pleasure of playing chess with Papa or Lord Crayton." She whispered this last bit to the ladies for good measure.

"Of course." Lady Penninghurst nodded her understanding. "My niece is the most thoughtful of creatures," she stated to Lady Crayton, who agreed wholeheartedly before discarding a card.

Triss sat back in her chair, doing her very best to suppress a self-satisfied smile.

Chapter Ten

The next morning was clear and bright at Penninghurst Park as Lady Beatrice breezed into the large and formally appointed breakfast room.

She was humming a happy little tune as she first kissed her mother's cheek, then moved to her father and kissed him on the top of his head, as he was engrossed in his newspaper.

Continuing to hum, she went farther down the highly polished table to kiss her uncle good morning and give a cheery wave to Tommy.

Just as the footman was about to pull out a chair for her, Lady Triss suddenly gave such a piercing shriek that her mother dropped her teacup and Tommy covered his ears.

"Good heavens! What is the matter with you, Triss?" Lord Penninghurst shouted at his only offspring as she stood staring at her astonished uncle with an expression of growing horror.

"Uncle Alfred! What are you doing here?" she exclaimed.

Alfred looked from his niece's horrified expression to his brother and sister-in-law, then back to his niece.

"What has you so upset, my dear?"

"Never tell me that you did not return home last night!"

"No, I stayed here last night," her uncle said calmly. "Our chess game went quite late, and as the duke is staying at the Park, I decided I might as well stay too."

"Oh, no! Oh, no!" Triss sank down into the side chair as the enormity of the disaster began to sink in.

Lady Penninghurst slowly rose from her chair, now quite worried at this unprecedented behavior from her daughter.

"Triss, you are worrying us. What is the matter?" her mother begged.

"The duke . . . The duke . . ." Triss stopped, for she did not even know how to begin.

"The duke has not rung yet this morning. Aunt says to let him rest," Tommy informed her in an attempt to be helpful.

Drawing her hands up to her cheeks, Triss looked at each one of her relatives. They in turn were looking at her as if she were a Bedlamite. Her thoughts went in circles until she was almost dizzy with trying to come up with some story—any story, save the truth.

But after a moment she realized there was nothing else she could do but confess her shocking behavior.

"I thought you would return home last night," she began a little desperately. "I thought I would give Bella and the duke an hour or two to speak with each other." She paused for a breath.

"Triss, whatever are you babbling about? Just tell us what is wrong," her father demanded.

"I saw no harm. . . . I never thought you would stay the night, Uncle Alfred," she stressed.

"Get to the point, young lady," Lord Penninghurst cut in with uncharacteristic harshness.

Taking a huge breath, Triss plunged ahead. "I sent Bella and the duke home in the coach after dinner last night. I told a whopping falsehood when I said the duke was upstairs. But truly, it never occurred to me that Uncle Alfred and Tommy would not go home as well," she said in a rush.

Complete silence fell on the room as each of her relatives took in her statement.

Triss looked at the dawning shock and accusation on their faces. Her eyes silently beseeched them to understand and forgive.

In the dead silence, Uncle Alfred laid his napkin very precisely next to his plate. Then he pushed back his chair and slowly stood. He looked at his niece, and she saw the red flush rising from his cheeks to the tops of his ears. "Do you mean to say that my daughter has spent the entire night alone with the duke?"

His tone was so sharply cold that Triss shivered. She could only nod her response. For once in her life, her voice failed her.

"David." Alfred turned to his brother. "Please have a horse waiting for me in five minutes." He began to stride to the breakfast room door when Tommy jumped up and started to follow. "No, Thomas, you must remain here," his father told the boy.

Tommy sat back down in his chair and looked at Triss with tear-filled, reproachful eyes before turning to look pleadingly at his aunt. "Is Bella in very bad trouble, Aunt Elizabeth?"

Lady Penninghurst did not answer her nephew, but instead turned to her husband. "David, go with him," she urged. "You must try to keep tempers from getting out of hand."

"Of course I'm going with him," the earl said, and quickly followed his brother out of the room.

"Aunt Elizabeth?" Tommy said again, beginning to sniffle.

Lady Penninghurst turned outraged eyes to her daughter.

"Why, for the love of heaven, would you want to do something like this? Do you want to see Bella ruined?"

"No, Mother, of course not! I just wanted Bella and the duke to have a chance to talk. I am so sorry."

"Sorry! I can listen to you no longer. Leave my sight!" her mother said vehemently. "You have always been spoiled and selfish, and that, I admit, is the fault of me and your father. But until this moment I never thought that you were actually bad. Go to your room, and for once do not think of yourself and make excuses. Think on what your foolish actions have wrought."

Triss stood before her mother with her head bowed. She was thinking of Bella as she closed her eyes in shame. A moment later she lifted her head and looked again at her mother's outraged face. "Yes, Mother," she said quietly, and fled the room.

Chapter Eleven

Bella awakened that morning a little later than was her usual time. Sitting up in bed, she smiled at the bright morning sunlight streaming into the bedchamber.

For reasons she refused to examine, Bella felt happier than she had in months. Maybe because she sensed a hint of spring in the air, she decided.

After rising and donning a plain gray dress, she left the room without bothering to put her hair up, simply tying it back with a ribbon. Entering the kitchen, she decided to make everyone a hearty breakfast, and set about rattling pots and pans. But upon hearing a noise coming from the other room, she went to investigate.

It was the duke, dressed in breeches, white lawn shirt, blue waistcoat, and shiny black Hessian boots.

"Good morning, your grace," Bella said a little shyly as she curtsied.

"Good morning, Arabella. Please forgive my lack of a neckcloth." He gestured to his sling ruefully. "I still find it difficult to tie the blasted thing."

"Not at all." Bella waved away his concern. "You should know by now how informal we are. Please sit down." She gestured to the dining table. "I am about to make us all breakfast. Would you like to start with a cup of chocolate and toast, your grace?"

"If you will join me." He smiled lazily at her and seated himself at the table.

He looked much better this morning than he had when they had returned to the cottage last night, Bella observed as she poured the chocolate into her late mother's delicate cups. Last eve, after she had helped him to his room and assisted him in removing his boots, he had lain back on the bed and had been asleep almost before his head had reached the pillow. She had shaken her head over his stubborn unwillingness to heed her warning that he was attempting too much, too soon.

"Papa and Tommy must have returned from the Park very late last night. I did not even hear them come in," Bella told the duke, more to make conversation than anything else, for something about the expression in his gray eyes was making her exceedingly nervous.

She could not explain her own feelings at this moment. She had spent hours upon hours alone with the duke, she reminded herself, and in much more intimate circumstances than sharing toast and chocolate.

Yet her heart still fluttered. She felt a flush rising to her cheeks and did not know where to look. Maybe it was the way he was looking at her now that caused her to view him so differently. Or was it the way he had looked at her over the candles last evening? She recalled how his gaze had swept her from head to toe before they had gone into dinner.

Rather desperately, she reminded herself that he was only trying to stave off his growing boredom. She reminded herself that he must want to return to his ladies in atriums.

"What is it, Bella?" the duke asked quietly.

Bella almost jumped out of her chair at the sound of his deep voice. "Nothing," she said a little breathlessly.

Westlake shifted to a more comfortable position in the chair, leaned back, and crossed his legs at the ankles. "I have come to know a little of your character, Arabella. Something is disturbing you."

For one wild moment Bella almost said, *You*. Desperately, her mind searched for a way to change the subject.

"I must get Papa and Tommy up. It is unlike them to sleep so late," she said in a rush before jumping up and heading down the hallway to the staircase. After receiving no response to her knock at her father's door, Bella opened the door and poked her head in.

"Papa?"

Opening the door all the way, Bella stepped into the room and immediately noticed the perfectly made bed. She stood stock-still as her eyes scanned the room. "What on earth?" She turned and left the room, a puzzled expression on her face.

As she was making her way down the hall to Tommy's room, she heard a knock at the front door and wondered if Papa and Tommy had risen very early and were now returning home. But they wouldn't knock, she thought, dismissing the notion.

Her mind searched for some logical reason for the unslept-in bed.

She went back downstairs and found the duke had answered the knock and was now standing in the middle of the room with Robert Fortiscue.

"Mr. Fortiscue," Bella said in surprise.

The gentleman doffed his brown beaverskin hat and stared at the duke's bare neck.

Bella crossed the room to stand next to Westlake, and continued to look at Robert with a questioning look on her face.

Mr. Fortiscue switched his assessment of the duke to Bella's unbound locks.

"Miss Tichley!" Mr. Fortiscue said, placing a hand on his hip. "I take leave to tell you how shocked I am at your behavior. This is outside the bounds of all decency."

A dreadful feeling washed over Bella as Mr. Fortiscue's harsh words and expression of contempt began to sink in. Papa and Tommy must not have come home from Penninghurst Park last night, she surmised. How could this have happened? And how could Robert know? Her mind raced to solve this terrible puzzle.

Mabry Green was a small village, and she knew very well that news, especially gossip, traveled quickly. She also knew that the housekeeper at Penninghurst Park was the sister of the butler at Oakdale.

That's it! Bella thought in horror as she made the connection. What on earth could have prevented her father and Tommy from coming home last night? she wondered desperately.

"And you, *your grace,*" Mr. Fortiscue continued shrilly. "A man in your position, taking advantage of—"

"Stop your idiotic prattling, you jackanapes." The duke's icy tone stopped Mr. Fortiscue midsentence.

"Oh, your grace," Bella choked out, turning to the duke. "A terrible misunderstanding has occurred. My father and brother did not return home from Penninghurst Park last night."

"The devil you say," the duke said.

Bella saw the astonishment in his eyes as he bit out the words.

"Do not play coy." Mr. Fortiscue's voice had grown even more shrill as he turned on Bella. "To think that I ever considered you suitable to take my mother's place at Oakdale."

"Get out." The duke barked the order at the blustering gentleman.

"How dare you speak to me so, when you are grievously beyond the pale!" Robert put his hand dramatically to his chest.

"Get out before you find yourself on your backside in the drive." The duke took a threatening step toward the blond man.

Gasping, Mr. Fortiscue widened his eyes in fear. With one last outraged sputter, he turned on his heel and practically ran from the room, leaving the front door open.

A moment later Bella and the duke heard his horse leaving at a fast trot. She sank down on the settee, her mind reeling from the possible ramifications they were facing.

The duke sat down in a chair opposite Bella and looked at her intently.

"Am I to understand that we have spent the night without anyone else in this house?" he asked her quietly.

"It appears so," Bella said helplessly.

"And how would Mr. Fortiscue be privy to this information?"

Bella explained the connection between the housekeeper at Penninghurst Park and the butler at Oakdale.

Nodding, the duke said, "I am quite familiar with how servants can gossip."

Bella agreed, and they both fell into silence for some minutes, while Bella tried to recover from the shock of Robert's attack.

"Your father will be home soon," the duke continued after some thought.

Bella felt a bubble of hysterical laugher rising in her throat. How could he be so calm? she wondered. This was beyond horrible. Within the hour, she knew, the entire village would be apprised of the shocking fact that Miss Arabella Tichley and the Duke of Westlake had spent the night quite alone.

Of course, she also knew it would not matter to the village gossips that the event was completely innocent.

"Arabella."

Bella's head went up at the sound of her sharply spoken name, and she looked at the duke with anxiety-filled eyes.

"No matter what happens today, I want you to know that everything will be all right," he told her.

Bella was too distraught to take in his words.

At the sound of fast-approaching hooves, Bella jumped up from the settee and rushed to the window.

"It is my papa and my uncle," Bella informed the duke in growing alarm. "How could this have happened?" She practically groaned the question.

Suddenly galvanized into action by panic, she turned and looked at the duke sitting in his shirtsleeves. "I'll get your neckcloth and jacket! I'll put my hair up," she said in sudden inspiration. "Get up! We can't be seen lounging," she said as she moved across the room with frantic movements.

The duke remained seated. As she passed by his chair, he reached out and put a restraining hand on her arm. "Arabella, it is too late. We have done nothing wrong, but that does not matter under the circumstances."

Bella looked down at the duke's hand on her arm as she listened to his words. "What are you saying? Of course it matters. We will talk with Papa and Uncle, and all will be explained. There will be gossip in the village because of Robert, but that does not signify."

The duke did not respond and only gave her a slight, enigmatic smile.

Bella sat down again, feeling as if it took an eternity for her father and uncle to cross the last few yards of the drive.

Her father was the first to enter, and she immediately saw that he had again forgotten his hat. He strode quickly into the middle of the room shouting her name.

"I am here, Papa," Bella said quietly from her chair.

Her father turned to her, and Bella saw an expression on his face that she had never seen before. It was a combination of anger, disappointment, and deep concern.

Bella rose slowly, and so did the duke.

"His grace and I have just discovered that you and Tommy did not return last night. Was something amiss?" she asked, deciding to take the initiative.

The duke, standing next to Bella, looked at her with admiration at her willingness to try to brazen the whole thing out.

Uncle David entered then, and Bella saw that his expression was as grim as her father's.

"We thought that the duke stayed at the Park last night," her father informed her in a flat tone.

"But why? Triss knew we were returning to the cottage. She said she would make our apologies to my aunt and uncle, and send you and Tommy home later."

"We will talk about Triss another time," her father replied. "The fact of the matter is that Tommy and I were at the Park and you and the duke were here."

"I want you to know, Mr. Tichley, that nothing remotely improper occurred here last night," the duke broke in, his tone firm.

"Thank you, your grace." Alfred Tichley inclined his head briefly to the younger man.

Bella let out a sigh of relief at her father's acceptance of the truth.

"But you know as well as I do, your grace, that this is very serious business," her father continued.

From the corner of her eye, Bella saw the duke incline his head in agreement. Bella looked at her father in renewed alarm.

"Yes, Papa," Bella said quickly. "But no harm has been done."

"No harm!" Alfred and his brother shouted in unison.

Uncle David stepped forward when it became obvious that his brother was at a loss for words.

"Arabella, we as a family have always spoken plainly to each other. And I will speak plainly now." He paused to look at the duke briefly for a moment, and then turned back to his niece. "You are ruined. In a matter of days your name will be a byword for all that is unsavory."

Bella stared at her uncle in stunned silence, almost unable to comprehend the ugliness of his words. "Oh, no, Uncle," she was finally able to choke out. "Surely that is an exaggeration. Everyone in Mabry Green knows me. Everyone knows I would never do anything sordid."

Her father regained his voice and threw up his hands before starting to pace the room. "Bella, shortly it will be known throughout the county that you spent the night with a rakehell of the first consequence. No offense, your grace," her father bit out to the duke.

"None taken, Mr. Tichley," the duke stated quietly, with a slight inclination of his head.

Bella was peripherally aware that since her father and uncle had started speaking, the duke had not taken his eyes from her face.

She cast a quick glance at him and saw his formidable expression. Her heart began to beat even faster. "But Papa, I don't care what anyone says. I know the truth."

Her father stopped his pacing for a moment to point his finger at her angrily.

"Of course you care. Think, Bella. From this moment on no one will receive you. How will you bear the whispers when you venture to the lending library?" He laughed bitterly, and continued. "Do you recall all the offers I have rejected on your behalf? Do you not think those families will gloat at your downfall? This kind of scandal is never forgotten. You shall be shunned and despised."

As hard as she tried, Bella could not prevent the tears from coming to her eyes and spilling over at her father's harsh words. "Papa, please," she said, as she began to cry.

"Mr. Tichley, it is time to call on the vicar," the duke broke in with a note of quiet authority. "I shall arrange for a special license, which will naturally take a few days. The nuptials can take place Friday morning."

Bella turned to stare at the duke in complete shock. She seriously doubted that she had heard him correctly.

"We shall be ready on Friday, your grace." Bella saw her father's expression change to grim satisfaction. "Bella, you will return to the Park with your uncle until the ceremony. Your aunt will attend you."

"No, Papa, wait," Bella said desperately, raising her hands in supplication. "This is ridiculous. There has been a miscommunication and nothing more! Your grace"—she turned pleading eyes to the duke—"you cannot be serious. You must see how preposterous this whole notion is. This is unnecessary."

"On the contrary, Miss Tichley. It is very necessary," the duke said in a deep, decisive tone.

Chapter Twelve

"It is time, Bella," Aunt Elizabeth said quietly to her niece.

Seated at a dressing table, Bella lifted her head and looked at her aunt with anxiety-filled yet tearless eyes.

Without saying a word, or even glancing at herself in the mirror, Bella rose and followed Aunt Elizabeth out of the pretty blue-and-cream bedchamber she had been occupying for the last four nights.

The two women silently made their way through the long hall, down the staircase, and across the foyer to the front door.

Lady Penninghurst looked at her niece with a great deal of worry evident on her patrician features. "Wait, Bella." Aunt Elizabeth put a hand on Bella's arm as the solemn girl was about to descend the wide steps leading to the graveled circular drive.

Bella paused, and looked questioningly at her aunt.

"Let me straighten your bonnet ribbon," Lady Penninghurst said. Not that the bow under Bella's chin needed adjusting, but Aunt Elizabeth needed a moment of normalcy during this very trying morning.

"You look beautiful, my dear," Aunt Elizabeth whispered.

Bella's eyes closed for a moment as she stood before her aunt. She was dressed in a lavender gown and matching pelisse with blond lace at the neck and at her cuffs. Bella had fervently resisted wearing this ensemble today, but her aunt had insisted.

"Arabella, I will not have you looking like a waif on your wedding day," Lady Penninghurst had said earlier, when Bella had stated she would be wearing her old gray gown.

"This is not my wedding day," Bella had responded hotly, pausing in her anxious pacing for a moment. "The duke and I are being forced into this sham marriage because of archaic and barbaric notions of propriety."

"Bella, please let us not argue this again." Aunt Elizabeth sighed. "We must be at the church in less than an hour. I insist you wear your lavender gown and let my maid do something with your hair."

She had looked at her niece's stricken features and softened her tone. "Do not you see that your honor is at stake? There is no other answer but to wed the duke and have the protection of his name. You should be pleased that he is a man of principle and is willing to do the right thing."

Bella snorted derisively at this, and resumed her pacing. "With my father and uncle looking as if they would call him out if he didn't, I doubt the duke felt he had any choice in the matter," Bella replied.

But Bella knew that no amount of pleading or arguing would do any good. She had tried everything she could think during the last few days to get everyone to see reason. She had written letters to her papa and uncle, which they ignored. She had cried and pleaded with her aunt to make her uncle David put a stop to this nonsense, again to no avail.

Yesterday, in a last desperate attempt to prevent this travesty, Bella had hastily written a note to the duke. In it she beseeched him to just leave Mabry Green and ignore her father and uncle. After charging one of the servants to take the note to the manor and wait for a reply, Bella had sat in her room and waited with the feeling that her nerves were stretched beyond her endurance.

It had seemed to take an interminable amount of time before the servant returned. She had torn the duke's note in her haste to read it, and to her dismay he had stated that they both must do the honorable thing. He had concluded the note by writing that he would see her at the church on Friday morning.

She had balled up the missive and thrown it across the room in desperate anger and frustration. At that moment she seriously contemplated running away—but very soon realized that there was nowhere for her to go.

In that moment Bella knew her fate was sealed. She was being forced to wed a man who was a gentleman by birth and rank, but whom she knew to be a rake.

Bella could not recall ever feeling so bereft or frightened.

So she had pressed her lips together and given in to her aunt's desire that she wear her best gown to this mockery of a holy ceremony.

"There," her aunt said, giving the bow a last tweak, bringing Bella back to the present.

Bella finally lifted her eyes and looked at her aunt.

"Please do not be so angry with us, Bella. We truly have your best interest at heart," Aunt Elizabeth said softly to her niece.

The short journey to the place where Bella and her family had worshiped all their lives was made in silence until the carriage pulled up to the wide wooden doors of the church.

"Bella, before you enter I should let you know that your uncle and I have given Beatrice permission to attend the ceremony," she told Bella with some trepidation.

Bella heaved an angry sigh. "Why not? She might as well see the culmination of her handiwork. But if she thinks I shall forgive her because we are in church, she is quite mistaken," Bella told her aunt with quiet vehemence.

After Bella had learned of Triss's deceitfulness, Triss had tried to explain and beg forgiveness numerous times. She had pleaded with Bella to open the bedroom door. She had banged on the bedroom door. She had slid notes under the bedroom door. But Bella would have none of it.

Her cousin's duplicitous behavior had cut so deeply, Bella could not imagine anything Triss could say that would make her feel any different toward her.

The most painful part of this estrangement was that Bella, though she would never admit it, missed Triss terribly. *How ironic,* Bella thought bitterly. The one person she would normally look to for comfort was the person who had caused this nightmare.

The carriage door opened and Bella saw that her father was standing outside the church doors, evidently waiting for them to arrive. Before exiting the carriage, she paused a moment and turned to look at her aunt. "My last remaining hope is that the church is empty," Bella said with a remnant of her old humor.

"I somehow doubt it, Bella, dear," Aunt Elizabeth said with a tight little smile.

Her father approached and first helped Aunt Elizabeth from the carriage. She whispered something to her brother-in-law before quickly slipping into the church.

Bella's father turned to her, and she met his solemn gaze before taking his outstretched hand, allowing him to assist her exit from the carriage.

Breathing in the crisp morning air fortified her as, without a word, he led her up the church steps.

Suddenly an icy calm descended over Bella's roiling emotions. For the first time since that horrible moment four mornings ago, Bella found a little hope. Somehow, some way, she would find a way out of this horrible mess, she vowed to herself resolutely.

It occurred to her that she certainly must have an ally in the duke.

Her heart lifted a little more as her father opened the church door and they entered the vestibule.

Bella latched on to the idea that the duke would help find a way to extricate them from such a misalliance. She had heard of the Church granting annulments under certain circumstances. Surely, together they could find a solution. Despite his stated willingness to do the honorable thing, the duke must be as eager as she to be free. After all, he had ladies to meet in atriums, she thought with some asperity.

She was pulled from her musings when she became aware that her father had stopped just inside the open doorway of the church.

His eyes were resting on her, and though his expression was still very solemn, there was something else in his gaze. "I am deeply pained that you should feel this animosity toward me, Bella, but I have faith that someday you will see that this was the honorable course to take."

Bella, with a bitter explanation, threw up her hands in dismay. "Oh, Papa, what does honor matter when I shall be miserable the rest of my life? It is not too late to stop this charade," she finished on a plea.

Her father's expression grew stern, and he put a hand on her elbow and drew her to the nave of the church. "No, Arabella. Do not make this more difficult than need be. After being in his presence for the last few days, I am assured that the duke will treat you with care and respect. He has accepted the necessity of this marriage with great dignity. You must try to emulate him on this," he said firmly, and moved forward.

Bella held back and again thought about picking up her skirts and running out of the church as fast as she could. Taking another deep breath, she dismissed the idea almost instantly. She knew in futile acceptance that there was no real solution in fleeing.

So Bella started the long walk down the aisle with her father. A moment later she heard the strains of a faint but familiar hymn being played on the church organ.

Looking down the long aisle of the beautiful Gothic church, Bella felt her heart clench at the splendor of the morning light streaming through the numerous stained-glass windows that graced her childhood place of worship.

Of all the dreams she had had over the years about her wedding day, Bella had never dreamed of a day like this. As they continued moving slowly up the aisle, Bella saw her aunt and uncle, Tommy, and Triss standing in the front of the church to her left. She quickly averted her eyes, lest they meet Triss's.

Keeping her gaze firmly fixed ahead, Bella saw that a profusion of ivy, white roses, and lilies covered the chancel rail. Their sweet fragrance reached her, and Bella wondered how her aunt had procured such a display this time of year, and why she had bothered.

Avoiding the inevitable as long as possible, Bella looked beyond the chancel rail to the vicar. He was staring fixedly down at the prayer book he held in his hands.

Closer they drew to the front, and Bella found herself

gripping her father's arm, trying to hold on to the calm that had so blessedly enveloped her earlier.

To her right, on the groom's side, a single female guest caught Bella's attention. As she and Papa passed the pew, Bella flicked a surreptitious glance to the lady. Bella took in her fashionable ensemble of a bishop's blue velvet pelisse over a paler bluish-pink gown. The lady's bonnet was an exquisite confection of blue velvet and exotic feathers, tilted at a fetching angle above a classically beautiful face.

In an instant, Bella's eyes met the lone guest's, and she felt a mortifying blush heating her cheeks at what this unknown woman must be thinking.

Bella had steadfastly avoided looking in the duke's direction, and now was a little surprised to see another man standing next to him at the altar. He was as tall as the duke, with coffee-colored hair and a handsome face with a short, jagged scar on the high plane of his cheek, which gave him the look of a pirate, despite his stern expression. Evidently this man was to act in the role of supporter to the duke, Bella concluded.

As the vibrating notes of the organ music faded to silence, Bella finally looked up at the duke as she and her father finally reached the steps of the altar. Still clutching her father's arm, she smelled the poignant scent of the roses and lilies all around her as she bravely looked at the man who was about to become her husband.

Her frightened gaze took in the duke. She immediately noticed that no sling marred the perfection of his bottle-green colored coat, but he held his left arm stiffly to his side. His nearly black hair only accented the extreme pallor of his complexion.

Frowning slightly, Bella thought he looked worse than when she had seen him last.

His expression was unreadable, but his intense gaze met and held hers for a moment before he moved to stand next to her, facing the altar.

The vicar cleared his throat and the ceremony began. Everything became a blur. Bella felt, rather than saw, when her father gave her away and moved to the front pew with the rest of her family. She was aware of repeating words after the vicar, but paid no heed to what they were until she heard the vicar say, "Repeat after me: I, Arabella Cornelia, take thee, Alexander Arthur Henry George, to be my wedded husband."

Her gaze flew to the duke's grave profile as she muddled his two middle names. A smile touched the corner of his mouth.

It was only when the duke placed a simple gold band on the third finger of her left hand that Bella feared her hard-won composure would fail her.

"With this ring I three wed, with my body I three worship, and with all my worldly goods I thee endow." The duke said these ancient words in a deep, firm voice, and Bella felt her hand shake in his.

In a daze Bella heard the vicar announce them man and wife, and she gulped in disbelief. There was brief, awkward pause, during which Bella prayed the duke would not attempt to kiss her. After a moment the vicar suggested that they remove to an anteroom to sign the papers.

The duke nodded, and he, Bella, the man with the scar, and the elegantly dressed lady all moved silently to a side door that led to a tiny room.

"Let's see, I believe everything is in order," the vicar said nervously as he handed Bella a quill.

Pausing before she signed her name, Bella scanned the documents and saw that the duke would be one and thirty in August. It was a good thing to know one's husband's age, she thought with a suppressed urge to laugh.

After the duke took the quill from her and signed "Westlake" in the proper place, he straightened, turned to her, and said, "Arabella, I would like you to meet my very good friends, the Duke and Duchess of Severly."

A little taken aback by the duke's use of her given name, Bella said hastily, "How do you do?" and managed a curtsy in the small room.

On her way back up, it suddenly occurred to her that a duchess probably did not curtsy to another duchess.

"We are very pleased to meet you," the Duke of Severly told her. Bella wondered at the sincere tone in his voice.

"We are indeed," the Duchess of Severly added with a gentle smile.

"Thank you," was all Bella was able to say.

She stood mutely next to Westlake as the duke and duchess added their signatures as witnesses to the papers. Dismally, Bella wondered if she would ever again have anything to say for herself.

After the formalities were completed, the five of them returned to the main part of the church, where Bella's family stood waiting, each with a solemn expression.

Westlake paused and looked down at Bella. He then offered her his arm; Bella looked at it for a moment before placing her fingers lightly upon it.

They proceeded to walk toward the back of the church, with the Duke and Duchess of Severly following behind.

Moments later the two couples emerged into the bright morning sunlight, leaving the haunting scent of roses and lilies behind.

Aunt Elizabeth and Uncle David soon came out of the church with Mr. Tichley and Tommy. Bella noted that Triss was the last to exit, and that she hung well back from the rest of the solemn group.

"If you would care to come to Penninghurst Park, I have breakfast awaiting us," Aunt Elizabeth hesitantly said to the group.

"We'd be delighted," the Duchess of Severly spoke up after a quick glance to her husband.

A barouche Bella had never seen, pulled by four perfectly matched bays, rolled up next to them. As the duke handed her into the vehicle, Bella was immensely relieved to see that the Duke and Duchess of Severly were joining them in the plush interior of the conveyance.

Glancing across the carriage to the other couple as they settled themselves, Bella could not help wondering what this noble pair must be thinking about the extremely odd ceremony they had just witnessed.

After all, her thoughts continued, the marriage of a duke should take place at Westminster Abbey, or some equally illustrious site, witnessed by hundreds of people, not just seven.

The tension was palpable as the four of them rode in complete silence for some minutes.

"My dear Duchess," the Duke of Severly said in a very formal tone.

Bella jerked her head up, startled to be addressed by the title.

"My wife and I," he continued, "wish to express to you our very deep gratitude for your care of our friend."

"Yes," the Duchess of Severly seconded, leaning forward a little. "Alex has told us how you and your brother saved his life."

Bella looked at the beautiful duchess and thought her smile was encouraging.

"Please call me Bella. But it was Tommy who found his grace. I just did what anyone would have done," she said simply to the imposing couple.

"But it was you who removed the slug. I think there are few women who would be brave enough to act so swiftly," Westlake inserted.

"I agree, you are a very brave lady, Bella," the Duchess of Severly said.

Looking over at the beautiful duchess, Bella thought there was a look of understanding in her gaze. Bella had the feeling that the duchess was not just referring to Bella's act of removing the ball from the duke's shoulder. "Thank you," she said in a whisper.

Casting a quick glance to Westlake's pale, gaunt features, Bella thought again how tired he looked.

Because she had refused to even accept that there would be a wedding, Bella had been unable to look beyond this day. Now she was eager to have a quiet moment with the duke so that she could share her idea of an annulment.

Annulment! She could not even comprehend that they were actually wed, much less contemplating an annulment. She dejectedly sank back in her seat.

The small group remained silent for the rest of the journey to Penninghurst Park, and was just as silent as they all filed into the breakfast room and took their seats.

What little conversation there was during the meal was very stilted. The sounds of forks and knives clinking against china seemed very pronounced to Bella. Pushing her food around on her plate, she kept her eyes averted from everyone.

As the meal was ending, Bella's panic grew. What was going to happen next? Maybe the duke would depart and leave her here in Mabry Green; she gave this new thought a great deal of hope.

At that moment the duke rose from his chair, and Bella held her breath.

"Mr. Tichley, Lord and Lady Penninghurst, I have much to be grateful to you for, and I thank you for your care and your hospitality," Westlake stated with obvious sincerity. "I beg your leave, for it is time that Bella and I depart for Autley."

Bella's stricken gaze went to his face. *Depart! No, no, no,* Bella repeated in her heart over and over; it was much too soon to depart.

Lady Penninghurst saw Bella's frozen expression, and turned to the duke with great concern.

"Surely, your grace, your departure can wait until the morrow? I am sure Dr. Pearce would advise you against such a long journey after so trying a day," she appealed to the duke.

"Thank you for your concern, Lady Penninghurst, but I believe it best that we, leave." His tone made it clear that he would not be dissuaded from his plan.

Bella finally looked at her uncle, and then to her father. Her heart sank as she saw by their expressions that neither one intended to oppose the duke.

"Very well, your grace," Aunt Elizabeth said very calmly, nodding to the servants to clear the plates. "Shall we all go into the drawing room? Bella, you should change your gown. I shall send one of the maids to pack for you."

Bella found she had no voice. Rising from the table, she forced her trembling bottom lip between her teeth before starting for the door.

"Excuse me?" a young, quavering voice spoke up as everyone was rising from the table.

Bella turned at the question and saw her little brother looking around the room at all of them with confused, fearful eyes.

"What is it, Tommy?" Alfred Tichley asked his son.

"Should not we make a toast? At all the other weddings I have been to, the bride and groom are toasted."

No one in the room made a sound.

"Why don't you do us the honor, Tommy?"

Bella was surprised to hear the supportive note in the duke's deep voice.

After a shy moment, Tommy nodded. Straightening his shoulders, he picked up his glass, pausing while the others followed suit. "To Bella and . . . ?" Tommy's face fell as he realized he did not know the duke's given name.

"Alex," the Duke of Severly leaned over and supplied, giving the boy an encouraging smile.

Tommy nodded and began again. "To Bella and Alex! May your happiness grow from this day forward, and God bless you both."

The resounding chorus of *"Hear, hears"* so touched Bella that she could only lower her head against her sudden tears. As quickly as she could, she fled the room, with the toast still ringing in her ears.

Chapter Thirteen

Bella, sitting at the head of the immensely long dining table, lifted the etched crystal goblet and took another sip of the excellent wine the wine steward had chosen for her. As one footman removed the plate in front of her, another replaced it with a dish of savory hothouse vegetables covered in a French sauce.

It was her fourth night at Autley, and the first she had spent dining alone in this cavernous blue-and-gold-appointed room. In spite of the elegant surroundings, Bella felt a keen sense of dismay and annoyance.

Since her arrival, a frown seemed permanently on her brow, and the three servants attending her in total silence wondered at the haunted look in the new Duchess of Westlake's eyes.

As Bella took small bites of the delicious dish, her confusion and distress grew as her mind again went over the events that had occurred since she'd come to Autley.

Situated on a rise in the midst of vast acres of forests, fields, gardens, and lakes, the duke's home had caused her to catch her breath at its beauty upon her first sight of it.

She could hardly believe that anyone actually lived in such a massive place, she had thought as the carriage passed through the imposing iron gates. Looking out the carriage window, she could see brief glimpses of a huge mansion with massive gray stone spires and towers as they drove through the turns on the road.

As they drew nearer, she could see that Autley was built on a quadrangle around a courtyard. She found the place beautiful and awe inspiring.

When the carriage had pulled up the miles-long drive to the grand columned entrance, it had been late evening on their wedding day. Bella was thankful the duke had slept for most of the journey, giving her time to think and formulate some sort of plan to remove herself from this untenable situation.

Surely, given some time, Papa and Uncle David would eventually soften. She had consoled herself with this thought as she had watched the duke slumbering across from her, deciding that she was much more comfortable with him this way.

I am certainly more familiar with him asleep, she thought with an ironic twist to her lips.

When the coach door had opened, Bella had emerged first to see a score of servants lined up on the wide marble steps. She glanced back to see the duke following stiffly and looking positively ashen.

After the duke greeted his butler, and all the servants had bowed, they were led into a cavernous entry hall. The huge hall ended at a wide marble staircase that split at the landing of the first floor, diverging in opposite directions to a gallery visible from the hall below.

Standing on the bottom of the staircase had been the duke's mother. Next to her stood a younger, prettyish red-headed lady, garbed in a peach-colored silk gown boasting a multitude of bows, puffs, and gathers. Standing next to the redhead was a boy perhaps a year or so younger than Tommy. He had very dark hair and light eyes. Bella instantly knew that this must be Henry, the duke's nephew.

As she and the duke drew near, the redhead curtsied, the boy bowed, and the dowager stepped forward. Bella was again impressed by the dowager's stately manner.

"Arabella, you are most welcome to Autley. This place has been too long without a mistress." She had smiled warmly at her new daughter-in-law and offered her cheek to be saluted.

Bella felt the heat of a blush surging to her cheeks. *What must his mother be thinking?* she wondered in great dismay.

Despite the dowager's imposing demeanor, Bella had instantly admired the lady when she had come to the manor. Bella wondered how, under the circumstances, she could ever behave normally in her presence.

With a tentative smile, Bella kissed the dowager's cheek. When she pulled back, her eyes met the older lady's, and for a brief instant Bella saw a look of such gentle understanding, it almost made her cry.

Stepping forward, the duke brought Bella's attention to the other lady. "Arabella, I would like to make known to you my sister-in-law, Margaret."

The redheaded lady dropped a deep curtsy to Bella, and then met her gaze with wide brown eyes.

"My dear Duchess, when Mama shared the news that Westlake was bringing home a bride, I cannot express to you how excited I was. Was I not terribly excited, Mama?" Margaret looked to the dowager for confirmation of the state of her emotions.

"Yes, Margaret, you were very excited," the dowager offered in a neutral tone.

"See? Welcome to Autley, your grace," Margaret said with another quick curtsy.

Instantly Bella recalled the duke's telling her how his brother had come to regret his marriage to this woman.

After greeting Henry with great affection, the duke had then presented his nephew. The handsome little boy looked at Bella with very solemn eyes that showed a maturity beyond his young years.

"I am pleased to meet you, Henry." Bella smiled gently down at the boy.

"Are you really married to my uncle?" the boy asked in reply.

Bella straightened and cast the duke a quick, harried glance. How to answer such a question?

But before the duke could step in, Margaret tousled her son's hair and gently rebuked him. "Now Henry, you know I explained it to you earlier. Do not ask silly questions."

Henry looked from Bella to the duke and back again, his eyes still inquisitive.

"I am very glad to meet you both," Bella had said to mother and son.

"I am sure you both are hungry after your long journey.

I have arranged for a light repast to sustain you until breakfast," the dowager had informed them.

"Thank you, *ma mère,* but I am quite fatigued and shall go straight to my chambers," the duke said, turning to Bella and giving her a slight bow.

"Forgive me for deserting you on your first night at Autley, my dear, but my mother will see to your comfort."

With an expression of growing concern and confusion, she watched the duke's back as he ascended the stairs.

After sharing a light meal with her new mother-in-law and Margaret, Bella had been shown to the largest, most exquisitely appointed bedchamber she had ever seen. A huge canopied bed dominated the room, with voluminous swags of brocaded fabric, in the colors of spring, hanging from the rails.

Bella walked farther into the room and saw that there was a settee and two chairs by the fireplace. The marble-mantled fireplace was so large, Bella was sure she would have been able to stand in it if a fire were not already crackling away.

The dowager had shown her around, indicating a dressing room on the north side, and a private salon on the south.

Bella could only nod, and was embarrassed to see that two maids were unpacking her few belongings.

"This was never my chamber, my dear," the dowager duchess had told Bella in a conversational tone. "My husband and I always preferred the south wing of the house. But my son has made improvements to the west wing, and prefers having his chambers here. This room also has a balcony that overlooks the garden, and, of course, has a wonderful view of the sunsets."

Bella had been enormously relieved when the duchess had shooed the maids out and wished her a good night, saying, "I know you shall be happy here at Autley. It is a bit daunting at first, but it truly is a magical place."

Bella had thanked the dowager for her kindness, and once the door closed she allowed herself to collapse on the bed. Finally she gave way to a flood of tears, brought on by fear and fatigue. She was completely overwhelmed by the sudden sweeping changes occurring in her life and wept with a sadness she had never felt before.

* * *

The next morning, Bella had taken herself well in hand. During the night, as she tossed and turned in the huge bed in the vast bedchamber, she had determined to make the best of her circumstances. Surely without the pressure of her father's and uncle's presence they could come up with a plan, she decided hopefully, sitting up in the large bed.

There was a light tap on her door, and Bella bade whomever it was to enter. One of the maids who had unpacked her clothing the previous night came in with a breakfast tray and placed it on the table next to the bed.

Bella thanked the woman, who bobbed a curtsy before leaving the room without a word.

Looking at the beautiful porcelain tea set and dishes, Bella prayed she would not be clumsy—it all looked priceless.

A note nestled next to a small flower vase on the tray caught her attention. Curiously she picked it up and broke the seal. It was from the duke.

My Dear Arabella,
  I must beg your forgiveness, but I am called away on urgent business.
  You will be well taken care of here at Autley, and I urge you to treat my home as you would your manor in Mabry Green.
  I shall do my best to hasten my return, for I know that there is much for us to discuss concerning our future.

                                        Your servant,
                                        Westlake

"Well," Bella said aloud in mild surprise. After reading the note again, she could not decide if she was relieved that he was gone or not. Even though she was anxious to have things settled between them, his presence had become so disturbing, some time to sort out her thoughts would be a relief.

A little later, her curiosity about the duke's home drew her from her bedchamber. After some minutes of going up and down hallways, Bella realized that she was hopelessly lost. Though there were innumerable footmen and maids to direct her, she would turn down another corridor and lose her way again.

Since she had nothing to do, she did not really mind. After all, how lost could she get? she mused with a little smile.

Autley was beautifully decorated, and Bella owned herself impressed with the antiques and rare artwork that filled the place. Gainsboroughs and Van Dykes filled the gallery, and when she had wandered into one of the formal drawing rooms, she stopped to stare in awe at the gilded mural depicting a romanticized scene of heaven, taking up all four walls.

It was only by opening one door after another that Bella was able to find a room that seemed lived in. On her fifth try she stumbled into what was apparently a sitting room, and found Margaret Westlake perusing a fashion magazine while seated on a settee by a large bay window.

"Good morning," Bella said with a little laugh. "I have been wandering this vast place for what seems like hours. What a relief to find another living soul!"

Margaret laughed a little too hard and long at Bella's attempt at humor, especially since Bella did not think the mirth reached her brown eyes.

"Come and sit with me, my dear sister-in-law. We must become acquainted."

Bella moved across the room to sit in a chair opposite Margaret and took in the peach confection of the morning gown she wore.

From neck to hem, there were graduating sizes of puffy peach bows. The largest one, at the hem, was probably a foot wide. Bella wondered if Margaret was considered fashionable or if others considered her attire as absurd as she did.

"So how do you like your new home?" Margaret asked once Bella was seated.

"I do not know yet. It is certainly beautiful here. And large," she told the redhead in an attempt to ease their conversation.

"Yes, it certainly is that. But you would be hard-put to find a grander house in all of England."

"I am sure."

"I must say we were all quite bowled over by the news that Westlake had married." Margaret smiled, but Bella noticed the redhead was watching her keenly.

"It was very sudden, was it not?" she continued.

Bella did not intend to discuss her marriage to the duke with his sister-in-law. "Yes. I suppose it was." She smiled politely. "Your son seems to have recovered very well from his accident. And he seems a very bright boy," she offered in hopes of changing the subject.

Margaret looked at Bella with her head slightly tilted before responding. "Yes. At the time I thought his fall was more serious than it turned out to be. But yes, my Henry is very bright. He takes after my poor departed James." Margaret pressed a bit of lace to her eye to convey her still-fresh grief.

"I am very sorry for your loss," Bella said gently.

"Thank you, your grace." Margaret sniffed. "It is very difficult to be a widow, especially at so young an age. I just thank heaven that I have my Henry. He is my only comfort." Margaret heaved a heavy sigh.

Bella made a sympathetic noise, for she really had no idea what to say to the young widow.

At that moment the door burst open and young Henry came bounding in.

"Look, Mama, I have found some of Uncle Alex's old toy soldiers in the nursery." The little boy held out his hand to his mother and showed her the small figures. He then saw Bella and stopped, turning to look at her in wide-eyed surprise.

"Good morning, Henry. How are you today?" Bella inquired gently.

The boy continued to stare at Bella with a confused frown forming on his little brow.

"Make your bow, Henry," Margaret encouraged.

"Good morning, Aunt Arabella," the little boy finally said after making a very practiced bow.

"I have a little brother who also likes to play with toy soldiers," Bella said in an attempt to bring the boy out of his shyness.

He said nothing to this.

Bella glanced to his mother, who was beaming at her son proudly.

"Are you going to have a baby?" Henry burst out as he clutched his toy soldiers.

Bella stared, speechless, at the dark-haired little boy.

"Henry! Watch your manners!" his mother chided.

Henry did not even glance in his mother's direction, but continued to look at Bella. "Well, are you?"

Bella overcame her immediate shock and smiled at the precocious little boy. Obviously the answer was very important to him.

"Well, I expect I shall someday."

Frowning, Henry turned to his mother.

"But Mama, you said she would not have a baby," he said anxiously.

Not knowing what to make of this odd conversation, Bella looked at Margaret with raised brows.

"Hush, Henry! Go back to the nursery and play with your toys," Margaret admonished her son, blushing to the roots of her red hair.

With another anxious look at Bella, Henry reluctantly left the room.

"Children!" Margaret tittered after the door closed. "One never knows what will come out of their mouths. He is a very curious boy by nature. He asked me the other day if you would be having a baby. I, of course, said no, as you have only just married. You know how confused children can get," Margaret explained hurriedly. "I hope he did not embarrass you."

"No," Bella said with a light laugh to put Margaret at ease. "I do know how precocious little boys can be."

Margaret continued to blush.

"If you will excuse me, your grace, I . . . I need to finish some letters so they can go out in the post today."

Without waiting for Bella to reply Margaret jumped up from the settee and quickly left the room, leaving Bella to look after her with a curious frown.

On her second full day at Autley, while dining with the dowager and Margaret, the dowager had informed Bella that she, Margaret, and Henry would be leaving for London.

"When?" Bella had asked, startled by this sudden news.

"It has been planned for some time that we leave tomorrow," the dowager had supplied. "We shall be staying at the town house of my oldest daughter, Lady Edgeton. My younger daughter, Louisa, is there now. She is to marry the Duke of Malverton this June. Because of my son's disappearance, the wedding plans were halted, of course. But now that everything is fine we must catch up. We have six hundred guests!"

"Oh, my!" Bella had said, finding it hard to imagine the enormity of the preparations to be made for such an event.

"You shall have to come visit us while we are in London; it is vastly diverting. We shall go shopping together," Margaret had offered.

Bella had looked at Margaret closely then. She was not one to rush to judgment about a person's character, but she had come to a conclusion about the duke's sister-in-law. There was definitely something about her manner that revealed an effort at artifice. No matter how gushingly Margaret spoke to Bella or the dowager, the look in her eyes did not match her tone.

But still, the thought of their going to London and leaving her virtually alone in this cold house was distressing to Bella.

But they had left the next morning as planned, with Bella waving after them from the wide marble steps of the entrance. She returned to the main salon and asked the butler, Hollings, if he knew when his grace would be returning. It was very embarrassing to have to ask a servant such a question, but as the duke had not given any real indication of when he would come home, she felt there was little choice.

The very correct man had looked down at Bella with an expression that could only be described as haughty.

"I do not know, your grace," was all he said before bowing and backing out of the room.

When the door closed, Bella had flopped down on a settee in complete vexation. She could understand the duke's desire to take care of estate matters, but she was growing anxious to speak to him about her idea to free them both.

Even if she had wanted to take on such a daunting role as the Duchess of Westlake, which of course she did not, he had to be aware that she had no notion of how to behave. Granted, she was the granddaughter of an earl, but that was no help under these circumstances. As her father was a second son, they had always lived quietly and simply, and there had been no need to learn anything of protocol, court life, or entertaining on a grand scale.

Annulment seemed the only way out for both of them, she concluded with a deep sigh. Certainly the duke did not want to be saddled with a country girl who had no idea of how to conduct herself among the nobility.

She already missed her family and the comforting routine of her life in Mabry Green. As she sat in the luxurious room, Bella experienced a deep, almost painful desire to return home.

Later, sitting alone at the dining table in a state of deep frustration, Bella wondered again how long the duke would be away from Autley. Glancing up at the young footman, she decided to try her luck with him.

"Do you happen to know when his grace is expected to return home?"

The young man froze at her unexpected question and looked at her uncertainly.

"Er . . . yes, your grace. I believe his grace returned this eve and is in his library," he supplied a little nervously.

One of Bella's dark brows went up at this information. "Thank you," she said, coming to a decision.

Placing her napkin down, she did not wait for the footman to pull her chair back before rising from the table. The footman nearest the door had to take a quick step to reach it before the new duchess opened it herself.

Bella headed down the hallway with rapid determined steps, past numerous works of art, tapestries, and antiques, until she reached the duke's private library. It felt as if she had walked for miles before she came upon the large double doors with a liveried lackey standing in front of them.

Seeing that she intended to enter, the lackey adroitly blocked her way.

"May I announce you to his grace, your grace?"

Bella stood before the burgundy-and-black-clad man and resisted the urge, with some difficulty, to kick him in the shins.

Taking a very deep breath, her eyes flashing blue fire, Bella pushed past the footman and opened one heavy oak door herself. As soon as she was in the room, she turned and slammed the door shut.

The duke, seated behind a massive desk, rose immediately at her unexpected entrance.

"Hello, Arabella. I see you are learning your way around Autley." His tone was very polite but his eyes held a hint of amusement.

Now that she had achieved her goal in locating him, Bella found that she did not know how to begin.

Stalling, she looked around the very attractive room with its leather-lined walls, two-story bookcases, and air of masculinity. It seemed a fitting atmosphere for the duke, she thought.

Finally she turned to him and looked him squarely in the eyes.

"Your grace, I desire a word with you."

The duke came around to the front of the desk, leaned his hip against it, and crossed his arms.

"I apologize for not informing you at once of my return, Arabella. I have been tending to some papers, as I have been away from my affairs for too long. Several of my estates have needed my immediate attention. But now I am at your service."

At his explanation, Bella took a deep breath to cool the anger she had been fanning all day.

"Your grace, I can understand the sense of honor that forced my father to expect this marriage. I can also understand the sense of honor that caused you to agree to it," she began. "But I don't think there is anything to prevent us from pursuing every possible avenue to try to rectify this situation."

She saw one dark arched brow go up as he casually leaned against the desk.

"And what avenues are you speaking of?" he questioned politely.

"Well, I think the most obvious and logical step is to investigate the process of an annulment."

The duke straightened, his expression completely changing, and took a step nearer.

"Arabella, I agree that the situation we face is far from ideal. But let me make something unequivocally clear: There is not going to be an annulment."

Bella looked at him with a stunned expression.

Marshaling her thoughts, she tried again, thinking he had not understood her clearly. "Not immediately, I know," she conceded, wringing her hands a little nervously, "but after some time has passed, and if we go about it quietly I see no reason why it will not work."

"Go about it quietly?" he repeated, before giving way to a deep laugh. "My dear innocent, there would be no such thing as a *quiet* annulment if a Westlake were involved."

"But your grace—" she insisted.

"Call me Alex," he put in.

"Your grace," she emphasized, ignoring his invitation to use his given name. "You are being unreasonable. This *is* an untenable situation, and I cannot understand why you will not help me put it right."

The duke's expression hardened. "You are not a child. Even if I would consent to an annulment, it would put nothing right. We both must make the best of this."

"Make the best of this? We do not even know each other," she said in disbelief.

She would never have imagined that the kind man whom she had nursed would behave in this autocratic manner, and finally her temper snapped. Thrusting her chin up, she looked at him scornfully. "I will have you know that besides not wanting to be married to you, I find it horrible here! I have been completely alone since your mother and sister-in-law left for London. Your servants let me do nothing for myself and treat me with veiled contempt. And I have continually gotten lost in these endless corridors."

The duke watched this show of anger with very little change in his expression, but she saw some hint of unidentifiable emotion flicker in his eyes before he spoke.

"I know Autley can be daunting. But you shall soon become familiar with the inner workings of my home. And as for the servants, I shall speak to them," he said dismissively.

"As for not wanting to be married to me," he continued, "I would remind you of a conversation we had not so long ago, when you specifically said that you believed common interests and respect for each other were the most important ingredients in a marriage. I would put it to you that we have those ingredients, Bella."

During his speech, Bella had begun to pace on the Turkish carpet. At this last statement, she turned on him with angry eyes.

"How dare you throw my words up at me at a time like this? You know very well that those standards could never apply to us."

She saw his expression close as he pushed himself away from the desk and returned to his chair.

"I have a different opinion on the subject," he said in a very neutral tone. "But I am not prepared to continue this discussion."

Bella marched up, leaned forward, and placed her hands forcefully upon his desk. "I have no intention of making the best of anything, your grace. And I shall do everything in my power to extricate myself from a future I know will be filled with misery."

His gray gaze seemed to ice over. "You overstep yourself, Arabella. The simple fact is that we are married. And nothing shall change that."

Something in his intractable tone caused a frisson of fear to travel to her heart. She had never seen this side of him and she was at a loss as to how to reach him. As she continued to stare into his unreadable eyes, she knew there was no use in continuing to goad him.

Lowering her head, she turned to leave the room. As she reached the door the duke's voice halted her steps.

"Bella," he said in a softer tone. "I told you once that everything would be all right. If you could grow to trust me, I still believe that is possible."

Without turning to look at him, Bella opened one heavy door, stepped into the hallway, and slammed it shut behind her as hard as she could. The startled footman was so caught off guard that he actually uttered an exclamation as the new duchess darted past him and ran down the hall.

Once Bella gained her bedchamber, she threw herself on the bed. But she remained dry-eyed as she pondered what to do next.

Chapter Fourteen

Four days later, Bella found herself wandering around the large sitting room, holding an unread book in her hand. She could not recall her emotions ever being in such a state of confusion. Life at Autley was even worse than she had feared it would be. There was nothing to do! Back home she had run her father's house just as she pleased, she thought dismally as she sat down in a petit-point-covered chair.

Right now, if she were back at Mabry Green, she would be helping her aunt plan the spring garden party that took place on the lawns of Penninghurst Park every year.

It had been apparent to her from the moment of her arrival that Autley was run with formal precision; the servants took care of even the smallest task. Mealtimes never deviated from a centuries-old schedule. Even some servants had servants to wait upon them, she had learned to her amazement. So on top of her confusion and distress over the forced marriage between herself and the duke, Bella was growing increasingly bored. And now, to her further distress, the duke was gone from Autley again.

Not that she had seen much of him since their encounter in his library. What little she did see of him was usually while the length of the dining table separated them at mealtimes. Conversation between them was awkward at best, and this saddened Bella even more.

Where was the witty, good-natured gentleman whom she

had gotten to know at the manor? Where was the man with whom she had had lively discussions over their favorite books? Where was the man who had on occasion made her blush with his flirting? She even missed him. *This* duke was remote and forbidding.

Last night during dinner, Bella had been startled when he had broken the oppressive silence and addressed her from the other end of the table.

"Arabella," he had begun, looking across the table at her, over the multitude of crystal goblets of varying sizes and shapes. "I shall be leaving for Derbyshire in the morning. I have an estate there in need of my attention. I shall be back at Autley in a fortnight or so."

She had regarded him for a moment, taking in how elegant he appeared in his formal evening attire as he gazed back at her with an unreadable expression.

For an instant Bella thought of asking Westlake to take her with him, but she had immediately discarded the notion.

Now, as she sat in this beautiful room with its gilded cornices and breathtaking view of the lake, Bella thought about her future. How could they continue in this fashion? Surely the duke would want to be married to a woman who would give him children someday.

His words, spoken to her in his library the other night, now came to mind. Did he really believe that having a few common interests and some mutual respect could possibly overcome the differences they faced?

These disturbing thoughts were interrupted by a knock on the door and the immediate entry of Hollings carrying a silver tray.

"A letter, your grace," he intoned with a bow.

"Thank you," she said with a slight smile, which the butler did not return.

As the butler closed the door behind him, Bella looked down at the folded vellum curiously. Instantly she recognized the hand as belonging to her aunt and opened the envelope eagerly.

Her eyes scanned the note and took in the news of Mabry Green and the goings-on at Penninghurst Park.

A particular passage caught her attention, and she read that segment again.

Although I understand that it is unfashionable to be in town so much before the Season, I thought it best to arrive soon enough for Beatrice to procure a suitable wardrobe.

Please do not perceive this visit to London as a sign of forgiveness of Beatrice on the part of your uncle and me. Indeed, how could such a wicked trick ever be forgiven? But your uncle believes it best to find Beatrice a husband as soon as possible.

We shall be in London within the week.

Glancing back to the date at the top of the page, Bella made a quick calculation and determined that her aunt and Triss would have arrived at their rented town house by yesterday, today at the latest.

She finished reading the letter and sat for some moments with her eyes on the lake beyond the French windows, without really taking in the beautiful view.

A look of determination settled on her features, and her expressive deep blue eyes were less troubled than they had been in weeks. Rising, she set the book that had been in her lap on a side table, refolded her aunt's letter, and left the sitting room. As she climbed the steps of the wide Italian-marble staircase, she espied a footman in the hall below. She caught his eyes, and he stopped and bowed.

"Please send my maid to me," she directed, hoping that her tone sounded firm.

Since she had arrived, she had noticed that the servants at Autley were an imperious lot. They were nothing like the good-natured family retainers at Penninghurst Park. They were much too well trained to have been outright insubordinate to her, but they certainly did not make an effort to do her bidding promptly. So it was somewhat to her surprise that by the time she had gained her bedchamber, Jones, the middle-aged woman appointed as her maid, was waiting in the room for her.

Bobbing a curtsy, the maid waited for Bella to speak.

"Please have a trunk packed with my belongings, and inform the head groom that I require a coach to be ready to depart in the morning. I want to be in London before nightfall."

Bella saw a look of surprise cross the older woman's face.

"Very good, your grace," Jones said, and bobbed another curtsy before leaving the room.

As soon as she was alone, Bella finally gave way to a very satisfied smile.

"So this is London," Bella said, more to herself than to Jones, as she looked out of the coach window onto the crowded, noisy street.

Hearing this comment caused the maid to mentally reiterate the comment she had made to the housekeeper the night before: that the new duchess was one step removed from being a turnip

"Yes, your grace," Jones said with strained civility.

Ignoring the surly maid, Bella continued to look out of the window with great interest. Her heart quickened its beat every time she thought about her departure from Autley. She had never done anything so bold in her life, she thought, still marveling at her own temerity.

"Would you please give this letter to his grace when he returns?"

The butler had taken the note and looked down his very long nose at her.

"Perhaps your grace would have me send it to Derbyshire?" he had hinted in a censorious tone.

"No. When his grace returns will suffice," she had tossed over her shoulder as she stepped into the luxurious traveling chaise.

Now, as they wended their way through the twisting streets of London in search of her aunt's town house, Bella wondered what the stuffy old majordomo had thought of her actions.

Very soon, the carriage had entered a less busy street and turned up a drive.

"This is the address, your grace," the coachman informed her.

Bella allowed him to assist her from the carriage. She looked around the pleasant tree-lined street before going up and knocking on the black-painted door. An ancient, stooped man answered her knock.

"Would you please inform Lady Penninghurst that her

niece, Arabella, is here?" she asked, unable to bring herself to use her new title.

The decrepit butler peered up at Bella before he stepped back and let her enter the modestly proportioned foyer.

"A moment, miss. I will inform her ladyship," he said before shuffling off.

Bella cooled her heels in the foyer, a feeling of excitement at the thought of seeing her aunt bringing a soft smile to her lips. It was a pity that the thought of seeing her cousin again did not bring about the same feeling.

"Arabella!"

Bella's head went up at the sound of her name being called, and she saw her aunt descending the staircase.

"Aunt Elizabeth, how well you look," she replied with pleasure, ignoring the distressed expression on her aunt's face.

"Bella!" Lady Penninghurst said again as she reached the bottom of the stairs. "Never tell me you have run away from the duke?"

"No, of course not. His grace is off in Derbyshire tending one of his estates. So I have decided to come to town and renew my wardrobe," she explained, deciding not to tell her aunt that the duke was unaware of her excursion.

Her aunt frowned at her. "It is wonderful to see you, Bella, and I own I have been worried. But to come to town so soon after being married?"

"Oh, it's perfectly all right, Aunt," Bella said with a confidence she did not feel. "The duke shall be coming to London presently."

Bella refused to feel bad about this fib, as it caused the worried expression to instantly lift from her aunt's brow.

"Well, then, that's wonderful," Elizabeth responded with relief. "Where is the duke's town house?"

Bella looked at her aunt with a mildly startled expression, for she had never given a thought to the idea that the duke would have a town house.

"Er . . . his town house? I thought I would stay here until Westlake arrives. I have a trunk and my maid outside. That is, if you do not mind . . ." she manufactured quickly.

Lady Penninghurst gave her niece a sharp, suspicious

look. "Bella, answer me true. Is all well with you and the duke?"

Bella met her aunt's anxious gaze for a brief moment before looking away with ill-concealed sadness.

"As well as can be, under the circumstances, Aunt Elizabeth," Bella replied.

A long, tense moment passed before her aunt's look softened.

"Of course you may stay, Bella."

Sagging with relief, Bella thanked her profusely.

"Come to the sitting room. I shall have your trunk brought upstairs, and Hobbs will tend to your coach and servants."

Bella thanked her aunt again, and followed her into the sitting room. "How are Papa and Tommy?" she asked as she removed her bonnet.

"They are quite well," her aunt said, giving her a reassuring smile. "Your papa misses you, though he won't admit to it. Tommy has been a little in the mopes since you left, but as he still has the duke's horse to tend, that keeps him busy."

Bella's hands stilled on the buttons of her spencer as she looked at her aunt with surprise-filled eyes.

"The duke's horse? That beast is still at your stables?"

"Yes." Her aunt nodded before indicating to Bella that she should be seated. "Tommy is growing terribly attached to the animal. I am afraid that it will break his heart when the horse has to be returned. In truth, the horse really won't let anyone else near him."

"I wonder why the duke has left him at the Park," Bella asked with a perplexed frown on her brow.

"Well, there have been other, more important things for the duke to attend to in the last few weeks," Lady Penninghurst opined before she returned to the door. "I shall only be a moment—I want to give Hobbs the order."

Nodding, Bella allowed herself to lean back and relax on the comfortable settee. Hearing the door open again a moment later, she turned, thinking her aunt had been very quick.

"Hello, Bella." Triss was standing in the doorway,

dressed in a sky-blue gown, wearing a very tentative expression on her face.

"Hello, Beatrice," Bella responded, a little surprised at the dark circles under her cousin's eyes.

"Mother says that you are to stay with us. I am very glad," she said.

"You are? I shouldn't be if I were you." Bella's reply was cold.

"Why not?" Triss came farther into the room.

"If you knew how angry I am with you, you would not want me here."

"I do want you here. I have missed you and have been worried about you. I would very much appreciate it if you would ring a peal over me. I know how much I deserve it."

"Do you really?" Bella questioned her contrite cousin.

"Yes, I do. I never thought my plan would go so awry. But I sincerely know that I should never have played so fast and loose with your future. I am thoroughly ashamed of myself and know that I shall never be able to make it up to you."

For once, Bella did not see a hint of mischief or mockery in Triss's eyes. But it was cold comfort. "You *should* be ashamed of yourself," she replied, giving no quarter.

"Bella, setting aside your anger for one moment, do you believe that I intended you any harm?" Triss seated herself in the chair across from her cousin and looked at her with anxious eyes.

"Well, no, but that is beside the point. I still do not know what possessed you to play such a trick."

Triss bit her lip and looked away from Bella for a moment. "In all honesty, I had noticed the way you and the duke had been looking at each other during dinner. I thought that it would be nice for the two of you to have a little while to speak to each other without Tommy or Uncle Alfred hovering close by. I truly thought Uncle Alfred would return home a little while later." She finished her explanation with an apologetic look.

Bella said nothing. She and the duke *had* been looking at each other frequently during dinner at Penninghurst Park, but she had not realized that it had been noticeable to anyone else. But whatever had begun that night between herself and the duke had been destroyed by the forced marriage, she realized.

"Since you admit that you know I did not intend any harm," Triss said hastily to fill the ensuing silence, "do you believe that someday you will be able to forgive me?"

There was a long pause in the quiet room, while Bella thought over Triss's words. "I expect I shall eventually find a way to forgive you," she grudgingly admitted.

"Then I will gladly bear your anger for now," Triss said with a new maturity.

Bella looked at her lifelong friend and decided that she would not continue to fan the flames of her resentment.

They sat together for some moments in silence, but this time the silence was not as strained.

"Bella, may I ask you a question?"

"Are you sure you would not be pressing your luck?" Bella cautioned with the merest hint of a smile.

"It is something I would like to know." Triss forged ahead. "Do you think it is so terrible to be married to a duke?"

Bella stared at her cousin for a moment before answering. "Do you think your mama married your papa only because he is an earl?"

"No, of course not," Triss responded with a note of confusion in her voice.

"Then do you think my mama minded that my papa was a second son?" Bella continued.

"No, Aunt Mary and Uncle Alfred were always very happy."

"Why, then, would you, who were raised with me, think it would matter whether my husband was a duke or a second son?" Bella said succinctly.

Nodding her understanding, Triss looked at her cousin a little sadly.

"And how do you believe you would feel to know that the only reason your husband married you was because of a sense of duty and social pressure?" Bella asked.

Triss's gaze dropped from hers, and Bella saw her swallow several times before she looked back up with tear-glazed eyes.

"Do not forgive me too soon, Bella," she said with quiet sincerity.

* * *

After spending a comfortable night, the three ladies enjoyed a leisurely stroll around Green Park the next morning. Bella felt better than she had in a month, and was very glad that she had made the decision to come to London.

Upon their return, the ladies were taken aback when Hobbs greeted them at the door with the news that the Duchess of Westlake and Lady Edgeton were waiting in the sitting room for the Duchess of Westlake.

"I am *sure* I heard her grace correctly," Hobbs assured Lady Penninghurst.

"I am surprised that they would come here in response to the note I sent over to Lady Edgeton's," Bella told the others as she removed her bonnet and pelisse. She had dashed off a note that morning, thinking the correct thing to do would be to let the dowager know she was in town.

"Please come with me," she requested of her aunt and cousin, for though the dowager was very nice, Bella still found something about her intimidating.

The three ladies all went to the sitting room, where the dowager and her eldest daughter were seated, both with very erect postures, in the two chairs by the window. Bella saw that the dowager was wearing a beautiful afternoon dress the color of green apples, with a matching spencer trimmed with a triple fall of lace at her throat.

Bella turned to look curiously at Lady Edgeton. She found her to be very much like her brother, tall and very distinguished-looking. Bella might have considered her pretty if her countenance did not bear a certain look of condescension.

The dowager and Lady Edgeton rose as the three ladies entered.

Lady Penninghurst and Triss curtsied as Bella presented her relatives.

"How nice to see you again, Lady Penninghurst, Lady Beatrice. I should like you to know my daughter, Lady Edgeton."

Bella was growing anxious, for there was definitely something disapproving in the dowager's tone, and Lady Edgeton looked positively cold. After they were all seated, the dowager looked at Bella.

"Arabella, I see no reason not to speak plainly," she began. "I was quite shocked to receive your note this morning."

"But why, your grace?" Bella asked her mother-in-law in a startled tone.

"To be informed that you are here so soon after the wedding, and without my son . . . well, it's just not seemly," she stated bluntly. "I believe it would be best if you returned to Autley before the Season gets under way."

"But I am to bespeak a wardrobe, your grace. And as Westlake is in Derbyshire on business, he could not come to London for at least a fortnight." Bella refused to let a hint of doubt enter her words. She did not care what truth she needed to stretch; she was not going to go back to Autley until she absolutely had no choice.

The dowager and her daughter exchanged surprised glances.

"And why, may I ask, are you staying here"—Lady Edgeton glanced around the pleasant, but by no means grand, sitting room with a haughty look and continued—"instead of Westlake House?"

Not wanting to get off on the wrong foot with her sister-in-law, Bella decided to take no offense at the lady's disparaging attitude.

"I saw no reason to stay at Westlake House by myself when I could stay with my aunt and cousin here." Bella's chin went up stubbornly; she was leaving out the simple fact that she had not even known that the duke owned a town house until yesterday afternoon.

"Definitely not good *ton*," Lady Edgeton said to her mother with a sniff.

Bella saw her aunt stiffen.

"Arabella"—the dowager was now looking at Bella a little more kindly—"I can understand your actions now that I have a better notion of your thinking. But this just will not do," she stated.

Bella cast a quick glance to her aunt's offended visage, and then to Triss, who just looked frightened. "I do not wish to give offense, your grace, but I am not taking your meaning." Bella turned confused blue eyes back to the dowager.

Sighing, the dowager attempted to explain. "Again, I shall speak plainly. No matter what the circumstances of your marriage to my son are, you are the Duchess of Westlake."

"I take leave to inform you, *your grace,* that it is through no fault of my niece that she finds herself wed to your son." Aunt Elizabeth quickly came to Bella's defense.

At this, Lady Edgeton gave another haughty sniff.

"Are you catching a cold, my lady?" Triss spoke up, and directed her sharp blue gaze at the dowager's daughter.

Bella could not hide her smile. How glad she was to be with Aunt Elizabeth and Triss at this moment. The Tichley ladies had always stuck together.

"Oh, please do not take offense," the dowager said impatiently. "When you understand the ways of the beau monde you will see that I am trying to help. As I was saying, you are the Duchess of Westlake, and as the wife of a leader of Society, certain behavior is expected of you. I shall send a note over to Westlake House and have the staff make the house ready. Of course, as there are more than twenty guest chambers, there is no reason why your good aunt and cousin cannot stay with you there."

The Tichley ladies exchanged glances, and waited for Bella to make her decision.

"If you think it best, we will move to Westlake House," Bella said, deciding not to further cross the imposing woman.

"Excellent," the dowager said with satisfaction, rising from her chair. "My daughter and I have another call to make, so we will take our leave. No, no, do not trouble seeing us to the door, Lady Penninghurst. Arabella, please walk with me to my carriage," she directed her daughter-in-law imperiously.

Bella jumped up quickly to do the dowager's bidding. Lady Edgeton had reached the front door first, and as Hobbs opened it she swept past the stooped butler without a word of good-bye to Bella, and entered the awaiting barouche.

Pausing on the front step, the dowager turned to Bella. "My dear, under the circumstances it is imperative that you behave with all propriety, so please do not hesitate to ask my advice on any matter." The dowager's tone was almost kind now.

Before Bella could respond, they both heard Triss's excited voice emanating from the recently vacated room. "Just think Mother, Westlake House! We shall soon be all the kick!"

With an inward groan, Bella turned chagrined eyes to the dowager.

"I apologize for my cousin, your grace; she is a terrible snob."

"Then she shall get along with my daughters famously," the dowager replied with a hint of a smile before she turned to enter the carriage.

Chapter Fifteen

After agilely jumping from the high-perch phaeton, the duke tossed the reins to Johnny. Taking the wide marbled steps two at a time to the front entrance, he handed his hat and gloves to Hollings.

Without a word to anyone else, he let his long strides take him up the grand staircase to the west wing. Rolling his sore left shoulder tiredly, the duke entered his bedchamber. He was glad to see that Wilkins, his valet, was waiting for him. Silently and with practiced efficiency, the valet helped him out of his formfitting coat of slate superfine.

Greeting his longtime manservant, Westlake took note that Wilkins was still wearing the injured expression he had nursed since Westlake had sent him home from the Tichley house. The duke smiled to himself as he began to remove his neckcloth, ignoring the sensitive servant's aloofness. He knew from long experience how protective his valet tended to be and how easily he could get his nose out of joint.

Wilkins had served his master since the duke had been a very young man. He had not even left Westlake's side during the war, when the duke had been only a marquess. When the duke had gone missing on the way to Tilbourne, Wilkins had been frantic with worry. Finally the duke had been located and everyone at Autley had rejoiced. Wilkins had set out immediately to tend his master while he recovered from his near-mortal wound.

When the dowager duchess had informed him that the duke would not need him and that he was to turn around and go right back to Autley, Wilkins could not believe he had heard the dowager correctly. It was inconceivable that the master would want to stay in some uncivilized backwater without him. But return he did, with his pride wounded and his feelings hurt.

The duke continued to remove his clothing in preparation for his bath.

"Wilkins, please have her grace informed that I will be available to dine with her this evening," he directed as he removed his waistcoat.

Westlake was eager to speak with Bella. During the entire time he was in Derbyshire, he kept going over the near argument that had occurred between them in his library. He regretted using such a peremptory tone with her when she had brought up the absurd idea of an annulment. It had not set well with him to be the cause of the frightened look in her beautiful dark blue eyes.

He had been away from Autley longer than he had intended, but had taken a couple of extra days to go to Tilbourne. A number of weeks ago he had dispatched several men to the area to investigate the shooting. He had wanted to speak with them personally about their progress in finding the assailants.

He hoped his absence had given Bella enough time to get over her temper so that they could speak to each other in a reasonable manner.

"The duchess has left, your grace," Wilkins informed his master in a stilted tone.

The duke's hands paused in the process of removing his shirt, and he quirked a questioning brow to his stone-faced valet.

"Left? Back to Mabry Green?" he asked sharply.

"I believe to London, your grace. She has left a note," the valet said, indicating an envelope lying on a silver tray on the table next to the duke's bed.

Westlake walked over and picked up the missive. Looking down at it, he studied the handwriting for a moment, admiring the elegant, upright strokes of his name on the front of the envelope.

"That will be all for now, Wilkins. Thank you," he said, not looking up from the letter in his hand.

"Very good, your grace," Wilkins said quietly before leaving the room.

Stretching his stiffening shoulder again, the duke moved to sit on the bed before opening the letter. When he did, he read the words once through, then again, slowly.

My Lord Duke,
I have decided to visit my aunt Penninghurst in London. She and my cousin have taken a house there for the Season. Under the very unusual circumstances we find ourselves in, I am sure that you can understand my need to be near my family.
Furthermore, I think it must be apparent to you, your grace, that I do not belong at Autley.
I hope that you will be willing to discuss our future very soon.
I trust your shoulder is continuing to heal well.
Sincerely,
Arabella

Westlake stared down at her signature for some minutes before folding the letter and placing it in the drawer in the table next to his bed. With a frown creasing his forehead, the duke rose from the bed and went to the room adjoining his chamber, where a large copper tub filled with hot water waited to soothe his tired muscles.

As he removed the last of his clothes, the duke contemplated what to do next.

Chapter Sixteen

"Bella, never say you are not ready! Do hurry; we do not wish to be late," Triss scolded upon entering Bella's sumptuous bedchamber and finding her still sitting at the dressing table. To her further annoyance, the maid was still fussing with Bella's hair.

With a brief smile and a nod, Bella dismissed Carter, her new lady's maid, and turned to Triss. Leaning one arm on the back of her chair, Bella gave Triss the once-over.

"Aren't you a vision," she said with a tease to her impatient cousin.

Always ready for a compliment, Triss stopped her badgering to pirouette in the middle of the room. "Am I? I so want to cut a dash at my first appearance in Society," she said to Bella with an anxious look in her clear blue eyes.

Bella admired her cousin's evening gown of frosty blue satin, with its overslip of silver net. There were tiny rosettes of silver satin dotting the pouf sleeves and the hem, and even a few sprinkled in her upswept blond hair.

"You are stunning, Triss, truly," Bella said sincerely. Bella thought Triss looked like a beautiful, dignified ice queen. How deceiving looks could be, she thought, with an ironic smile coming briefly to her lips. Rising, she gave her appearance one last glance in the large, silver-framed mirror on her dressing table before picking up her shawl and reticule.

"Oh, Bella, you're lovely," Triss said with an uncharacteristic tone of awe.

"Am I?" she said, repeating Triss's words with a smile. Despite her offhand manner, Bella was gratified to know that she was looking her best tonight. Out of the numerous new gowns she had acquired over the last few weeks, she felt the one she now wore was the most beautiful. The material was a luminescent blush-colored silk that did amazing things for her complexion and eyes. Madame Triaud, the modiste who had designed the deceptively simple gown, had told Bella that she had been saving this very rare, and very expensive, bolt of fabric for a most special client.

"Only a lady with your exquisite complexion, deep blue eyes, and dark hair could carry off this particular shade. Anyone else would disappear—it would wash them out. No, your grace, this fabric was made for you," the modiste had assured Bella.

Bella smiled a little wryly at the remembered trip to the very exclusive dress shop. She had not wanted to go. But Triss had pointed out that she had told her mother and the dowager duchess that having a new wardrobe was her express purpose for coming to London in the first place.

"Besides, Bella, you must have clothes befitting your new station," Triss had pointed out.

Bella did not tell her cousin about her hopes of convincing the duke to agree to an annulment. Instead she had reluctantly gone to the shop with her aunt and Triss and had ended up giving Mrs. Triaud her head, allowing the modiste to create an entire wardrobe for the new Duchess of Westlake. Every day boxes and boxes were delivered to Westlake House. Bella's head was spinning with the number of morning gowns, tea gowns, walking dresses, afternoon dresses, evening gowns, capes, spencers, pelisses, slippers, and bonnets.

"I can't possibly wear all of this," she had lamented to her aunt when yet another evening gown had arrived.

"Mrs. Triaud said this would barely be enough for the Season," Aunt Elizabeth had replied.

Now Bella was very pleased she had left it all to the

talented mantuamaker, for she never would have picked this gown for herself.

She also wore her hair in a new style. Instead of her thick, dark locks being pulled back in a simple twist, there was now a profusion of ringlets at the sides, with the back pulled up very high, calling attention to her graceful neck.

The new maid had proved very proficient at taking care of Bella. Finally losing her patience with Jones, who barely concealed her surliness, Bella had sent her first maid back to Autley.

"Bella, let us depart!" Triss's urgent tone pulled Bella back to the present.

"All right, I am coming," she said, and followed Triss out of the bedchamber and down the wide hallway, with its plastered and coved ceiling.

Westlake House had been a revelation to Bella. She had expected it to be as cold and unwelcoming as Autley, but it had proved quite the opposite. Where Autley was vast and full of antiques and strict attention to protocol, Westlake House was a new Palladian-style mansion with extremely modern Greek revival furnishings and décor.

"Bang up to the nines," Triss had stated with approval the day they had arrived.

The servants were highly efficient, but unlike those at Autley, they did not find little ways to show their disrespect to Bella; in fact, they seemed to go out of their way to please her. This had been a great relief to Bella, who was finding her stay in London more enjoyable than she would have thought possible.

Aunt Elizabeth was waiting for them in the black-and-white-marble foyer.

"I vow, we shall be the loveliest ladies at the ball tonight," Triss stated as they left the house and entered the closed carriage that was to take them to Lord and Lady Edgeton's house, which was only a short distance away. There, a ball was being given in honor of the engagement between the Lady Louisa Westlake and the Duke of Malverton.

What a very unusual world she found herself in, Bella mused, as the carriage turned down the drive. At first she had resisted the idea of attending the ball. Every morning, Graves, the majordomo, brought her stacks of invitations to every type of occasion, all of which she had politely declined. As things were so unsettled between her and the duke, she did not think it wise to enter Society.

But after being in London for more than three weeks, without a word from the duke in response to the letter she had left at Autley before she departed, she saw no polite way out of attending the engagement ball for his youngest sister. Besides, Bella found she liked the very pretty, if scatterbrained, Lady Louisa.

The day after Bella had arrived at Westlake House, Lady Louisa had called upon her. At first, as she, Triss, and Lady Louisa were sitting down to tea, Bella had been wary, lest Louisa behave in the high-handed manner her sister had. But she needn't have feared; the duke's youngest sister had been warm and friendly—and extremely curious about Bella.

"It has been driving me to distraction to not have met you before this, my dear sister-in-law!" she said with shining eyes as soon as she had made herself comfortable in the beautifully appointed drawing room.

Bella had decided that she had a fondness for this particular room, which was decorated in gold and pale blue. The servants kept the numerous Grecian-style urns filled with orchids. And it overlooked the expertly laid-out garden that was now in early spring bloom.

"When Alex sent us that maddeningly brief missive," Lady Louisa continued, "saying that he had recently married Miss Arabella Tichley, I thought he was hoaxing! Though why anyone would hoax about such a subject, I am sure I do not know. But, after having the devastating news that my brother had gone missing, and then to find out that he had been shot and almost lost his life . . . well, you can imagine what we all thought! So when we discovered that Miss Tichley was the young lady who had nursed my dear brother through this ordeal, it suddenly all made sense! Of course Alex would fall in love with you! 'Tis the most romantic tale in the world, next to my own romance with my darling Malverton. Though nothing as dreadful as highwaymen and fevers interfered with our courtship—we met at Almack's." Lady Louisa took a deep breath and reached for her teacup.

Bella stared, nonplussed, at the duchess-to-be. She had not the faintest notion of how to respond to such profuse outpourings. She sent a helpless glance to Triss, who only smiled, shrugged lightly, and drank her tea.

Bella was saved from having to think of something to say, for after another inhalation, Lady Louisa was off again.

"So then you show up in London without Alex! I thought Mama was going to have kittens! But, of course, it was all explained. And I am in complete agreement with you. You have to have a wardrobe, and if Alex cannot be bothered to come to town with you, well, then, what are you to do? I would have done the same, honeymoon or not. Though Alice says—you have met my sister, have you not? Of course you have! What was I saying? Oh, I recall now. Alice says that something is odd about this whole business. Your marriage to Alex, that is. And now the whole town is abuzz with rumors about you. Can you not hear the hearts breaking all over London? My brother is finally off the blocks! And every hunting mama is devastated. Though there are those who refuse to believe you really exist. Since you have not bestirred yourself to accept any invitations, the *ton* is simply mad with curiosity about you. Are you not very lucky to be so beautiful?"

Bella continued to stare at the young lady in silence, sure that she would resume her monologue after her next breath. But this time, the silence stretched and Lady Louisa looked at Bella expectantly.

"Oh . . . Well, yes, if I am beautiful, then it is pure luck," Bella finally responded with a smile at the younger woman.

"You are nice! Say you will be at the ball Alice is giving for me. It will be so much fun to watch the *ton* try to get a look at you. My ball promises to be a dreadful crush. I must be off! More wedding plans to attend. What a delight to meet you, dear Arabella, and you too, Lady Beatrice," she said, jumping up from the chair and leaving the room with a quick wave, her harried maid scurrying behind her.

Once she had left, Bella and Triss had looked at each other, mystified.

"Lud, she talks even more than I do," Triss had said in disbelief.

So, after a discussion with Aunt Elizabeth and Triss, Bella had decided that they had little choice but to attend the ball given by her sister-in-law.

Now Bella found that she actually felt a certain sense of anticipation regarding her first ball.

"We are here!" Triss said excitedly, as the carriage pulled in line with a string of other carriages waiting to unload their fashionable occupants in front of the very elegant town house belonging to Lord and Lady Edgeton.

Looking out the window to the lamplit scene beyond, Bella thought that Lady Louisa must be delighted, for if the number of carriages choking the drive was any indication, her ball would indeed be a dreadful crush.

Their own carriage had to wait a full twenty minutes before it could move from the bottom of the drive to the front entrance.

"We are so close now, why don't we just get out and walk the rest of the way? It is dreadfully stuffy in here," Bella suggested.

"Oh, no!" Triss looked horrified. "It would be too lowering to be seen *walking* up the drive. Besides, I wish to be seen exiting Westlake's coach."

"All right, you goose," Bella said with an indulgent smile.

With growing excitement, the three ladies were finally able to disembark and join the huge press of people ascending the staircase to the first floor, where the ballroom was situated. With a great deal of curiosity, Bella observed her surroundings as they slowly made their way up the staircase. She had never thought to see such a beautiful display of finery in the whole of her life. She admired the profusion of jewels glittering in the light of the chandeliers, and the rainbow hues of the ladies' gowns, shown to greater advantage against the black of the gentlemen's evening clothes. A secret smile touched Bella's lips. How Robert Fortiscue would have disapproved, she thought with some enjoyment.

It suddenly occurred to her that she would have liked to

share this private joke with the duke. As she continued to move up the staircase behind Aunt Elizabeth and Triss amidst the noisy, festive crowd, Bella paused to examine this disconcerting thought.

Could it be that she missed the duke? A frown immediately came to her brow at this unbidden thought.

What other explanation could there be for how often her thoughts went to him?

Well, they had spent a lot of time together at the manor, and she had grown to enjoy his company, she thought, trying to explain away this unnerving revelation.

If only I had not found those tryst notes, she thought with sadness. And if only her papa and uncle had not forced the duke to marry her, her life would be so different now.

But would it be better? A little voice in her heart whispered the question.

Bella's attention was abruptly pulled from her disquieting thoughts by her aunt, who was standing, immobile, on the step above Bella.

"What is it, Aunt Elizabeth?" Bella questioned urgently, for those behind were beginning to murmur about the delay.

Bella could see by looking past her aunt that they were almost to the entryway to the ballroom. She could also see the dowager, Lady Edgeton, a large man with a florid complexion next to her, Lady Louisa, and a handsome young blond man, who could only be the Duke of Malverton, greeting each guest as they passed through the receiving line.

"I do not know what to do," Aunt Elizabeth whispered in a frantic tone to Bella and Triss.

"Oh, Mother! Do not make a cake of yourself *now*," Triss whispered back fiercely.

But Lady Penninghurst did not move.

The two liveried footmen, one on either side of the entryway, glanced at each other in growing alarm.

"Aunt Elizabeth, just follow what the others are doing. There is such a commotion, no one will notice you anyway," Bella directed in an encouraging murmur, and gave her aunt a little push.

Straightening her posture, Aunt Elizabeth took herself in hand, climbed the last step, and handed her card to the majordomo, who then announced her to their hosts.

To Lady Penninghurst's relief, Bella's prediction proved true. Of the several hundred people already in the ballroom, only those nearest the entry paid any notice to Lady Penninghurst or her daughter.

Bella decided that she was going to enjoy herself this evening. In an odd, detached way, some of the excitement permeating the room transmitted itself to her, and she was enjoying the never-before-seen spectacle of the fashionables at play.

So this was the duke's world, she thought as she unfolded her fan and began to wave it in a desultory manner. After handing her invitation to the majordomo, she moved forward without a pause.

"Her Grace, the Duchess of Westlake."

She heard this announcement above the din, just as she reached her mother-in-law.

"Good evening, your grace," Bella said, raising her voice a little so that she might be heard over the laughter and chatter that surrounded them.

Only, to Bella's surprise, the chatter had ceased. After the noise a moment ago, this sudden silence was like an explosion.

Catching herself midstride, Bella looked around curiously, wondering what had just occurred. She was instantly confused and startled to see several hundred pairs of eyes aimed directly at her. Standing next to her mother-in-law, Bella found herself frozen where she stood. She could not imagine why they were all staring at her. She had the overwhelming urge to wipe her nose, in case a smut had found its way there.

The dowager smoothly stepped forward and slipped her arm through the arm of her stunned young daughter-in-law.

"Keep your chin high, my girl. We shall take a very leisurely turn around the room and meet a few notables," the dowager said in a very low voice, without disturbing the elegant half smile on her lips.

Taking a deep breath, Bella gave a slight nod to the dowager's plan, and the two ladies moved forward.

First the dowager presented Lord Edgeton. He greeted

her very correctly, but Bella noticed he had the same condescending expression his wife's face bore.

Next, Louisa stepped forward eagerly, the duke of Malverton in tow.

"My dear sister! I wish you to know my darling Malverton!" she gushed with great pride. Bella was touched by the genuine smile Lady Louisa beamed upon her.

Bella turned her own smile to the young duke. The Duke of Malverton, without so much as a word, made a passable leg to Bella while Louisa continued to chatter.

"Oh, I am beyond pleased that you are here! My ball would not be complete if you had not arrived, though we did have someone faint earlier! I told you my ball would be a complete crush! I was starting to worry, as it is getting late, and you still had not arrived. But my worry was for nothing, because you are now here. You look breathtaking! What an unusual shade your gown is. Is our new duchess not breathtaking, Malverton? Of course she is—my brother would not have it any other way, would he?"

"Louisa," the dowager cut in with just a hint of sharpness to her tone, "we must not monopolize Arabella."

Lady Louisa was undaunted.

"Of course, Mama. You must go meet everyone, and we will have a good coze later," Louisa said before turning to those waiting in line to wish her happy.

"Heavens!" the duchess said as they moved away from her youngest daughter. "That child never knows when to stubble it."

Bella was so taken aback by this comment she laughed aloud, thus giving everyone still staring at her the impression that the mysterious Duchess of Westlake was on the best of terms with her formidable mother-in-law.

The dowager led Bella to a small group of people, and presented Lord and Lady Sefton, Lady Cowper, and Sir John Mayhew.

Bella was about to curtsy, but the firm hand of the dowager on her elbow brought her to her senses. Bella threw a quick, grateful glance to the dowager. With so many eyes upon her, she would have burned up with embarrassment if it could have been reported that the Duchess of Westlake had been seen curtsying to those of a lower rank!

"My dear Duchess," Sir John crooned in a very supercilious voice, "you have us all aghast at your person. There have been so many rumors floating around town, few of us believed you to be real."

Looking at the elegant, sophisticated people in front of her, Bella felt completely out her depth, and could come up with no witty rejoinder.

"How lucky for Westlake that your grace is real," Lord Sefton smoothly inserted into the silence.

Bella smiled gratefully to the handsome lord, just as the dowager pulled her away.

"I must introduce my daughter-in-law to a few others; you will forgive us," the dowager said breezily.

"Arabella, you must have something to say for yourself, or everyone will think you are a nodcock," the duchess whispered when they were out of earshot of the group.

"I am sorry, ma'am. I have not been much in Society, and then only in Mabry Green." Bella felt the beginnings of a blush as she tried to explain.

"Well, pretend you are back there. What did you talk of in Mabry Green?" The duchess's impatient tone belied the correct smile she wore.

"We would often discuss books, or my father's research in Roman archeology. Sometimes we translate Latin phrases as sort of a game," Bella offered.

The dowager drew back from Bella with a look of growing horror. "Archaeology? Latin? Heavens, my girl, you are not a bluestocking, are you?"

Bella thought the dowager's tone implied *leper,* instead of *bluestocking.*

"I do not believe that the fact that I enjoy learning should be so shocking," Bella replied.

"Oh, don't bristle, my dear. There is nothing wrong with learning; just don't admit to too much of it," the dowager advised. "There are Margaret and Mrs. Drummond Burrell," the dowager continued. "At least you know Margaret. Let's try this again, my girl."

As they moved through the crowd, Bella changed her mind. She was not going to enjoy this evening after all. Her homesickness grew, and with a little throb in her heart she longed for her Mabry Green, where no one looked down his nose at her.

After Mrs. Drummond Burrell was presented, Margaret greeted Bella as if they were long-lost friends. Bella responded with a little less enthusiasm to the petite redhead.

"Finally!" Mrs. Drummond Burrell said, examining Bella keenly. "The mysterious Duchess of Westlake! The town is agog at the news. But why do we not have the pleasure of his grace's company also?"

Looking at the avidly curious expression on Mrs. Drummond Burrell's arrogant face, Bella desperately wished she had stayed at Westlake House this evening.

Glancing around the crowded room before she answered, Bella was gratified to catch sight of Triss and her aunt speaking with Lady Louisa and Malverton. Triss, at least, looked as if she were having a fine time.

"My husband was called away to Derbyshire, but should come to town any day now," she finally responded with the fib she had used to appease her aunt and the dowager.

"Derbyshire?" Margaret tittered, and cast what Bella could only describe as a sly smile to Mrs. Drummond Burrell. "Does not Lady Helen Bingley live in Derbyshire?"

By the way the dowager stiffened at her side, Bella took it that there was some significance to Margaret's question.

"Yes, as a matter of fact, Lady Helen does live in Derbyshire," Mrs. Drummond Burrell agreed with alacrity. "And I have yet to see her in town this Season."

Bella raised one arched brow and looked at the ladies coldly. It was obvious to her what they were suggesting. Bella again thought of the notes she had found in the duke's waistcoat. Was that why he had been so long in Derbyshire—to meet one of the authors of the tryst notes?

Her heart thudded dully at this conclusion. How had everything in her life gotten so mixed-up and confusing?

As soon as she returned to Westlake House she would write the duke again, and demand that he grant her an annulment. She did not care what he said this time, she thought, thankful that her temper was rising. She would not be dissuaded, even though she was unclear on how to even go about obtaining an annulment.

She was just about to turn from the ladies without a word when the noise from the hundreds of guests reduced by half again.

What now? Bella wondered, turning to look toward the entryway with everyone else.

There, standing by Lord and Lady Edgeton, were the striking Duke and Duchess of Severly. Bella's heart lifted a bit as she recalled their kindness to her in Mabry Green after the ceremony.

The Duke of Severly was speaking to someone Bella could not see. A moment later, the person blocking her view moved and Bella saw an extremely handsome man.

He was very tall, very tan, and fit-looking, and the expression on his face revealed complete boredom as he surveyed the assemblage. His black evening coat fit his broad shoulders snugly, and his sparkling white neckcloth was splendid in its mathematical symmetry.

Suddenly Bella sucked in her breath.

"There is my son now," the dowager duchess stated in a tone of great satisfaction.

Chapter Seventeen

Bella could not take her eyes from Westlake. He looked so different; it was no wonder that she had not immediately recognized him.

Gone was the pallor she had grown used to, and he had also gained back some of the weight he had lost during his illness, which enhanced the air of authority emanating from him.

Bella realized the main reason she found him so unrecognizable was the bored, worldly expression he wore. She could not recall seeing that particular look during his stay at her home.

Bella continued to watch him from across the ballroom floor as the duke took a few strides into the room. A number of guests approached, and he seemed to greet them all politely as his gaze still scanned the crowd.

Without a word, Bella moved away from Margaret and Mrs. Drummond Burrell, putting more space between her and the duke. A feeling of trepidation mixed with nervous excitement engulfed her at his unexpected appearance.

At least most of the assemblage was no longer staring at her, Bella thought with a little relief.

The two footmen standing by the entryway moved in unison to close the double doors and caught her attention. A moment later Bella heard the orchestra play the opening strains of a minuet.

Lady Louisa and the Duke of Malverton, both with

beaming smiles, took the dance floor and started the minuet alone. After they made a few graceful steps, several other couples joined them on the parquet.

Bella's eyes went back to the duke's tall frame as he continued to work his way through the crowd milling on the edge of the dance floor.

Taking a deep, steadying breath, Bella stepped away from the relative safety of her vantage point and moved to join Aunt Elizabeth and Triss.

"Bella, have you seen?" Triss questioned as Bella reached her side. "The duke is here! Doesn't he look madly dashing?"

"Yes, he does," Bella said, as she continued to track his movements across the room.

He stopped to stand beneath the large crystal chandelier, slowly turning his head to take in the entire room.

Bella knew that he would see her any second now, for she was sure he was looking for her. Still, when his gaze finally found hers, the expression in his slightly narrowed eyes sent a shock through her veins. Standing rooted to the floor between her aunt and cousin, Bella tried to decipher the look in his eyes as he slowly strode toward her. Surprise? Anger? It was hard to know. He had almost reached them, and Bella was trying to catch hold of her runaway heartbeat. Could it be possible that she was wed to this handsome near-stranger?

"Good evening, Lady Penninghurst," the duke intoned after a brief salute to her aunt's hand. "Lady Triss, how many hearts have you broken so far?" he asked, turning to her cousin. Triss only giggled at his compliment.

Bella released the breath she had not realized she'd been holding, and met his gray gaze, again noticing the tiny green flecks around the irises.

His gaze swept down her form, taking in her new blush-colored gown, and moving back up again. He then surveyed her new hairstyle.

"Good evening, Arabella," he said softly. "I almost did not recognize you."

Recovering a little from feeling overset, Bella could not help smiling at his unexpected words.

"I could say the same to you, your grace," she replied.

He then offered his arm without a word, and after the merest hesitation Bella laid her fingers through the crook of his elbow. The duke excused them both to her aunt and Triss, and led her away.

As soon as they had taken a few steps, Bella was again aware of how many eyes were drawn to them, though the duke seemed to take no notice.

Westlake deftly guided her through the throngs of guests across the room to a set of open French doors that Bella had not noticed before. Seconds later they were on a garden terrace with only the low illumination from the chandeliers in the ballroom lighting their way.

The duke obviously knew his way around, for he took her straight to a bench, where he stopped and turned to face her.

She felt, more than saw, his eyes upon her in the dimness as she listened to the distant notes of a waltz. But he said nothing.

"I hope you are well, your grace," she managed to say.

"Completely recovered, thank you."

"And your business in Derbyshire went well?" she asked, wondering again about the implication Margaret and Mrs. Drummond Burrell had made about his trip.

"Yes, very satisfactorily," he replied succinctly.

"Is there any news on the highwaymen? Have they been apprehended yet?"

"No. Not yet. But I am confident they will be. In fact, that is why I was away longer than I had intended. I had to take care of some matters regarding the attack."

Bella was gratified to hear this; she hated the idea of the men who had shot the duke being at large. Moving a few steps away from the duke's disturbing nearness, she took a moment to sit down on the bench and take a couple of fortifying breaths of the cool night air. There was so much she wanted to discuss with him, but she found herself unable to formulate her words properly. Even though it had been more than six weeks since they had been compelled to wed, Bella still felt it hard to accept that this formidable nobleman was her husband—even if it was in name only.

"You are a very curious girl, Arabella," he said after a moment, his voice deep and thoughtful in the relative quiet of the cool, dim terrace.

"What do you mean?" Bella asked, looking up at his shadowy figure, trying to read his expression.

"I thought you had little interest in coming to London for the Season. But here I find you enjoying a ball, looking so much altered. You've certainly acquired town polish in a short period of time," he said in a conversational tone.

Bella could not help but laugh in surprise at the duke's assessment of her.

"Looks can be deceiving, your grace," she said a little wryly. "Let us be frank. You know I came to London only to get away from Autley. When I arrived, I intended to stay with my aunt and cousin at their town house. I truly did not intend to accept any invitations, especially since things are so unsettled between us. But your mother found my arrival a shock, and tried to send me back to Autley. So I stretched the truth by implying that I was to come and have a new wardrobe, and that you would soon be coming to London. I had to follow through with having some gowns made—or be found out," she explained as best she could.

"And as I have now arrived, you can count your conscience clean," the duke put in, and Bella heard a hint of amusement in his deep voice.

"As for having town polish, I fear nothing could be farther from the truth," Bella continued. "Your mother was just admonishing me for having so little to say for myself. I fear if I continue in this fashion, your grace, I shall be an embarrassment to you."

Bella tried to keep her tone light, but in truth she did have a fear of making an anecdote of herself.

There was silence between them again, and it was a little while before Bella took her courage in hand and broached the subject that constantly nagged at her emotions.

"Your grace, we should discuss our future," she began in a hesitant voice, playing with the fan in her lap.

The duke took a step toward her and breached the space between them. He sat down next to her, and Bella could see his handsome face more clearly now. Her heart gave an odd thump at the mixture of amusement and sympathy she saw in his eyes.

"Yes, Arabella, we should. But first I have a very great favor to ask of you," he said.

"What is it?" she asked with hesitant curiosity.

"I read the note you left for me at Autley before you came to London. I understand why you were uncomfortable there. More importantly to you, I understand your desire for an annulment. But I would ask that we put off any further discussion on the subject until after Louisa's wedding. I'm sure you are aware of the scandal such an event would cause during this important time in her life," he finished in his deep voice.

Suddenly Bella felt very selfish for not having thought of this before. Of course the news of their annulment would ruin this very happy time for Louisa. The duke was as much a victim of circumstances as she was, she realized. But because the duke now seemed more amenable to at least discussing the prospect, Bella felt better than she had since coming to London.

"That is a reasonable request, your grace," Bella replied with a sincere smile. "Perhaps it would be better to wait until after the wedding before setting the process of annulment in motion."

"I believe that is the best course for us to take." The duke nodded.

Understanding the reason for his suggestion, Bella was pleased to think that there was a plan for resolving their dilemma. She watched him closely, for she still detected a gleam of amusement in his eyes, though it was hard to be sure in the dim light on the terrace. But her heart lifted at the knowledge that he was willing to discuss an annulment at a future date.

"Nil deserandum," she said more to herself than to him. She heard his deep chuckle in response.

"That is right, my little scholar, do not despair," he replied.

"Tell me, your grace, what does your family know of the situation surrounding our marriage? From conversation with your sister, I could tell she did not know the whole of it," Bella told him.

"The Duke and Duchess of Severly are the only people who understand the full circumstance of our marriage. My mother knows something odd occurred after she left Mabry Green, but has not pressed me for details. As for the rest of my family, I only informed them of the fact that we were married and that they were to welcome you accordingly," he replied. "I also have not discussed the shooting with anyone else, and have told my family not to do so either."

Nodding her understanding, Bella was silent as she thought over his words.

"I have the feeling that you have not enjoyed yourself while you have been in London. Am I correct?" he asked, changing the subject.

"Yes, you are," Bella agreed with dismay. "I do not know what all the fuss about London is, though everyone else seems to be having a gay time."

"Let us see if we can change that," the duke offered, rising from the bench to stand facing her on the dark terrace. "You have been to none of the museums. I am sure you will find Lord Elgin's marbles of interest. You have not been to the theater? Then we will go to Covent Garden soon. There are also a number of bookstores to visit. Have you been to the Tower of London?" he questioned.

Bella could only shake her head in the negative, for she was completely taken aback by his offer.

"Then we should start there. I predict that in a very short time, Arabella, you will be enjoying some of the delights London has to offer," he stated with conviction.

Bella had risen also, and of an accord they both started to walk back to the ballroom. Right before they were to enter, the duke paused, turning to Bella.

"One more thing, my dear. If you cannot bring yourself to call me Alex, then you must at least manage Westlake. This formality will just not do." He gave her a slight grin and offered his arm once again.

Bella swallowed hard as they stepped back into the noisy, brightly lit ballroom.

"Thank you . . . Westlake," she said, returning his smile.

Chapter Eighteen

A week later, the duke invited the three ladies residing in his home to take a drive in Hyde Park.

"We shall tool around at our leisure, and relax after all the walking we have done these last few days," he offered as they were all sitting in the bright and airy breakfast room.

"Famous! We shall be delighted," said Triss, hardly able to contain her excitement at the prospect of being seen by the beau monde in the duke's landau.

Bella gave her cousin a quelling look, for she thought Triss was much too coming where the duke's generosity was concerned.

Triss ignored Bella and continued to gaze at the duke with excitement.

"No, Beatrice, we are going shopping this afternoon," Aunt Elizabeth reminded her daughter. "And have you forgotten your appointment to have your new gown fitted? You said you wanted the pink one to be ready by Wednesday."

Triss bit her lip in indecision. She wanted to ride in the duke's landau very much, but she also wanted to have her pink gown to wear at her first appearance at Almack's.

The duke solved her dilemma. "Arabella and I shall go today. But we will all go to the park again soon," he offered generously.

"Promise?" Triss demanded.

"Triss! Really!" Bella had had enough of her cousin's impertinent behavior.

Laughing, the duke made the promise, and Triss looked as pleased as a cat with a bowl of cream.

Bella set her cup of chocolate back in its saucer and surveyed the scene around her with some amazement. A week ago she never would have believed that this kind of harmony could have been achieved. She had, at first, been worried about how the duke would react to having Aunt Elizabeth and Triss as his guests. Somewhat to her surprise, Westlake had been more than welcoming.

After Lady Louisa's engagement ball, Aunt Elizabeth had suggested that she and Triss return to their rented house. To Bella's amusement, Triss had looked as if she were going to faint at her mother's words, and waited for the duke's response with bated breath.

"I won't hear of it, Aunt Penninghurst," the duke had said, taking the good lady's hand in his and bringing it to his lips in a brief salute. "Besides, you and Lady Triss are all settled in, so why bestir yourself to move when I am pleased to have you as my guests?" he had asked with such a charming smile that Lady Penninghurst found she could not resist him.

So the four of them stayed at Westlake House, and to Bella's disbelief, she began to enjoy her stay in London.

In the following days, the duke had proved as good as his word. He had taken her to the Tower of London and the British Museum. Bella thought her papa would have found it interesting to view the marble friezes Lord Elgin had removed from the Parthenon and brought over to England.

Bella had been very much impressed with the well-rounded knowledge of art and history the duke displayed. But what surprised her most was how amiable and relaxed the duke seemed. She had fully expected him to be bored with such tame pursuits as strolling through museums and browsing through stalls at bookstores. But he had shown no such sign of ennui.

Last night had been exceptionally exciting for Bella, for the duke had escorted all the Tichley ladies to Covent Garden to see *The Barber of Seville*. Bella had never experienced anything like it. She had looked around in wonder at the theater, which resembled a fantasy version of a Greek temple. She raptly watched the opera from the duke's box, which afforded an excellent view of the stage. At first she had found it extremely distracting that half the people in the pit and in the boxes on the other side of the horseshoe-shaped opera house seemed to have their lorgnettes trained on her and the duke. It had also been annoying that Triss was paying little attention to the entertainment and kept whispering and pointing out the other notables in attendance.

Still, Bella had enjoyed the new sights and sounds immensely.

After such excitements, a ride through Hyde Park on this gloriously clear spring day would be a refreshing diversion, Bella decided as she left the breakfast room to change her clothes.

Later, as the duke handed her into his high-perch phaeton, instead of the landau, Bella was able to smile at him quite naturally. Everything would be wonderful if only the oppressive specter of their forced marriage were not hanging over them, she thought as he jumped in next to her and took the reins.

But the duke's proposal that they not discuss the annulment until after his sister's wedding had freed Bella from having to worry constantly, and for that she was grateful.

Setting his horses to a brisk trot, the duke expertly tooled them around his drive and onto Park Lane.

Bella chanced a sideways glance at him from under the brim of her new bonnet. His black beaver top hat accented his height, and she could not help but admire the cut of his coat. Now that he had fully recovered from his injury, there was no bandage or sling to mar the effortless perfection of his elegance. Though he had shown little interest in his appearance during his stay at the cottage, there was now no denying that the duke was a leader in masculine fashion.

They drove through the streets enjoying the bright spring day in silence, before Bella decided to bring up something that had been bothering her since his arrival to town.

"Thank you for offering to take Triss for a drive in the

park. It is very kind of you, under the circumstances," she said a little shyly as they turned in to the park.

"Not at all, Bella. A ride in the park is a trifle," he dismissed, giving her a brief smile as he slowed the horses to a walk.

"She does not deserve such trifles," Bella stated with asperity. "In truth, it embarrasses me how she has manipulated this situation she created to advance her cause. She is on the hunt for a titled husband and is using her connection to you to give her an air of consequence. I have no doubt that the only reason she received her voucher for Almack's so quickly is because of you."

"It matters not. The way you two squabble reminds me of my sisters." The duke shot her a teasing grin as they joined a crowd of carriages and horses as they turned onto Rotten Row.

"Squabble!" Bella looked askance at the duke. "*We* are the victims of her machinations. And *she* blithely plans her come-out next week at Almack's. You are much too generous in your attitude toward her," Bella said.

"It is my pleasure to see what your cousin will do and say next," he responded.

She could think of nothing to say and was soon diverted from her worrying thoughts by the sight of the most toplofty members of the beau monde showing off for each other in the spring sunshine. Shortly it became apparent that a number of people who had not met Bella previously were eager to be introduced to the new Duchess of Westlake.

The duke seemed perfectly at his ease, and was quite amenable to stopping his cattle every few yards, so that any number of people could be presented to Bella.

Bella had to squelch her growing nervousness as she met the duke's friends. Though she had agreed not to pursue an annulment until after Louisa's wedding, it seemed to her that the more people that she met, the more embarrassing it would be for the duke later.

Maybe she should have stayed in the country, she mused with a frown. But when she had arrived in London she had had no intention of entering into Society, she reasoned.

Who would have guessed the turn of events in the last week?

The words the duke had said to her in his library about trusting him came immediately to her mind. Though he sometimes made her nervous for reasons she refused to examine, there was no doubt about his sense of honor. He, at least, was certain that all would turn out well. Resolutely she pushed the niggling feeling of uncertainty away and turned her attention back to the conversation at hand.

After a few more shared pleasantries with some of the duke's friends, he drove the phaeton a little farther along Rotten Row.

"Arabella," the duke began once they were a little more private, "we have received an invitation from my good friends the Duke and Duchess of Severly. I know you are not fond of crowded events, but Drake and Celia rarely entertain on a large scale. They usually only have ten or twelve couples to dine. I think you might find an evening spent with them enjoyable."

Bella thought over the duke's words for a moment. She recalled her brief encounter with the duke and duchess at the marriage ceremony, and because of their kindness, she decided she would indeed like to meet them again.

Bella continued to watch the throngs of people enjoying the park in the warm afternoon sunshine.

Up ahead a vis-à-vis driven by a liveried coachman caught her attention. "There is Margaret," Bella told the duke.

Frowning, the duke's eyes narrowed as he surveyed the crowded lane before them. "Where?" he questioned.

With a little movement of her parasol, she gestured to the carriage. "Up ahead. She is with a very pretty blond-haired lady and they are speaking to a gentleman on horseback."

"I see them now," said the duke, maneuvering his team around a stationary carriage.

As he pulled the phaeton next to the vis-à-vis, Bella saw Margaret break off her conversation with the man on horseback as soon as she caught sight of the duke. Without waiting to acknowledge Westlake, the gentleman spurred the horse into a canter and left the lane.

"Westlake!" Margaret said with an odd note of alarm in her voice.

"Afternoon, Margaret," said the duke in a cool tone.

"May I present Lady Kendall, your grace?" she said, looking at Bella and twisting the handle of her beribboned parasol around and around.

It took Bella a moment to respond. "Oh, of course," she said, recovering quickly. She wondered if she could ever get used to being addressed so formally.

"I am so very glad to meet you, your grace," the blond woman gushed.

"Thank you," Bella said, with a slight inclination of her head.

"You will forgive us, won't you, my dear Duke and Duchess? Lady Kendall and I are shockingly late for our tea with Countess Lieven," Margaret said, tapping the bench with her parasol to signal the driver to be off.

Bella watched the duke touch the brim of his hat politely and watch the ladies retreat with cool, slightly narrowed eyes.

As they headed back to Westlake House, Bella thanked the duke for the outing.

"My pleasure, Arabella."

Something about the duke's manner made Bella sense that he was distracted.

"Is something wrong, Westlake? Has the drive been too much for your shoulder? I am sure it must still bother you at times," Bella asked.

"No. I am fine." He dismissed her concern with a brief smile. "Tell me, did you happen to take notice of the man on horseback who was speaking to Margaret as we drove up?"

"Why, yes," Bella answered in a slightly startled tone, wondering what he was getting at.

"Do you believe you have ever seen him before?"

Pursing her lips, Bella tried to recall something about the man that might seem familiar. "No, I don't believe so. Why do you ask?"

"It is nothing very important. But if you ever see him

again, I want you to inform me immediately," he said firmly, turning his disturbing gray eyes to meet hers.

Bella could not mistake his very serious expression.

"Certainly I will," she assured him as they turned up the drive leading to Westlake House.

Chapter Nineteen

"This is Almack's?" Bella whispered to Triss, looking around in disbelief as they stepped into the large, plain ballroom. "This is the place you have for years so wanted to gain entrance to?"

"Hush, Bella," Triss said crossly to her cousin. "It will be much better later in the evening. It is early yet."

Triss had insisted that they arrive at the hallowed halls of Almack's before the dancing began. The ball would open with a minuet, and it had been arranged that the Duke of Malverton's younger brother would partner Triss in her very first dance at the exclusive club. She had been adamant in her desire not to miss anything.

It had not been Bella's desire to attend the assembly tonight, but as Triss had wheedled the duke to act as escort, Bella decided it would look odd if she did not join her aunt, Triss, and Westlake.

Triss had been transported with excitement to finally have a voucher to Almack's, the most exclusive playground of the *haute ton*. In her desire for perfection, she had driven Bella to distraction with her endless fretting and fussing over her toilette until she had finally been satisfied that she looked her best.

Triss's new pink gown was scattered with a multitude of tiny seed pearls, and she wore a band of the same on the crown of her head, with her golden blond hair arranged in a riot of upswept curls.

Though the duke had accompanied them to the unprepossessing building, he had taken himself off to one of the antechambers as soon as he had delivered Bella, Triss, and Aunt Elizabeth to his mother's side.

Bella watched him stride away, relieved to be out of his disturbing presence.

"It is a very good thing you are married, Bella, or I would be quite jealous of you right now," Triss said, eyeing the jewels Bella wore with envy.

Glancing down, Bella admitted to herself that she felt odd wearing the diamond *demi-parure* the duke had given her before they had departed for the evening. She felt even more disturbed recalling the scene that had taken place between them in her bedchamber.

An hour earlier, after her maid had just finished helping her dress in her lavender-blue evening gown, there had been a knock on her bedchamber door.

It had been a complete surprise to see the duke enter. Dressed in formal evening attire, he presented an impressive picture. Carter the maid slipped from the room and closed the door softly behind her. Bella's questioning gaze immediately went to the large flat leather case the duke held.

"I thought you might enjoy wearing these this evening," the duke said, stepping farther into the room.

Bella could only raise a brow in surprise and watch as the duke placed the case on her dressing table and opened the lid.

Taking a step closer, Bella did not glance down at first, but continued to look at the duke. There was something different about his demeanor this evening, some indefinable emotion she could not put her finger on.

Finally she looked down at the open case. A gasp escaped her lips at the sight of the glittering jewelry lying against the deep blue velvet that lined the case.

"They would look very well on you," he said, his voice deep and gentle.

The necklace was made of a triple strand of graduated diamonds; the brooch was large, with three large diamonds dangling from the bottom of a round cluster of diamonds. A pair of diamond earbobs nestled between the necklace and brooch.

"Oh, no. I could not wear these," she said.

Reaching into the case, the duke picked up the necklace. "Of course you can. Don't all women like to wear jewels?" he responded with a slight smile on his firm lips.

"But, your grace, I already feel such a fraud. Somehow wearing these would just make it worse," she tried to explain, twisting her hands together.

The duke's piercing gray-green eyes met hers as he moved to step behind her. "Arabella, it is only jewelry. You are a beautiful woman on your way to attend a ball. The Westlake vaults are full of such trinkets. Why not enjoy their beauty?" he questioned as he brought the necklace around to rest on her neck.

Bella could see the duke's reflection in the mirror on her vanity as he stood behind her. Something about his nearness made her stand very still. She found it difficult to breathe as he fastened the heavy piece of jewelry around her neck. It lay cool and sparkling against her collarbone.

Their gazes met in the reflection of the mirror, and Bella saw a smile lurking at the corner of the duke's mouth. The warmth of his breath was on her nape, as he stood very close behind her. His long fingers still rested very lightly on her neck, and a shiver went down her arms as she stood, as if frozen, in front of him.

His piercing gaze held hers in the mirror, and she found that she suddenly had no desire to pull away. Again, an exquisite shiver danced down her spine.

Was this the same man she had cared for while he had been so weak? she asked herself in wonderment. It was almost impossible to recognize this broad-shouldered, disturbingly confident, and heartbreakingly handsome man as the one who had been so near death in her bedroom.

Slowly his fingers trailed down the sides of her neck to the tops of her shoulders. She felt the strength of his hands through the sheerness of her evening gown. All of a sudden the feel of his warm hands and the intensity of his gaze were too much for Bella to cope with.

Taking a ragged, deep breath, she let a feeling of self-preservation make her step away from him. With trembling fingers, she reached for the earbobs.

"Thank you. I shall enjoy wearing such lovely things," she said shakily, refusing to look at him.

"Thank you, Arabella," he said.

Holding the earbobs in her hand, Bella cast a quick sideways glance at the duke, and caught the speculative gleam in his gray gaze as he turned to leave without another word. When the door closed behind him, Bella moved on unsteady legs to sit on her bed, still feeling the warmth of his fingers almost caressing her neck. A feeling of near disorientation seized her emotions, and she closed her eyes against the onslaught of unfamiliar feelings.

It is what sophisticated men of the duke's ilk do for amusement, she told herself sternly. Since coming to London, had she not heard story after story about the duke's reputation as a rake? Had she not seen for herself the notes women had given him, so that he would meet them in private?

Bella felt confused and frightened, betrayed by her own thoughts and emotions. She had always prided herself on her good sense and judgment. From the time she was twelve, after the unexpected death of her mother, she had planned her life out very carefully. But since the day she had found the duke half-dead on her front drive, everything she had believed in and planned for was now gone.

If she allowed herself to succumb to his obvious expertise where women were concerned, she knew she would only be a fool.

It was horrible enough that they had been forced into this sham marriage, but how much worse it would be if she actually cared for him, she thought, clutching the earbobs to her chest.

Since the wedding Bella felt that she no longer truly belonged anywhere. Virtually rejected by her father and uncle, she knew she could not go home. So she had grasped at the idea of an annulment to save her from being a faceless nobody in one of the duke's homes. She would continue to be treated with contempt by his servants, because even they knew that she did not belong.

She recalled the duke's words about assignations in atriums being unimportant. The women who had written those notes had been guests in his home, ladies from good families, and it had meant nothing to him. She wondered how they felt. Had they been in love with him and felt the sting of his rejection?

If those women had meant nothing, Bella knew in her heart that she would mean less than nothing.

Oh, she knew that he was grateful to her for her care of him while he had been injured. He probably had no compunction in starting a flirtation with her. She could even believe that to save his family from the scandal of an annulment he might even accept this marriage. But he certainly would never have chosen her for his bride.

Even if they agreed to continue with the marriage, his life would not change. She would be the one to suffer the pain of his faithlessness, the shame of his flaunting his dalliances in front of the world.

No! She would not live that way, she vowed to herself, thankful that anger was now clearing her confused senses.

Once she obtained the annulment, Papa would have to take her back. She did not care if she lived the rest of her life as a pariah. She would not consign herself to this kind of misery if she could do something to prevent it.

Feeling relief at her new resolve, Bella had affixed the earbobs to her earlobes and clipped the brooch to the front of the high-waisted bodice of her gown. She then grabbed her shawl and reticule and left her bedchamber, determined to ignore the duke at all costs.

"Bella, are you well? You are awfully flushed."

Bella was pulled back to the present by her aunt's concerned question, and saw that the duke's mother was also looking at her with a frown.

"I am perfectly well." She forced a smile and opened her fan.

Looking around, she noticed that there were now scores of people milling about, and the room was becoming noisy as the musicians tuned their instruments.

Triss and Louisa came to her side, and for once Bella was grateful for their chatter. She thought the two younger girls looked enchanting together, Triss in her pink gown and Louisa in one of spring green.

It occurred to Bella that she had not seen Margaret this

eve, and she questioned Lady Louisa regarding the where-abouts of her sister-in-law.

"Oh, Margaret. She is at some rout or crush," Louisa said with a dismissive shrug. "More than likely somewhere with high-stakes faro. Margaret was always one for the cards."

Bella raised a brow at Louisa's cold description of her sister-in-law but made no comment.

"Arabella, you look stunning in Grandmama's diamonds," Lady Louisa told her a moment later. "Grandpapa had the set made for their wedding. I always remember Grandmama wearing them on special occasions. I wonder what kind of jewelry Malverton will give me? Do you think I should let him know that I much prefer diamonds and emeralds to rubies and sapphires?"

Bella left the answer to that question to Triss's expertise, turning to converse quietly with her aunt.

After the orchestra began to play, it suddenly became clear to Bella why Almack's was so popular. Besides the exclusivity created by the patronesses, the orchestra was very good. As she stood on the edge of the dance floor with Aunt Elizabeth and the Dowager Duchess of West-lake, Bella watched Triss as she performed the intricate steps of the minuet. Bella observed that the Duke of Malverton's brother seemed very young, but he partnered Triss well.

Afterward, the young man returned Triss to her mother, thanking her with a bow for the honor of their dance. Triss turned shining, excited eyes to Bella.

"Is not this the most wonderful evening? Just think, Bella, there are any number of eligible gentlemen from very good families, all under one roof!"

Bella could not help but laugh at her cousin's frank hus-band hunting. It certainly was difficult to stay angry at Triss for any length of time, she admitted to herself.

The music, the laughter, and the skill of the dancers helped a great deal in Bella's attempt to keep her mind from the disturbing scene earlier with the duke. At unex-pected moments, Bella's mind would conjure the feel of the duke's hands upon her neck and shoulders and the unsettling intensity of his gaze.

As Bella stood conversing with Aunt Elizabeth and the dowager, Lady Louisa again approached Bella, this time with a very beautiful woman in tow.

"My dear duchess, I would like to present Lady Bolton. She particularly wished to be made known to you."

Lady Bolton sketched a quick curtsy to Bella just as Lady Louisa's current partner claimed her hand for the next cotillion and led her away.

Bella smiled at Lady Bolton, admiring the beautiful blue gown that showed the swanlike length of her neck to advantage.

"Your grace, I have desired to make your acquaintance since hearing of Westlake's unexpected marriage," the lady said.

"I can understand that," Bella replied as noncommittally as she could after a moment's pause. Bella watched Lady Bolton as her gaze traveled over Bella's figure, lingering on the jewelry the duke had given her earlier.

"Yes, you see, Westlake has been a *dear* friend for any number of years, and I was a guest at the house party taking place at Autley when we received the dreadful news that he had gone missing," Lady Bolton continued.

Even though she was standing next to Aunt Elizabeth and the dowager duchess amidst a crowd of people, Bella was aware that she and Lady Bolton were relatively private, as her aunt and the duke's mother were deep in conversation.

"That must have been distressing," Bella acknowledged, doing her best to keep her expression serene.

"Oh, very!" the lady said. "Especially since the duke and I had *certain* plans. You and Westlake could have known each other for only a matter of weeks before you wed. Tell me, your grace, how did your romance blossom so quickly?"

"Yes. It did happen quickly. The ways of fate are so mysterious," Bella replied, growing increasingly nervous at Lady Bolton's line of questioning. Bella also had not missed Lady Bolton's comment about having *certain* plans with the duke.

Plans to meet at midnight in the lush atrium at Autley, no doubt, Bella thought with a pang near her heart.

"One wonders how the two of you had enough time to get to know each other," Lady Bolton continued, her eyes expressing avid interest.

"Yes, one does wonder," Bella replied, trying to imitate the polite half smile the dowager duchess constantly displayed to perfection.

Lady Bolton did not seem satisfied with Bella's answer. Her eyes narrowed slightly. She flipped her ornate fan open with a snap and began using it in a rapid motion to cool her flushed cheeks.

Bella decided the best course to take was to outwait Lady Bolton and remain silent. If the duke's friend wanted more information about their marriage, she could just ask Westlake, Bella thought with some exasperation.

At that moment Bella saw Lady Jersey coming toward her through the glittering throng of people. Bella was quite aware that Lady Jersey was one of the formidable patronesses of Almack's. Triss had explained this to her earlier. Along with the other patronesses, the lady ruled its hallowed ground with an iron fist cloaked in the proverbial velvet glove.

With an inward groan, Bella recalled what Triss had said earlier during their ride to Almack's: "If the patronesses find that someone is not up to snuff then they are banned forever from Almack's. No young lady could feel that her Season had been a success without a voucher."

Bella's nervousness grew as Lady Jersey bore down upon her.

"Is it the Duchess of Westlake? How terribly exciting!" the very grand-looking woman said to Bella without waiting for an introduction. "Your most unexpected union is the only topic upon everyone's lips this Season," Lady Jersey gushed. "How romantic, your grace. We shall take a turn around the room and you can tell me all about it. I cannot believe that sly boots, Westlake, did not tell me a thing about you!"

With a panicked look thrown over her shoulder to her aunt and the dowager, Bella saw no way out of going with the vivacious Lady Jersey.

They had not moved very far when, to Bella's great relief, she saw Westlake enter the assembly room from a side door. Over the heads of the other guests, she saw him scan the room and was immediately aware when he located her. She watched as he made his way through the crowd to intercept her path with Lady Jersey.

"Hello, Sally. I see you have met Arabella." The duke greeted Lady Jersey with the familiarity of long acquaintance.

"Yes, Westlake, and we are just about to have a nice coze," she told the duke with a smile. "I wish to get to know our new duchess."

"You will have to forgive me, Sally. But this is the first waltz of the evening, and it is my right as a groom to claim my bride before anyone else does," he said, flashing her an irresistible smile.

"Of course, of course," Lady Jersey responded with delight. "Who would have guessed that you would be so romantical? Well, they say reformed rakes make the best husbands!" she trilled before leaving the duke and Bella to take the dance floor.

Laying her fingers on the duke's arm, Bella looked up at him with an expression of unconcealed relief.

"Thank you, Westlake. I confess I do not know what to say when people start asking questions about our marriage. It is difficult to avoid it when everyone seems so curious about you," she finished with a sigh.

Looking down at her, the duke met her gaze with a smile. "You must just turn your nose in the air and stare them out of countenance. You are the Duchess of Westlake. You need not answer questions if you do not desire to do so."

Giving a little laugh, Bella shook her head. "It is all right for you to be so toplofty. But I find it difficult to behave with such condescension."

The duke quirked his brow at her.

"Then just pretend you are speaking to me. You have no such difficulty putting me in my place; why should you with lesser mortals?"

Bella could not help the laugh that came so easily at his remark, but made no response as the orchestra played the evening's first waltz.

Without another word, the duke placed his hand upon

her waist and swung her onto the floor to the opening strains of a Viennese waltz.

The duke proved an excellent partner as they gracefully waltzed among the *ton*. Feeling very aware of the duke's nearness, Bella kept her gaze firmly fixed over his right shoulder as they made another half turn in front of her smiling Aunt Elizabeth. She also noticed the approving looks given them by the dowager duchess and Lady Louisa. There were a number of other people watching them also, Bella noted—most of them being ladies, with less approving expressions.

As they danced, Bella was surprised at how well they moved together. It was as if they had been dancing with each other all of their lives.

"My compliments to your dancing instructor," the duke said with a smile in his eyes.

"I will thank you on his behalf," Bella responded, giving him a wry little smile.

In silence they continued to glide across the floor in perfect rhythm with each other.

With a growing feeling of self-consciousness, Bella became keenly aware of a fluttering feeling in her chest that was unconnected to the physical exertion of dancing.

The duke guided her through a smooth half turn, and Bella turned her gaze on the slight cleft in his square chin. Taking a deep breath, she concentrated on trying to calm the quivering of her nerves. This odd feeling had begun earlier in the evening, when the duke had entered her bedchamber with the jewel case.

"Lady Louisa told me your grandfather had the *demiparure* made for your grandmother," Bella ventured, trying to distract herself from the unfamiliar emotions assailing her senses.

"Yes. I have fond memories of my grandmother wearing the jewels."

"They are lovely," Bella said shyly.

"My mother is not overly fond of diamonds. She finds them cold," the duke continued. "But I think they look particularly well on you, Arabella. The sparkle of the diamonds complements the sparkle in your amazing eyes."

Bella's gaze met the duke's. The waltz was ending, and their gazes locked for a brief, heart-stopping moment. They stood motionless on the dance floor for a little longer than the other dancers.

Dragging air into her lungs, Bella forced her eyes from the duke's compelling gaze. "Thank you," she said breathlessly, still reeling from his unexpected compliment.

With a brief inclination of his head, the duke offered his arm and they made their way back to where his mother and Aunt Elizabeth were holding court with Triss and Louisa.

"There you are, Alex," Lady Louisa called as they approached. "Where have you been all evening? In the card room, no doubt. Aren't the stakes much too low for you? Oh, well, you are here now. I hope you have not forgotten that you promised to dance a reel with me." She looked up at her brother with smiling, confident eyes.

The duke looked down at his youngest sister with amused tolerance. "All right, Prattle. They are starting a reel now." He gave in with a chuckle. Giving a brief bow to Bella and the other ladies, the duke led his sister to the dance floor.

"I'll say this for you, my girl," the dowager called over to Bella above the din. "You are an accomplished dancer."

"Thank you, ma'am." Bella smiled at her stately mother-in-law.

"Are you enjoying yourself, Bella?" Triss asked as she stood at her mother's side.

"Yes. I believe I am," Bella admitted, somewhat to her own surprise.

The dowager stepped forward and began introducing a few "notables," as she put it, to Bella and her family.

Bella recalled the duke's words to her about keeping her chin up and not answering questions. So, when any of those she was introduced to became too inquisitive about her sudden marriage to the duke, she put his advice to use.

After a little while of this, Bella was given a reprieve from the onslaught of introductions when the dowager became involved in a deep conversation with her friend, Lady Pembrington.

Bella stood with her family for a few minutes, fanning herself and enjoying the sight of the dancers and spectators alike. She was only half listening to Triss chatter about the number of unattached gentlemen when she turned her attention to the duke dancing with his sister. The reel was lively, and Bella marveled at how well the duke had recovered from his injury. Bella found herself admiring the way he carried himself with such self-assurance.

After being at Autley, and now at Westlake House, Bella had to admit that it was much to the duke's credit that he was not completely insufferable. She considered the manner in which he lived—with hundreds of servants to see to his every need and whim, and numerous estates across Great Britain—yet one would never have known any of this by the way he behaved during his stay at her home.

In spite of his questionable morals, the duke certainly had impeccable manners, she mused, continuing to watch his movements.

The reel ended and Bella turned from watching Westlake to converse with her aunt. A moment later Triss caught her off guard by grabbing her arm.

"Bella, look over there," Triss whispered. "No. Don't look now."

"Heavens! What bee has gotten in your bonnet?" Bella gave a mystified smile to her cousin.

Her cousin's eyes were wide with concern as she stared at something across the room. Turning her head, Bella tried to follow Triss's gaze. She saw nothing out of the ordinary in the number of people crowding the assembly room. Triss continued to grip her arm, and Bella continued to scan the crowd for what was amiss.

The back of a blond male head caught her attention. Bella kept her eyes fixed on the blond as he turned around. She sucked in her breath as the man turned to face her fully. "Why, it is Robert Fortiscue!" Bella gasped in surprise.

Chapter Twenty

Standing with Triss in the midst of the crowded assembly room, Bella watched with a growing sense of foreboding as Robert Fortiscue approached them.

"How did *he* get a voucher?" Triss asked in a tone of great disgust.

"He cannot mean to address me, not after how horrible he was that morning," Bella whispered in astonishment.

But Robert Fortiscue continued to weave his way through the crowd toward her.

Bella could not help noticing how different her former beau appeared. His hair was coifed à la Brutus, very stiff and shiny. His shirt collar was so high that Bella thought it gave him the appearance of having a stiff neck.

"Lud, does he have egg whites in his hair?" Triss whispered behind her fan just as he was almost upon them.

Stopping a few feet away, Robert stared at Bella for a moment, with a trace of a sneer on his lips, before performing a flamboyant, sweeping bow.

Bella glanced around in panic, hoping that a way of escape would present itself. She did not know why she found his presence so shocking; she knew that he often came to London. So much had happened since he had found her with the duke that morning—she had never given a thought to meeting Robert by chance in London.

As he straightened, Bella saw his eyes traveling up her

form. She stiffened in offense as she saw his contemptuous gaze lingering on the jewels at her neck.

"Fancy meeting you here, Miss Tichley," he said to her in a haughty tone.

Before she could respond, Bella felt Triss bristle at her side.

"Are you, mayhap, addressing her grace, the Duchess of Westlake?" Triss said.

Shifting his weight to one foot and putting a hand on his hip, Robert turned his sneering visage to Triss. "Lady Beatrice Tichley. My! The patronesses are letting the guard down if they are giving hoydens like you vouchers," was his snapping response.

Triss gasped in outrage, and Bella put a calming hand on her cousin's arm.

"How dare you, sir," Bella said in a quiet, yet very firm tone. "If your only purpose in approaching us is to be insulting, then we shall take our leave of you." Bella lifted her chin, took Triss by the arm, and made to move past him.

Robert Fortiscue stepped smoothly in front of Bella, blocking her path.

Her progress halted, Bella looked up at him with angry astonishment. Short of shoving him aside, she had no choice but to stop. Glancing around, Bella could not help noticing a number of people looking their way with avid, curious faces. With burning cheeks, Bella wanted nothing more than to get away from Robert Fortiscue immediately.

"You forget yourself, sir," Bella said in a low, angry tone.

"You may be a duchess, Arabella Tichley, but you can be sure that I will make it known exactly how it is that you came to be one," he said in a slightly raised voice.

Without bothering to respond, Bella cast him a scathing glance before sweeping past him with Triss in tow. Desperately she looked around the crowded room for a familiar face. Aunt Elizabeth and the dowager had gotten separated from them in the last few moments, and Bella saw no one she knew in the immediate vicinity.

A little farther away, near the refreshments, Bella saw

Lady Edgeton and Lady Louisa. With relief, and with a great effort not to add to her conspicuousness by rushing, Bella and Triss moved through the throng to join the other ladies. As they drew near, Bella saw Lady Edgeton looking at her with an arrogant expression on her otherwise pretty features.

"Who was that man you were speaking with, Arabella? He certainly is quite the dandy," she said, looking at Bella keenly.

"Oh, that was just Robert Fortiscue," Triss put in before Bella could reply. "He used to be Bella's beau, until she had to marry the duke," she finished, her cheeks still flushed with anger from their encounter with Robert.

Bella's heart sank to her slippers. Unfortunately a number of people were close enough to have heard this indiscreet remark. Would Triss never learn to curb her wayward tongue? she wondered, trying to stifle the urge to run from the building.

Lady Edgeton straightened her shoulders as if a ramrod were thrust down her spine.

"Had to marry the duke?" she questioned Bella with angry, narrowed eyes. "I knew something was odd and amiss about this marriage. You will give me all the details of this sordid business at once," she demanded.

Bella looked from Lady Edgeton to Louisa, who stood next to her sister with her mouth open in astonishment. For once she seemed to have nothing to say.

The mere fact that her marriage to the duke had not been by her design was the only thing that saved Bella from a completely mortifying sense of embarrassment.

"The details of my marriage to the duke are none of your affair," Bella said, lifting her chin stubbornly in an attempt to stave off more questions.

Without saying another word, Bella turned on her heel and left the duke's sisters staring after her with varying degrees of astonishment plainly evident on their faces. She made her way as quickly as she could to the cloakroom. Triss caught up with her there.

"Bella, what are you going to do?" she questioned breathlessly. "Robert practically threatened to tell everyone about you and the duke!"

Completely out of patience, Bella rounded on her cousin.

"*He* threatened to tell everyone?" she said with anger sparking in her deep blue eyes. "*You* are the one who just told the duke's sisters that he *had* to marry me! Will you never learn to hold your tongue?"

Taking a step back in shock at Bella's unusual show of anger, Triss looked at her cousin in genuine confusion. "But I thought his sisters knew why you and the duke had to marry," Triss cried out after Bella swept past her, leaving Triss to follow with a hurt and baffled expression on her face.

Bella went to the entryway and told the doorman to have the Westlake coach brought around.

"But Bella, what about Westlake and Mother? Are we just going to leave them?" Triss asked Bella in a small voice.

"If you find Aunt Elizabeth within the next few minutes, she can return to Westlake House with us. I will send the coach back once we are home," she told Triss firmly. Nothing was going to make her stay a second longer than she had to, she thought, her cheeks still burning at the memory of Robert's insults.

"What I ever saw in that supercilious, odious fop, I shall never know," she said aloud, and in such an angry tone that the very well trained footman so forgot himself as to gape at her.

Triss was looking anxious, clenching and unclenching her fingers. "Bella, have them hold the coach a moment. Let me find Mama," she begged Bella before quickly leaving to search for Lady Penninghurst.

When the butler at Westlake House opened the door to the three dejected ladies, Bella immediately headed for the staircase.

"Please send the coach back to Almack's and inform me the moment his grace returns," she told the expressionless servant as she took the steps.

"Bella, please let us discuss what has happened."

Hearing the concern in her aunt's voice, Bella looked down at her standing in the foyer below, next to Triss.

"Please, Aunt Elizabeth, I would rather not," she said,

trying to keep the anger and panic she felt from reaching her voice.

She gained her room and instantly began to pace the floor. A moment later she stopped to take off the diamond jewelry and place it back in its case.

What would she do now? she wondered, putting her hands to her cheeks in misery. Taking another turn around the room, she tried to think of somewhere to go. The realization that there were no more places to run caused her to speed her pacing. She had fled Autley to seek refuge with her family in London. Now, after the mortifying scene at Almack's, London was no longer a solace against the recent, frightening changes in her life.

How long she fretted and paced she did not know, but when she heard a knock at her door, she ran to it and flung it open. To her relief it was the duke.

"Oh, please come in," she said, opening the door wide.

He strode into the middle of the room, still in his evening attire, and turned to look at her with an unreadable expression. Shutting the door, she moved to stand in front of him.

"Did you see Robert Fortiscue at Almack's?" she asked without preamble.

"No, he departed before I had the chance. But I gather from the gossip buzzing around the room, and from what I could glean from my sisters, that there was a bit of a scene," he said with a dismissive shrug.

Bella stared at him for a moment with troubled, beautiful eyes. It was frustrating that she could not discern from his words or expression what he was thinking.

Of a sudden, the weeks of turbulent, stressful changes seemed to crash down upon her weary shoulders. Her eyes welled with tears and her lips began to tremble with unspoken pain, sadness, and fear. She hunched her shoulders against the hurt and turned from him to face the fireplace.

"Tell me what is amiss, Bella," the duke said behind her.

She could tell by his voice that he had moved nearer to her, but she could not look at him. Nor could she answer him, for her throat felt clogged with tears trying to force their way out all at once.

The duke did not move, but waited patiently for her to speak. After a few moments he took another step nearer and began to speak to her, as if he were trying to gain the trust of a frightened, wild animal. "Before that morning, when we discovered that we had unknowingly spent the night together unchaperoned, I was under the impression that a friendship was developing between us. Was I mistaken?"

Bella was very still for a moment while she thought over the duke's words. With her back still to him and the tears slipping down her cheeks, she hesitantly nodded her agreement.

"In the light of that developing friendship, do you think you could speak to me as if we are friends now?"

His unexpected, gentle words caused a dam to burst within Bella. Turning, she looked up at him, no longer hiding her tears. "I do not understand how everything could suddenly go so terribly wrong. I have always been so careful to do the right thing. I have always tried to be wise about the decisions I have made. But, forgive me, ever since you came into my life, everything has been chaos." She sniffed, giving him a tearful smile to soften her words.

As the duke looked down at her, she saw the concern, mixed with amusement, in his eyes.

"And now," she continued, "that loathsome popinjay, Robert Fortiscue, comes to town and threatens to tell everyone why we had to marry. It is too horrible! We have done nothing wrong, and now there will be even more gossip about us," she said, ending with a tearful sniff.

A moment later she found herself wrapped in the duke's warm arms, her cheek on his chest. Stunned, she stood against him, very stiff and still, until she heard his deep voice rumble above her head.

"It matters not. After all, what is a London Season without a hint of scandal?"

At the gentle humor in his tone, Bella allowed herself to relax fully against his broad chest. The tears started to flow down her cheeks, unchecked.

They stood this way for some moments, in front of the fireplace, the duke gently rocking her back and forth as she cried.

Deep inside, as the jumble of her emotions finally found release, Bella realized that she had never before felt anything like this. To be held securely by strong arms while she wept her heart out was oddly comforting. It was such a rare occurrence for Bella to cry. She tried to avoid it, for when she did cry, Papa and Tommy acted as if she were dying. She had always been the strong one, but for once crying did not make her feel weak.

After a little while her crying abated, and she was able to look at the events of the evening with a clearer head. Wiping her tears away with her fingers, Bella raised her head slightly and looked at the duke with a tearful, mystified smile.

"I do not understand you either," she said to him. "Robert Fortiscue comes to town and spreads this gossip about us, and you do not seem bothered at all."

The duke still held her in his arms, their heads close enough for her to see the green flecks in the gray of his eyes. His gaze held hers, and Bella decided that she liked the feel of her body relaxing against the strong length of his.

"You mistake the situation, Arabella. I am bothered," he replied.

"You are?" she questioned, sensing that it was not Robert Fortiscue who was bothering him.

"Very much so," he said, as he lowered his head toward hers.

He stopped, his lips hovering just above hers.

Bella's heart seemed to catch in her throat and then began beating again in a wholly new way.

The duke did not lower his head any further; nor did he close his eyes. Somehow, instinctively, she knew that he would not be the one to bridge the slight gap that separated them.

Suddenly feeling safe after the cathartic intimacy of crying on his chest, Bella stood quietly within the warm shelter of his arms. Feeling as if it were the most natural thing in the world, she relaxed against him even more. She felt his warm breath on her lips, and something in the intensity of his gaze made her lift her head slightly and close the space between them.

Closing her eyes, she felt his firm, warm lips against hers, and became aware of a sensation of heat dissolving through her limbs and into her heart. She pressed herself a little deeper into his embrace and felt the taut muscles in his arms as he pulled her body closer to his. How different he felt, she hazily marveled.

While growing up, she had imagined that her first kiss would elicit a soft, happy feeling. This intense, almost frightening escalation of new sensations was completely unexpected.

His hand slowly, firmly moved up the side of her body, coming to stroke the hollow of her neck with tantalizing, gentle fingers. The woodsy scent of him assailed her senses, somehow enhancing her feelings.

His lips moved over hers, growing more insistent as she allowed her hands to steal up his broad chest. So caught up was she in the response his kiss was stirring within her, Bella's normal feelings of self-consciousness where he was concerned completely vanished. Dizzily, she did not think she could get any closer to him, until his hand moved to her waist and began to caress the small of her back, pressing her body even more intimately against his.

Swirling deeper into the melting sensuousness of his kiss, Bella did not, at first, hear the knock at her door. It was only when she felt his body stiffen and pull away from her slightly that she became aware of her surroundings.

"Bella, it is me. Are you all right? Please open the door. I wish to speak to you."

Bella almost groaned aloud at hearing Triss's muffled voice coming from behind the closed bedchamber door.

Her gaze flew to the duke's. She looked in dawning mortification at her hands splayed upon his chest.

"Yes, Arabella, I am most definitely bothered." The quiet intensity of his voice belied his slight smile as he released her.

Chapter Twenty-one

Bella squinted at the late-morning sun beaming into her sumptuous bedchamber. Her lady's maid had just flung open the curtains, and Bella rolled over, burying her face into her down pillow.

Last night she had slept fitfully after feigning a headache to get Triss to leave. Even though she rarely slept so late, she was in no mood to rise. After the maid left the room, Bella burrowed deeper under the covers. The memory of being in the duke's arms, and the feel of his lips on hers, kept repeating itself over and over.

Groaning, she turned over onto her back and pulled the pillow over her head. A moment later she tossed the pillow aside. Staring up at the rich, brocaded fabric that draped the canopy of her bed, Bella tried to sort out the chaotic emotions crowding her thoughts.

Too many changes had happened too quickly over the last few months. She had not enough time to adjust to one change before another one came along and bowled her over.

Pushing herself up onto her pillows, she brushed her long dark hair off her shoulders. The duke's words of last night came back to her. The words he had spoken before the kiss.

She admitted that he had been correct about her feeling the beginnings of a friendship developing between them during his recovery at the cottage. But that was before that horrible morning her father and uncle had confronted them. That was before they had been forced to marry. How would the friendship have grown if it had been allowed to blossom of its own accord? She would never know, she realized with sadness.

Across the room, on the little table by the chaise that overlooked the formal garden, Bella saw that the maid had left a tray with toast and chocolate. Rising and stretching, she moved to sit on the chaise. After pouring the chocolate into a delicate porcelain cup, she pensively contemplated the view from the high arching window.

Trying to push away the memory of how the duke's lips felt upon hers, Bella reflected on the scathing words the duke's sister had said to her last night. With a bit of a wrench in her heart, Bella knew the Lady Edgeton was right: The circumstance of her marriage to the duke was beneath the Westlake name.

During her brief stay at Autley she had toured the gallery, which was in actuality more of a museum of English history. There had been a direct succession of Westlakes unbroken since the year 1224. She had been astonished and impressed to learn the first Alexander Westlake had been created a duke in 1485. The family was aligned, in one way or another, with most of the other noble families of Great Britain.

She recalled the paintings and other artifacts depicting the glorious accomplishments of past Westlakes. Great soldiers and scholars and respected political minds were scattered throughout the Westlake family tree.

Putting the cup down, Bella began to pluck distractedly at the fine lawn of her negligee. In truth, as painful as it was to face, the duke had certainly gotten the bad end of the bargain when he married her.

To his credit, he had been willing to make the best of this bad bargain. A frown creased her brow when she recalled the argument they had had in his library at Autley. He had said then, and in no uncertain terms, that there would be no annulment. But upon his arrival in London, he had agreed to discuss it after Louisa's wedding. She wondered what had changed his mind on the subject. Probably after thinking over the idea of an annulment, he had concluded that it was the only way out of this misalliance.

And now, this kiss.

Her fingers stole up to her lips. She felt so different. Could it be possible that one kiss could change her whole view of her situation?

She felt she did not know herself any longer. Before the duke had landed at her doorstep, she had had supreme confidence in the decisions she had made regarding her future. She had been planning for three years to marry Robert Fortiscue. Planning to have children with him, she remembered with astonishment at her own blindness.

Never once had she thought of kissing him; never once had she contemplated the intimacy that would be required to create those children.

How completely different it was with the duke, she owned, with the beginnings of a blush coming to her ivory cheeks. It was now very clear to her that ever since he had come out of his fever, she had been fighting to suppress her overwhelming awareness of him as a man.

She realized it was not just his physical attributes, though considerable, that attracted her to him. It was his intelligence and sense of humor as well. She also liked the way he treated her family. She admired his military experience and thought him the most gentlemanly man of her acquaintance.

It was so lowering to know that the sense of duty and honor that she admired so much was the very reason she cringed with mortification every time she thought of their wedding.

So what to do now? she wondered dejectedly, just as she heard a knock at her door. Looking over, she saw the door open, and a moment later her cousin's blond head poked in.

"Oh, good, you are up," Triss said, crossing the room to flop down at the foot of the chaise.

Bella thought she looked charming, and deceptively innocent in her blue morning gown.

"I know you told me last night that we are to do nothing about Robert, but I wondered if you told the duke what happened. And if so, what did he say?"

"Yes, we were discussing what had occurred at Almack's

when you came in," she said vaguely, picking up her tea-cup again.

"And?" Triss asked.

"The duke thinks it does not signify," Bella replied with a little shrug.

"How like him. So lofty and dismissive of lesser mortals." Triss sighed and picked up a piece of toast from the tray.

Bella frowned at her cousin's words. "Is that how you see Westlake?" she asked over her teacup.

Triss glanced up from her toast with a look of mild surprise. "Of course. How can he help it? He has been all the kick since coming home from the war. Everyone gossips about him and tries to duplicate how he ties his neckcloth. And with every eligible miss, and a good many of their mamas, chasing after him, how could he not be arrogant? In a most attractive way, of course."

Bella contemplated her cousin's words. Triss's opinion of the duke did not quite agree with her own. Oh, he was definitely imposing and supremely confident. She had even seen his arrogance on occasion. But she recalled the time he had told her of his brother's death. He had revealed a depth of feeling that she somehow sensed was not often shared with others.

She also had to admit that his treatment of her had been above kind, under the circumstances. Who would have blamed him if he had shown resentment toward her because of this unwanted marriage? But he had been nothing but amenable, to the point of indulgence, toward her from the moment they had married.

No, she did not completely agree with Triss's assessment of the duke.

"We are quite dull," Triss opined while stretching her arms over her head and yawning. "Let us have a walk in the park and plan our revenge on that weasel-face, Robert Fortiscue."

Bella could not help but laugh at her incorrigible cousin. "All right, let me have a bath and I will be with you in less than an hour," she said. Rising from the chaise, Bella moved to the bellpull to summon her maid.

Still lounging on the chaise, Triss looked at Bella with curious eyes. "Bella, lately you seem to be different somehow," she said.

"Well, goose, my life has undergone a few changes in the last couple of months," Bella said in dry understatement.

"I *know* that," Triss replied. "I mean, you are prettier, and until last night I think you were beginning to enjoy the Season. I can't put my finger on it exactly, but you are different."

Bella said nothing. She was thankful when the maid entered, for the memory of being in the duke's arms was causing a blush to rise again to her cheeks.

It was a fine warm day, and Bella was glad to be out-of-doors—and appreciative of her cousin's chatter, for it diverted her from troubling thoughts of the duke.

They strolled along with their sunshades shielding them from the sun, while Bella admired the beds overflowing with beautiful fragrant flowers. She was pleased that they had come out before the fashionable hour, for they had the park almost to themselves. Glancing to a tree at the sound of a baby bird's call to its mother, Bella decided she liked this side of London after all.

"I believe I shall make a list," Triss stated, swinging her sunshade to and fro.

"A list of what?" Bella asked as they strolled along.

"Of eligible gentlemen, silly," Triss replied.

"Oh, of course. What other kind of list is there?" Bella responded with mock seriousness.

"I have very high hopes for Lady Louisa's wedding," Triss continued, ignoring Bella's levity. "Everyone of any importance shall be there. And as weddings are so romantic, mayhap my own romance shall be spurred on by the atmosphere."

"You really are a nudgeon," Bella said with a shake of her head and a little laugh.

They ambled on, and Bella felt better for the exercise. A few more people had entered the park, and Bella enjoyed watching the growing parade of fashionables taking the air.

"Is that not Margaret Westlake over there, by the very large tree?" Triss asked a few moments later.

Bella looked in the direction Triss indicated.

"Why, yes, and there is Henry, too."

"Do you recognize the gentleman with them?" Triss asked, still looking in the distance to where Margaret stood under the tree.

"I do not believe so. Let us go and greet them. I have not seen Henry since coming to London."

The two ladies changed their direction and walked across the grass. As Margaret looked over toward them, Bella saw her start with surprise.

"Good afternoon, Mrs. Westlake. Good day, Henry. I believe you have previously met my cousin, Lady Beatrice Tichley?" Bella smiled at the little group, closing her sunshade.

Margaret stared at Bella with a slightly open mouth.

Bella tried not to stare at the lady's attire. Margaret wore a very bright yellow walking gown with a spencer of yellowish green. The whole ensemble had a profusion of braids, gathers, and bows.

"Er . . . why, yes, I have had the pleasure. Ah . . . may I present Mr. Fitzdowning? The Duchess of Westlake," she said in a breathless voice.

Bella could not help noticing that Margaret was casting nervous glances at the gentleman. Henry, after making a hasty bow, wandered off, kicking divots into the grass.

Turning to the gentleman, Bella saw he was of a medium build, thickening around the middle. His features were blunt, though not unattractive. Bella thought his beaver hat had seen better days. Something about him seemed familiar. As he bowed to her, she wondered where they could have met. She had not been very much in Society since coming to London, so there were few choices for an encounter.

Introducing Triss to the man, Bella wondered at the significant glance she caught flashing between Mr. Fitzdowning and Margaret.

"Your servant, your grace, Lady Beatrice," he intoned stiffly as he bowed to Bella and Triss.

"Henry and I were taking some exercise when we saw our dear friend, Mr. Fitzdowning. He knew my poor late husband very well. We were just catching up on the news from Tilbourne," Margaret spoke, ending her little speech on a note of tittering laughter.

"You are from Tilbourne then, sir?" Bella questioned politely.

Mr. Fitzdowning cast another quick glance to Margaret, and Bella would have sworn that she saw anger in his expression.

"Yes, your grace, in town on some business matters. What a surprise to come across Mrs. Westlake and Master Henry," he offered.

"Has not the weather been very kind of late?" Margaret said, smiling broadly at them all.

Bella caught Triss from the corner of her eye giving Margaret a quizzical look.

"Lovely," Bella agreed.

"Oh, my, it must be getting very late," Margaret continued, her eyes going wide with surprise. "You must forgive me for rushing off in this fashion. The dowager duchess is expecting Henry and me for tea. We must not be late. Come, Henry," she called her son over, and grabbed his hand.

Mother and son were already moving away when Mr. Fitzdowning also recalled a previous appointment. With another bow, he turned and walked away in the opposite direction from Margaret and Henry.

Bella and Triss stood under the tree and looked at each other with perplexed expressions. After a moment they turned and headed back toward the carriage.

"Margaret Westlake is an odd fish," Triss stated.

"Indeed," Bella agreed with a frown. "I have the notion that I have seen that fellow before."

"Do you? Where?"

Bella shook her head, for she could not yet place him.

After a few more yards, Bella stopped in her tracks and grabbed Triss's arm.

"I remember now," Bella said, looking down at Triss with excited eyes. "When the duke had taken me driving in Hyde Park, we came across Margaret speaking to Mr. Fitzdowning. He was on horseback and trotted off before Margaret could make the introductions," she explained.

"So? What is there in that to get you in such a pet?" Triss asked as they resumed walking.

"Westlake specifically told me to inform him if I saw the man again," she told her cousin.

"Good heavens, why?" Triss asked as she hurried her steps to keep up with Bella.

"I haven't a clue," she said as they moved swiftly to the carriage. "But I am going to find out."

Chapter Twenty-two

Westlake walked into his club, handed his hat and cane to the majordomo, and looked around the richly appointed room.

Though it was late in the evening, the club was crowded, and it took him some moments to find what he was looking for. At the far end, ensconced in a wide alcove, the Duke of Severly was lounging in a leather chair. At the table with Severly were a number of other peers. Westlake moved toward the table, nodding to a few gentlemen on the way.

Severly looked up from the cards in his hand and was pleased to see his oldest and closest friend. But after taking in his friend's very composed expression, Severly folded, though he had a good hand, and left the game. Those who knew Westlake well recognized this expression as an indication that trouble was brewing.

The two men moved to a pair of club chairs strategically placed by the fireplace to afford some privacy.

"What has got your jaw set so firmly, Alex?" Severly queried.

"Actually, I would like you to help keep me from killing someone," the duke said, turning his cool gray eyes to his oldest friend.

"Again?" Severly asked, raising his brow.

Severly was fondly recalling a particular incident from their days at Eton. Only the two of them knew the exact details of what had happened on a certain night they had sneaked away from their rooms. If the headmaster had been able to uncover the full facts, there was no doubt that they both would have been sent down for their youthful prank. To this day, that wild night was legend among the men who had attended Eton at that time.

But a moment later Severly could tell by Westlake's closed expression that he was a little more than half-serious.

"What has occurred?"

"A former, and unimportant, acquaintance of my wife has insulted her publicly," Westlake explained. "I have directed a couple of my men to ascertain his whereabouts. He is, as we speak, at a hell on St. James Street. It is my intention to have him leave town. At once."

Severly leaned back in his chair and contemplated his friend with a frown. This was serious business. Being quite protective of his own wife, he fully appreciated Westlake's feelings.

"Let us take care of it," Severly said, displaying a grim smile.

With a nod Westlake rose from the chair. Severly followed suit, and the two men headed for the door to retrieve their gear.

Once outside in the cool night air, Severly whistled for his coachman, who trotted up the gaslit sidewalk a moment later.

"Stay here until I return, Stevens. Take the cattle around the block if they become too restless," Severly instructed before entering the duke's coach. When they were moving, Severly looked over to his friend, noting the pulse beating in Westlake's jaw. "How is the search for the bastard who shot you coming?"

"Fortunately, very well. I wish to thank you again, Drake, for sending out the runners as soon as you had received my mother's letter. They have uncovered some very pertinent information. We are closing in."

"Good," Severly said with satisfaction. "Personally I'd like to see him hang."

Westlake looked over to his old friend as the coach

rolled swiftly through the darkened streets. He gave a one-shouldered shrug, an affectation he had taken on, since his left shoulder still nagged him on occasion.

"Deportation with his partner will suffice," Westlake stated.

"Partner? I thought you shot the other assailant?"

"I did. But through my investigations I have discovered that the man who shot me has a collaborator."

Severly could tell by the thinly concealed anger in Westlake's tone that the investigation into the shooting had revealed some unexpected facts. He did not question his friend further, knowing Westlake would reveal what he knew in his own time. The two men made the rest of the short journey in silence.

After entering the narrow entryway to the Pigeon Hole, the two men strode through the room, which was crowded with tables and gamblers, in search of Robert Fortiscue. Westlake espied him playing near the back of the room.

All the men seated at the table with Fortiscue looked up at the two dukes as they stopped in front of their table. Westlake noted a few titled though notorious gamblers in the group. One was Sir John Mayhew, a friend of Westlake and Severly's from their school days. Westlake knew that Mayhew binged at gaming on occasion, and tended to be enormously lucky.

"Westlake. Severly. Don't often see the two of you slumming in these parts," Sir John said cheerfully. "Care to join us?"

"Thank you, no. I wonder if you gentlemen would not mind suspending your play for a moment, while I take care of a certain matter?" Westlake's drawling tone was the epitome of politeness.

Not one of the men seated around the table gainsaid him. Almost in unison the gentlemen laid their cards down and stood from the table, all looking at Westlake with expressions of curiosity.

Severly leaned against a nearby wall, his face impassive, and crossed his arms over his chest.

Robert Fortiscue turned nervous eyes from one duke to the other. He pushed his chair a good way back before rising in a transparent attempt to put distance between himself and Westlake.

Without taking his eyes from Fortiscue's, Westlake tossed his ivory-tipped cane to a nearby chair. Fortiscue jumped as the cane clattered against the wooden chair back. He swallowed several times and looked back at Westlake uncertainly.

Westlake's icy gaze held Fortiscue where he stood.

"Mr. Fortiscue, I find your neckcloth an eyesore."

Putting a delicate white hand to his throat, Robert gaped at the duke.

"I . . . I beg your pardon, your grace?" He could not believe what he had heard.

The other men standing around the table perked up considerably. Though most of them were inveterate gamers, they would gladly forgo a hand or two to watch this scene play out.

"Your neckcloth offends me. I wish never to see it—or you—again," Westlake reiterated slowly.

The half of the room nearest Westlake grew dead silent. By his statement, everyone realized that this was no mere demand of satisfaction for some trivial slight.

Looking around at all the keenly interested faces, Fortiscue lost some of his color. Feeling cornered and confused, he drew himself up and waved his hand around defensively. "See here, your grace, I do not know what this is about, but I would have you know that I am a relative of Lord Castlereagh. As he is our foreign secretary, I do not believe that he would take kindly to your attitude toward me."

Westlake cocked an amused brow at the blond man. "Egad, I am not inciting a diplomatic incident. I just want you and your neckcloth to take yourselves off to the country," he drawled, causing a wave of masculine laughter throughout the room.

"You may laugh, your grace, but my relative is a powerful man in our government, and—"

"Severly"—Westlake cut Fortiscue off midsentence and turned to his friend—"did I not see you at cards with Castlereagh not twenty minutes ago?"

"Stewart?" Severly said from his place against the wall. "Yes, you did."

"Thought so." He nodded with satisfaction.

"Mayhew." Westlake turned to his grinning childhood friend. "I would be indebted to you if you would be so kind as to take my coach, return to my club, and beg Lord Castlereagh to attend me here."

"Not at all, Westlake. My pleasure," Sir John stated congenially as he maneuvered his way from behind the table. As he was leaving, he paused a moment to make a bet with Lord Hillcrest that Mr. Fortiscue would be leaving London at first light.

"See here." Fortiscue sputtered his words as panic began to seize him. "There is no need to bother his lordship regarding some inconsequential matter that can be taken care of between the two of us."

"Inconsequential?" The duke turned his cold eyes to the flustered man. "You mistake the situation, Fortiscue. The offense your neckcloth gives is not inconsequential. But we shall leave the matter until Lord Castlereagh arrives," he stated in an offhand manner.

"Lord Kennymere, I believe I heard that you recently purchased a prime bit of blood at Tattersall's last week," Westlake stated to the man nearest him.

"Indeed, your grace. A real goer," Lord Kennymere replied affably.

Perfectly polite conversation ensued while the gentlemen waited for Sir John to return with Lord Castlereagh. Mr. Fortiscue said nothing and only grew paler with each passing moment. Somehow the fact that the duke was being so genial at this moment was just as alarming to Robert as having the duke's ice-cold eyes leveled at him.

In a remarkably short period of time Sir John returned. Following a short distance behind him was Lord Castlereagh. As usual, his expression was sour, and he eyed the group of men with great distaste.

"So, Westlake, to what purpose have you beseeched me to attend you in this illustrious place?" he asked sarcastically of the younger man.

Mayhew had told the lord what he knew during the drive back to the Pigeon Hole. Obviously this was pertaining to a matter of honor, Lord Castlereagh had easily surmised. Though he was a good twenty years older than Westlake, the lord had a fondness and respect for the younger man.

Though he would never admit to it, Lord Castlereagh was a bit flattered that such a blade of the first consequence would call upon him under such circumstances. Lord Castlereagh was also of the opinion that it was vital that the upper ten thousand, as it were, police themselves. It would not do to have upstarts causing gossip and trouble. Though he would not go so far as to condone a duel, sometimes it was best to call a chap out on his offensive behavior and see what he was made of. If he was less than a gentleman, then it was best to send him off with his tail between his legs.

Westlake gave the statesman an appreciative smile. "I am in your debt, my lord. We have here Mr. Fortiscue, who ties a very rude neckcloth. I have stated my desire that he take himself from London. Out of my great respect for you, and as you are claimed as a relative by Mr. Fortiscue, I would not want you to be offended by my request," Westlake explained to the older man.

Lord Castlereagh raised both brows at this before turning to examine Mr. Fortiscue with a critical eye.

Despite his very pale features, Robert still managed a defiant expression.

Lord Castlereagh knew well the language of the challenge. By insulting some aspect of another gentleman's person, the challenger was making it clear that the offense was of a serious and personal nature. Lord Castlereagh admired the duke's adroitness.

"What is the nature of our connection, Mr. Fortiscue?" he asked.

Robert cleared his throat. "My great-aunt, Gertrude Fortiscue, was married to the brother of your—"

"Bah!" Lord Castlereagh cut in with a dismissive wave of his hand. "I pay no heed to such distant relations. From my knowledge of Westlake, I do not believe I would take offense even if we were *closely* related."

Robert swallowed several times at the lord's pronouncement. But such was his opinion of himself that he still thought he could brazen the situation out.

"Do not think that I am incapable of defending myself, my lord duke," Fortiscue said, turning toward Westlake, his tone taking on a nasty edge. "I will not turn tail and leave just because you are annoyed at what I said to Arabella."

Severly pushed away from the wall to stand close to Westlake, casting a quick glance at his friend to see if he really did need to stop a murder.

The generally affable and sporting atmosphere in the room disappeared. Many of the eyes that a moment ago were only showing interest at a scene so rich in gossip, now turned cold at a lady's name being mentioned in a gaming house.

"Who?" Westlake said with deceptive calm.

By this time, Robert was beginning to sense the undercurrent of danger emanating from the duke. "Ah . . . the Duchess of Westlake?" he said, in the hopes that part of the duke's anger was at his familiar use of the duchess's given name.

"Good God, man!" Lord Castlereagh fairly shouted at Robert. "What maggot has possessed you to mention the duchess's name? I have a mind to call you out myself."

"Obliged, my lord," Westlake said to the older man. He turned his cold eyes to Fortiscue and took a menacing step closer.

"Name your second."

Robert Fortiscue stared at the duke, his eyes wide with horror. He truly thought he was going to be sick. "Your grace! Please allow me to . . . to apologize for the offense I have given you. Truly! I see now that my jealousy has caused my tongue to run away with me. I . . . I beg your forgiveness!" he pleaded, putting his hands out in a supplicating manner.

"I said name your second." The duke's tone was even harder.

Robert Fortiscue bit his trembling lip and said nothing. He knew, without a doubt, that he was ruined. The tenuous hold he had on the fringes of Society was gone. All the years he had spent using his distant connection with Lord and Lady Castlereagh were gone. The only reason he had ever received a voucher to Almack's was because Lady Castlereagh was one of the patronesses.

From this night forward he knew he must rusticate in the country, for to accept the duke's challenge would cause him grave personal injury at the very least. To decline the challenge would show himself in the wrong and a coward to boot.

He also knew the *ton* never forgot. If he ever showed his face in London again, the entire beau monde would give him the cut direct. Fighting back tears, he blanched at Westlake's annihilating look of contempt.

"Make no mistake, Fortiscue, I shall be in Green Park at dawn. If I do not see you, I am sure the reason will be that you have decided the country air suits you better."

Westlake turned on his heel and gave a brief salute to the gentlemen surrounding the table. "Good evening and good luck, gentlemen," he said, his face impassive once again.

The men, except Robert Fortiscue, resumed their seats and picked up their cards. None of them looked at Mr. Fortiscue again.

"So, my lord, how do you find the situation on the continent?" the duke of Westlake was heard to say as he, Lord Castlereagh, and the Duke of Severly leisurely took their leave.

Chapter Twenty-three

The wedding day of Lady Louisa Westlake to the Duke of Malverton started off with a few black clouds, but the sky showed a promise of clearing before the appointed hour.

Bella was making her way down the sweeping marble staircase to meet her family in the grand, oval-shaped foyer. In her excitement, she skipped down the last few steps. With a smile she greeted her father and brother, who were already waiting for her.

It had been delightful and totally unexpected to have returned from an afternoon of shopping two days earlier to find Papa and Tommy having their tea in the sitting room. She had rushed across the room, dropping her bonnet, and thrown herself in her father's arms with a cry of joy.

"How come you to be here?" she had asked, looking at them both with a joy she had not felt in a long while.

"For the wedding," her father explained. "Tommy and I received an invitation from the Dowager Duchess of Westlake. The duke sent his carriage to Mabry Green and here we are." He spread his hands to encompass the room.

"Uncle David has come with us," Tommy put in.

"How kind of Westlake," Bella said, unaccountably pleased that the duke had made it possible for her family to come to London.

Now, as they waited for Triss and Lord and Lady Penninghurst to join them, she noted how well her father looked in his morning coat.

"Aren't we a merry group!" Triss called from the first-floor landing.

Bella looked up to see her aunt and uncle following behind Triss in a more sedate manner than their daughter exhibited. She allowed her gaze to wander around the foyer as they waited for Triss and Lord and Lady Penninghurst to descend the staircase.

In preparation for the wedding breakfast taking place at Westlake House, the duke had directed the servants to decorate the house with a breathtaking profusion of flowers. The entire length of the balustrade was roped with garlands of ivy and sweet-smelling spring flowers. The footmen had been kept busy carrying in numerous, large Grecian-style urns that the maids filled with enormous bunches of beautiful blooms.

The mood in the house during the last few days had been festive, growing more and more exciting as the wedding day approached. After all, Triss had pointed out, a daughter of a duke marrying a duke was very much out of the ordinary.

This morning Triss had brought the paper into Bella's room while Bella was having her breakfast. She had read aloud a report that stated that the impending marriage between members of two such illustrious families was almost akin to a royal wedding. Her cousin had sighed over her envy of Lady Louisa's capturing such a plum title.

As she prepared for the wedding, after Triss had rushed off to begin her toilette, Bella examined her own sense of excitement. Now that the day of Louisa's wedding had arrived, Bella knew that she and the duke would soon be discussing their future. Her heart fluttered at the mere thought of this impending conversation.

She had seen very little of the duke in the last week or so. He had left Westlake House the day after their kiss. The note from the duke that the butler had given her had stated that pressing and unexpected estate business had called him away from London. Bella had not known whether or not she was disappointed that there was no reference to the kiss in his note.

When the duke had returned to London, he had not been

much at home. Bella had finally directed one of the footmen to take a note to the duke. In it she informed Westlake that she had again seen the man that he had pointed out to her during their first drive in the park. The duke sent a note back thanking her for the information.

In an almost feverish effort to keep from having to examine her confused feelings about Westlake, Bella kept herself as busy as possible. She read books. She took long walks. She had attended a small dinner party given by the dowager. She had spent time with Lady Louisa, who seemed to be almost exhausted from her excitement over her impending wedding.

"I do not know how I shall have time to make all my fittings," Louisa had lamented. "My trousseau is not nearly complete! And the cards I must send out! Every day box after box arrives, and the salon at my sister's house is filled to the rafters with wedding gifts already. I cannot keep up with sending out cards to half the *ton*. Thank heavens we are having the wedding breakfast at Westlake House. We are expecting almost six hundred at the church and almost three hundred for the breakfast. I so wish that Malverton's brother were not making the speech for his family; he is a wretched mumbler. And you, my dear sister-in-law!" she said, changing the subject without a pause. "I know for a fact that you and my brother have received dozens and dozens of invitations. You accept none of them. Everyone quizzes me constantly about the two of you. You need to give a ball or something, so that everyone may see how in love the two of you are. I vow this feverish gossip is about to overshadow my wedding."

"No one could overshadow a bride as lovely as you, Louisa," Bella had said with a warm smile.

But even Lady Louisa's prattle had done little to divert Bella from her growing anxiety regarding the duke. She had no idea how the path before her would unfold. It was frightening, yet somehow exhilarating at the same time.

Feeling oddly disappointed, she knew she would not see Westlake this morning. He had gone to Lord and Lady Edgeton's town house earlier so that he could drive with Lady Louisa to the church.

"Are we ready?" Triss asked, giving a last tug to her gentian-blue kid glove.

"You look very pretty, Triss," Bella told her cousin as the butler opened the front door for them.

"Oh, Bella, please do not call me Triss today," her cousin pleaded as they all descended the wide front steps to the awaiting carriages.

"All right. Beatrice it is. Be warned; I do not think I can 'Beatrice' you for more than one day," Bella teased, eliciting a laugh from the rest of the family.

Bella, along with her father and Tommy, stepped into one of the duke's stately town coaches with the Westlake heraldic arms boldly displayed on the doors. Triss and Lord and Lady Penninghurst followed a short distance behind in a similar coach. Riding ahead of the two coaches were four liveried footmen on horseback to aid the carriages' path through the crowded streets of London to Saint George's Church in Hanover Square.

Bella smiled fondly over at her brother. His awestruck expression as he looked out of the window touched her.

She had missed her father and brother so much, she thought with a poignant catch in her heart.

Looking at her papa sitting next to her, Bella could not help but smile at how tightly he held his hat. She knew he did so lest he set it down somewhere and forget it, as he was often wont to do.

"Your aunt tells me that you get on very well here in London," her father said with a hint of gruffness in his voice.

"Indeed I do, Papa," Bella said smiling into her father's gentle blue eyes.

It was true, she thought in surprise. She was enjoying herself, except for one or two incidents, more than she had thought would be possible.

The scene that met them as the coach pulled up to the church was one of festive commotion. Londoners had come out in force to goggle at the most toplofty members of the beau monde as they entered the place of worship.

It took some time for the coach to inch its way closer to the impressive columned facade of the church. Tommy did not mind the delay, for it afforded him a chance to look at all the prime horseflesh on display.

Finally they came to a stop, and the footman opened the door and helped Bella alight. She looked up at the sky and was glad for Louisa that the clouds were receding. Once inside, Bella looked around with admiration at the flowers and candlelight that added a romantic feel to the solemn beauty of the church. There were a number of guests ahead of Bella and the rest of her family, waiting to be escorted to their seats. Eventually a gentleman approached and introduced himself as Lord Danforth, a cousin of the Duke of Malverton. With her family following behind, Lord Danforth escorted Bella very slowly up the center aisle of the church.

Gazing around, Bella observed that the pews were almost full. The pervasive feeling of excited anticipation was evidenced by the hundreds of elegantly dressed guests chattering and waving across the aisles to one another. Bella fought the urge to hurry her escort along as she began to notice heads turning in their direction as she and Lord Danforth passed each pew. She was glad that she had decided to wear the ensemble Madame Triaud had sent over to Westlake House specifically for this occasion. The pelisse was made of a frosty lilac *gros de naples*. It was styled as a fitted open robe that revealed a slightly paler lilac gown beneath. Peeking through the pelisse, the bottom of the gown was gathered in swagging drapes. Her slippers, gloves, and reticule were in a summery shade of green. Her bonnet was small, with an angled brim that did not hide her face. There were bunches of rosettes made from *gros de naples* in shades of lilac and green festooning the crown.

The only jewelry she wore was a brooch with an enormous emerald surrounded by diamonds. Carter, her maid, had brought the jewel case in to Bella that morning with a note from the duke. The note stated that it was a shame for such a pretty piece of jewelry to be hidden away. Now, as they continued to make their way up the aisle, Bella noted more than one pair of eyes turned to the glittering jewel on her shoulder.

Close to the front, Bella caught sight of the Duke and Duchess of Severly. They were smiling at her warmly, and she returned their greeting with a sincere smile of her own. She recalled Westlake informing her of the Severlys' invitation, which was for a night next week. Bella wondered where she would be in a week's time.

Lord Danforth halted their progression for a moment and politely directed her family to the third pew from the front. Bella glanced back and briefly met her cousin's shining sky-blue eyes before Lord Danforth continued on with Bella. In the next pew, Bella saw Margaret, Henry, and what she assumed were other members of the Westlake family. She smiled, inclining her head slightly in greeting.

Lord Danforth stopped at the opening of the front pew. Bella saw that Lord and Lady Edgeton were already seated with three very pretty and beautifully dressed little girls next to them. Bella assumed these were Westlake's nieces. Lady Edgeton, in a rose-colored ensemble with gray bonnet and gloves, looked very much like her mother. Bella thanked Lord Danforth, who bowed and returned down the aisle to continue his ushering duties.

Turning back to Lord and Lady Edgeton, Bella said a very polite good morning. The couple returned her greeting, but did not move farther down the pew. With a mental shrug, Bella quickly slipped into the pew and passed in front of them, trying not to tread on their toes. The three girls stood, and though they bobbed quick curtsies, they did not budge from their places either. That left Bella to find a place at the end of the pew.

The Edgetons said nothing more to Bella. She spent the remaining minutes before the ceremony watching the Duke of Malverton's relatives being delivered to the corresponding pew across the aisle.

As organ music began to play softly, Bella listened to the vibrating notes that were enhanced by the effect of the high ceiling.

Soon the number of guests being seated had dwindled and the conversational chatter reduced greatly.

Bella glanced back, and between the myriad of colorful bonnets she saw the dowager duchess coming up the aisle on the arm of Lord Danforth. The doors of the vestibule closed behind them.

The dowager and the lord moved slowly forward. Her

grace's tall figure was displayed to advantage in a gown and pelisse of mauve. She nodded to friends on each side of the aisle until reaching the pew her family occupied. The dowager paused before taking the seat nearest the aisle and looked down the pew with a frown.

"Arabella, what are you doing down there? Come take your place next to me," she commanded in a clear, carrying voice.

Hesitantly Bella stood and glanced quickly over at the frozen expressions on the faces of Lord and Lady Edgeton. As she moved in front of Lady Edgeton, Bella met the lady's eyes briefly. Lady Edgeton visibly stiffened when Bella lifted her chin, refusing to be cowed by the duke's imposing sister.

The dowager smiled approvingly at Bella as she settled in next to her mother-in-law. "How lovely you look, my girl. You do my son proud," the dowager said, leaning her head toward Bella so that her compliment could be heard only by the two of them.

"Thank you, ma'am. You are very kind," Bella said in a low tone, feeling extremely touched by the dowager's words.

"Nonsense, my girl. 'Tis the truth," the dowager replied just as the music stopped and the hundreds of guests grew hushed.

Bella saw the Duke of Malverton enter with his younger brother from a side door. The two young men walked in silence to the chancel steps and stopped. They stood in front of the Archbishop of Canterbury, who wore a beautifully embroidered miter and cope.

The organ music rose again in a joyous fanfare. The doors opened. The dowager stood and turned toward the back of the church. Entering the nave of the church, the beautiful Louisa was escorted up the aisle by her brother, the Duke of Westlake. The congregation followed the dowager's lead and rose as one.

After a brief look to Louisa, who looked resplendent in her gown of oyster white silk under a slip of silver net, Bella looked to the duke and did not take her eyes from him.

Something in her heart tripped at the sight of him. His

tall, broad-shouldered frame moved with athletic grace up the long aisle. As he drew closer she saw his classic features and admired the squareness of his chin.

But the feature that struck her most was his complete and clearly apparent air of confidence. This was his world. He was a leader of Society and never stepped a foot wrong. In a room with members of the nobility and aristocracy in attendance by the carriageful, he more than held his own.

With a sharp sadness, she knew she would not likely be a part of this world for much longer. She was and always would be *The Correct Miss Tichley* of Mabry Green. She mentally thrust aside the reason why this fact would suddenly cause her such grief.

Westlake and the bride-to-be continued up the aisle, and as they came parallel with the first pew, Louisa leaned slightly forward to look at her mother with such an expression of happiness that Bella felt her eyes begin to mist. The dowager beamed at her youngest child and dabbed her eyes with a handkerchief.

Bella could not help recalling the very different ceremony that had taken place between herself and Westlake.

Louisa and her brother reached the chancel steps, and the organ music faded as the wedding ceremony commenced. At the proper moment the duke performed the ancient ritual of giving the bride away. Once his duty was completed, he kissed his sister's cheek, turned, and strode to the pew, moving smoothly past his mother to stand next to Bella.

The ceremony continued, and Bella stood listening to the beautiful words that joined the two young people together. As the Duke of Malverton started to speak, Bella became instantly aware that Westlake had turned his head and was looking down at her while the bridegroom repeated his vows. Bella turned her head up toward him very slowly. A shiver of anticipation and complete awareness constricted her throat so that she found it difficult to breathe.

As Malverton placed the ring on Louisa's finger, Westlake's gray-green eyes met Bella's dark blue, troubled gaze. His expression was somber, but there was something so compelling in his gaze, she could not lower her eyes.

Finally, as the archbishop asked the congregation to join

in song, Bella pulled her gaze from Westlake's, feeling shaken to her soul.

After that, as in her own wedding, everything became a blur.

Soon the new Duke and Duchess of Malverton were walking back down the aisle, and each of the pews began to empty one at a time. It had been arranged for Westlake to return to his town house in the carriage that had brought Bella, her papa, and Tommy to the church. As she entered the aisle with the duke, he offered his arm. Bella was mortified to see that the hand she placed upon him shook ever so slightly. For a brief moment the duke placed his other hand over hers as he turned to acknowledge a guest who greeted him.

It took some time to make their way out of the church.

Bella waited in silence with the duke for the coach to be brought around. Excitement swirled around them as the other guests chatted with one another during the wait. They all proclaimed it a beautiful, perfectly executed wedding.

The duke's coach finally pulled up and he handed Bella in before seating himself next to her. Once Tommy and her papa had made themselves comfortable, the duke signaled the coachman to depart.

"There sure are a lot of prime horses in London, your grace," Tommy stated to the duke.

The duke smiled at the boy and agreed with his opinion.

"Sir," Tommy began with a note of hesitation in his voice, "Zeus has been at Penninghurst Park for a very long time now. I tried to bring him to London to you, but your coachman said not to."

"That is because Zeus is now yours, Thomas," Westlake offered, smiling at the expression of complete stupefaction on Tommy's face.

"Thank you, your grace, but we could not possibly accept such a generous gift. Could we, Thomas?" Alfred Tichley interjected with a strong hint to his son.

Tommy's face fell at his father's words. "No, thank you very much, your grace, but I could not accept." Tommy choked out the words.

Bella almost laughed out loud at her brother's conflicted

expression. She looked at the duke, deeply touched by his kindness and generosity.

"Alfred, you agreed not two days ago to call me Alex, or Westlake at the very least," the duke said good-naturedly to Bella's papa. "Tommy saved my life. Zeus is but the smallest token of my gratitude. Please accept him. I would be greatly gratified if you would."

"Well . . ." Alfred hesitated, turning from the duke to look down at his son. "Will you continue to take very good care of the horse?"

"Oh, yes!" Tommy almost shouted his excitement. "There will not be a better cared-for horse in all of Kent. All of England!" he vowed. In his joy, Tommy threw himself across the carriage to hug the duke.

After the sound of air coming forcibly out of the duke's lungs, Westlake hugged Tommy back while the boy thanked him over and over.

Bella had to turn her face away from the touching scene, for she did not want Westlake to see what she suspected was plainly evident in her eyes.

Chapter Twenty-four

Bella carefully stole up the staircase, glancing behind her to make sure that no one enjoying the festivities would see her sneaking away.

It was midafternoon, and the sumptuous wedding breakfast the Duke of Westlake had provided for his sister and her new husband showed no signs of slowing down. If anything, it was only growing more festive.

After the very formal breakfast, during which the groom's brother did mumble through his entire speech, the gaiety had moved to the grand salon and spilled out into the gardens. Westlake had commissioned two orchestras to entertain the hundreds of wedding guests. One played on a dais in the salon, and the other was positioned under a canopy in the garden.

Upon returning to the town house after the wedding, the dowager had taken Bella aside and made it implicitly clear to her that she should remain at the duke's side as his hostess. Bella had done her best to behave with poise and grace, but had found the task colossally difficult. Feelings she had never thought herself capable of enveloped her in a thrilling, confusing cocoon as she and Westlake moved about, seeing to the comfort of their guests.

As various people spoke to her, she assumed she responded normally to them, for no one reacted to her as if she were a Bedlamite.

Bella observed that the duke seemed supremely in his element while he hosted the beau monde. As they moved from room to room, Bella almost shivered at the touch of his fingers on her elbow.

From the moment she saw the duke returning her brother's hug with such natural affection, her entire world turned inside out. These feelings of longing and passion were so new, she could almost not put names to them. She desperately needed a moment alone, and had stolen away, praying the dowager would not catch her. When she finally gained her bedchamber, she sat on the chaise and reclined with her legs stretched before her. Closing her eyes, she took several deep breaths.

She knew she could not leave the party for very long. It would be a terrible breach of all that was proper. But she was afraid that if she did not have a few moments to think, she would go mad.

Opening her eyes, she looked out of the window. Below, she saw Tommy, Henry, and the three Edgeton girls chasing each other across the smooth green lawn in the middle of the garden. She observed dozens of other guests enjoying the unexpectedly fine afternoon. The distant strains of a lilting melody reached her as she lay quietly in her room.

Her thoughts again, seemingly for the thousandth time in the last few hours, went to Westlake.

As she had gotten to know him a little over the last few months, it seemed to her that there were two very distinct sides to him: the confident, almost aloof side that he showed in public, and the gentler, though equally confident side he reserved for in private.

The public duke could intimidate her with a glance. The private Westlake, the one who had just given Tommy the horse, stirred the soul of her emotions.

Suddenly she was pulled from her thoughts as her bedchamber door burst open. Bella turned her head to see Triss rushing in.

"Oh, good, I found you! Bella, I must speak with you!" she gushed.

Bella swung her legs to the floor and sat up, noticing that Triss held a small wooden box in her hands.

"Triss, dear, I really cannot have a coze with you right now. We can discuss the wedding later," Bella told her cousin.

"I do not wish to speak of the wedding," Triss replied.

Halting in the process of rising, Bella raised both brows and sat back down.

"You *don't?*" she asked in disbelief. "Well, then, I do not have time to discuss the eligible titles that are downstairs."

"I do not wish to speak about that either, Bella," Triss said with asperity. "I wish to give you something, but first I must tell you the most amazing *on dit.* I have just had it from Louisa, who has it from Malverton, who has it from Sir John Mayhew, who was . . ."

"Triss! You are making my head spin. What are you rattling about?" Bella interrupted.

"Will you please just listen?" Triss demanded.

"Oh, go on," Bella said.

"Westlake challenged Robert Fortiscue to a duel!"

Bella jumped up from the chaise and stared at her cousin with wide eyes. "A duel? What on earth are you saying?"

"Westlake confronted Robert at some gambling den. He told Robert that his neckcloth was rude, and that unless he took himself off to the country, Westlake was going to shoot him at dawn."

Bella stared at Triss in disbelief, finding her cousin's words almost incomprehensible.

"Is it not too delicious?" Triss continued. "Louisa said that Malverton said that Mayhew said that Robert was practically whimpering by the time the duke was done with him."

Bella felt completely stunned. Slowly she returned to the chaise and sat down. "But why would Westlake do such a thing?" Her voice was almost a whisper.

"Because of you, silly," Triss said, moving across the room to stand next to Bella. "Louisa said that Malverton told her that even though gentlemen never discuss the real reason a challenge is made, it is most always a matter of personal honor. After the way Robert was so nasty to you at Almack's, it is no wonder that Westlake sent him off to rusticate."

Bella put her hands to her head. She remembered that

Westlake had seemed to dismiss Robert when they had spoken of him before their kiss. What could this mean? Her mind cast about for an answer. But she wanted answers to many things regarding her strange relationship with Westlake.

"You must try to get Westlake to tell you about it. I would so love to hear all of the details," Triss said.

Bella made no comment to this and only lowered her hands to her lap. "We have been away from the party too long."

"Yes, but before we return I wanted to give you something," Triss told her.

Bella glanced up in curiosity at the uncertain tone in her cousin's voice.

Triss handed Bella the small wooden box she had been holding. Bella accepted it from her and set it in her lap. Opening the lid, she saw what appeared to be a bunch of dried flowers and greenery tied together with an ivory silk ribbon.

"What is this?" Bella asked after a moment.

"They are from your wedding, Bella. After the ceremony I went back, pulled some of the ivy and roses from the chancel rail, and dried them. I have been waiting for the right time to give them to you."

Bella's brows came together in confusion. "I thought it was very kind of Aunt Elizabeth to have placed flowers in the church, but you needn't have done this, Triss," Bella stated softly.

"Mother?" Triss questioned. "Mother did not provide them. Westlake made arrangements to have the chancel rail draped in flowers."

Bella's head snapped up. "Are you sure it was Westlake?" she asked, her voice almost a whisper.

"Of course. It has seemed to me that of late you and the duke are in more accord. So I thought now would be a nice time to give you the flowers," Triss explained.

Bella stared down at the flowers for some moments, her heart very full. "Oh, Triss! How will I ever know what really could have happened? How can he ever forget that Papa and Uncle David demanded that he marry me?"

Triss knelt down next to Bella and placed her arms

around her cousin. "I am so sorry that I am the cause of all this pain, dearest Bella. But it is clear to me that you and Westlake at least respect each other."

"Somehow that is not enough."

Triss pulled back and looked at her cousin keenly. "But Bella, respect was enough when you had planned to marry Robert Fortiscue. You made no pretense about feeling anything other than respect for *him.*"

"Please do not remind me how foolish I was concerning Robert Fortiscue," Bella said with a pained smile.

Triss looked at Bella in silence for a long moment. "Arabella! Do you know what your problem is?" Triss demanded.

"I am sure that you are about to tell me whether I want to know or not," Bella replied dryly.

"You are refusing to be truthful with yourself. That is very unlike you."

Bella almost laughed aloud at this comment. Be truthful with herself? How could she be truthful when she no longer even knew her own mind?

"Triss, I cannot discuss this any longer," Bella said, her tone bordering on desperation. "Please leave me to freshen up a bit and I shall join everyone in a few moments."

Triss sighed and stood up from the chaise. "All right, Bella."

When Triss had reached the door, Bella called to her. "Thank you for saving the flowers, Triss."

"You are welcome." Triss smiled before leaving the room.

Bella sat on the chaise for a few moments, her thoughts in a confused whirl.

Suddenly galvanized into action by the intensity of her emotions, Bella jumped up from the chaise and set about tidying her appearance. It was imperative that she speak to Westlake. She left her room and walked quickly to the top of the landing.

The flowers Triss had saved presented a whole new set of questions. Why had the duke bothered to arrange for flowers at their ceremony? She determined that as soon as she could manage a private word with him, she would ask him. Suddenly the answer to this question in particular was of vital importance to her.

As she made her way down the first few steps, she mentally cursed the circumstances that had caused this sham marriage. It had prevented the possibility of something real developing between herself and the duke, she thought with deep regret.

The sound of feet quickly approaching caught her attention. Thinking Triss must have gone to her room to freshen up and was now trying to catch up with her, Bella slowed her steps.

Turning to look back up at her cousin, Bella suddenly felt a sharp push against her back.

Catching her breath in shock, Bella grabbed for the balustrade, frantically trying to regain her balance. Her left foot missed the next step and her hand missed the handrail. Pitching forward, she felt herself falling. A second later she was tumbling down the wide marble staircase.

She was aware of the moment when she finally came to a crashing stop halfway down. With a great effort, she lifted her head slightly and saw that her foot was caught between two balusters. In a daze of shock, Bella realized that her foot becoming stuck more than likely saved her life. She marveled at such a miracle.

Laying her head back down on the cold step, Bella thought it extremely odd that she should be seeing stars.

Her last thought, before the stars faded to blackness, was that she hoped her fall did not ruin the party.

Chapter Twenty-five

Slowly Bella's lashes flickered open. She lay listening for a little while to a rhythmic scratching sound coming from close by.

Turning slightly, Bella winced at the dull throb emanating from the back of her head. Staying still, she allowed her eyes to wander, and soon realized that the room was unfamiliar. The huge, four-poster bed she now occupied had no canopy, and she noticed that the coverlet over her was made of some deliciously soft material in a dark blue color that bordered on violet.

Her gaze continued to move around the dim, cool room, taking in the dark wood furnishings by the fireplace. The upholstery was all the same shade of deep blue, with silver accents. On the other side of the room, in front of a tall window with the curtains almost completely drawn, was a desk and chair.

The duke sat in the chair writing a letter. The scratching of his quill was the cause of the noise that had awakened her. She watched him in silence, her eyes scanning the classical lines of his profile. His aquiline nose and square jaw, with this room as a backdrop, gave him the appearance of a Roman emperor—especially since he was wearing a black robe, she noted.

Suddenly it was all so very clear and simple. She loved him. Though it had taken her until this moment to fully realize it, she now knew she had loved him almost from the moment he had awakened from his fever.

She loved the Duke of Westlake! She felt the beat of her heart quicken.

This realization explained her confusion over the last few months. It explained why she seemed to no longer know if she wanted to laugh or to cry most of the time.

She had done her best to resist the feelings he evoked in her, but no longer. Now that she had admitted to herself that she loved him, she could not continue to pretend that her heart did not soar every time he looked at her.

Knowing she loved him made the pain she felt over their forced marriage even worse. For the Duke of Westlake would never have chosen Miss Arabella Tichley as his bride. This thought stung even more, now that she knew she loved him so deeply.

At that moment he looked up from the desk and turned his gaze to her. In the dim light of the deep blue and silver room, his darkly lashed eyes appeared icy and arresting.

Laying his quill aside, he rose and came to sit next to her on the bed. "You have given us quite a scare, Arabella," he said with a gentle smile.

"I hope I did not ruin Louisa's reception," she said in a shy voice, overwhelmed by his unexpected nearness so soon after the realization of her love for him.

"Not to worry. This day will be the talk of the *ton* for years to come, and that, of course, delights Louisa."

An unbidden smile came to her lips at his gentle quip. "I am not exactly sure what happened. For an instant it felt as if someone pushed me from behind. But that cannot be so," she stated a moment later, her eyes growing troubled.

"Unfortunately it is so," Westlake began, his jaw tightening. "I shall never forgive myself for not being there to protect you from an assault that I should have known would happen. It was Margaret who pushed you."

She stared up at him in shock, seeing the anger flashing in his gray-green eyes.

"Margaret! But why?" She gasped in her astonishment.

Westlake turned his head away from her for a moment.

He then shifted closer to her on the bed. "Are you sure you are strong enough to hear this? You have a worrisome bump on the back of your head. Your ankle is also wrenched rather badly, and I suspect that by tomorrow you will be black and blue all over."

"My head does hurt a little. But I really would like to know what happened," she said as firmly as she could.

He nodded briefly but said nothing for a moment as he looked down at her with a grim expression. "I shall start from the beginning so that it will all make more sense," he began. "In February I received a note from the vicar of Tilbourne stating that Henry had had an accident and was near death. I set out immediately for Tilbourne. Two highwaymen accosted my groom and me, and I was shot. This much you obviously know," he said.

"Yes, of course," Bella replied.

"After I regained consciousness, my mother came to your home. During our conversation she explained that Henry was not seriously hurt. That seemed very odd, so as soon as I was able, I set into motion a very discreet investigation."

He paused to look at Bella closely. "Is there anything I can get for you? A glass of water, perhaps?"

"No. But would you help me sit up?"

"Of course."

Rising, he leaned forward and very gently slipped his arm beneath her shoulder. Bella felt herself tremble at the feel of his strong arm around her, and she inhaled the heady scent of him. Picking up a pillow lying next to her, he placed it behind her back and lowered her down.

"Better?" he asked, leaning back to look at her.

"Yes, please continue," she said, determined to ignore the pain in her head and in her arm.

Glancing down, she was suddenly aware that she wore nothing but one of her thin lawn nightgowns. A hazy recollection surfaced of her aunt and one of the maids helping her from her clothes. With her left hand, she pulled the bedclothes up to her chin.

"First, I learned that the vicar had not sent me the note. Then I discovered that Margaret had not been paying the tradesmen in Tilbourne. She is provided with a very generous allowance, so this was curious. I also learned that Margaret was keeping company with a man named Joseph Fitzdowning."

"The man on horseback!" Bella interjected in her surprise.

"Yes, the same. Mr. Fitzdowning had a brother who recently died in an accidental shooting. He died, not coincidentally, around the same time I was shot," he said with a wry twist to his lips. "Mr. Fitzdowning and his brother were from Derbyshire. That is why I went there shortly after our arrival at Autley. I had people watching Margaret closely. It was reported to me that she was losing large sums of money at cards."

Bella did not take her eyes off his face as he continued his story.

"Margaret planned with the brothers Fitzdowning to murder me. Upon my death, Henry would then inherit the entire estate, which would give Margaret and Mr. Fitzdowning control of the Westlake holdings. Margaret was planning to marry Fitzdowning. But I lived and managed to shoot the brother. With their plan foiled, Margaret and her accomplice had to regroup."

Bella could not comprehend such evil and felt shaken to her core that a family member could deliberately arrange for a relative's murder.

"I insisted that Margaret and Henry stay in London, where it would be easier to keep an eye on her. Fitzdowning showed up shortly after. They were getting desperate. The fact that I am now married complicated the situation for them. I believe that Margaret saw you going down the stairs and seized the moment. They could not take the chance that you would have a baby and then Henry would no longer be my heir."

"That explains Henry's questioning me when we were all at Autley," Bella told him, recalling the event.

"Yes. I have spoken to him. He had overheard his mother saying that she would make sure you did not have a baby," he explained.

"What is going to happen now?"

"Margaret and Fitzdowning will be transported to Australia. Henry will be living with Alice and Charles. I had discussed this with my sister and brother-in-law before Margaret had made the attempt on your life. They both want him, and think it best for the boy to become a part of their family."

"That is good," Bella said, relieved that Margaret and her accomplice would no longer be able to harm anyone else.

"I am so sorry that this occurred, Bella. If anything had happened to you—"

He stopped midsentence, and Bella saw that he seemed to be trying to gain control before he continued.

"I recall telling you that *my* family was eccentric. I certainly shall never make that claim again," she told him, attempting a note of humor.

He laughed, and she could tell her comment surprised him. He looked at her intently, searching her deep blue eyes until she lowered her gaze.

"Only you could be so brave, Bella."

"Brave? I only fell down the stairs," she said softly, touched and embarrassed by his praise.

"I should let you rest," he said, and made a move to get up from the bed.

"I really am not at all tired," she said.

She saw him raise a brow and resume his place. She watched him a moment, thinking how devastatingly handsome he looked in his black velvet robe.

"We previously decided that we would wait to discuss our future together until after Louisa's wedding," he said in his deep voice.

Bella's heart stopped for an instant.

"I have something important to ask you, Bella," he continued. "I realize that you are in no condition to answer me now, but I would like you to consider what I am about to say." He waited until she gave him a hesitant nod to continue. "Over the last few weeks, we have come to know each other a little better. I believe that we have the respect and common interests that you deem essential to a marriage. You know my feelings. Would you consider starting again, and giving our union a chance at success?"

His words seemed to repeat themselves over and over.

How naïve and foolish she had been when she had told him her opinion on marriage, she realized. That conversation seemed like a lifetime ago, when nothing was more important to her than an uneventful, safe life with someone as ridiculous as Robert Fortiscue.

She did not want that kind of life now! She wanted something completely different—his love. She wanted to waltz in his arms, to meet him at midnight in an atrium and have him kiss her the way he did the night he had given her the jewelry.

But something he said caught her attention.

"You say I know your feelings, but I do not," she said, her voice almost a whisper.

She saw him go very still, and his gaze scanned her face intently.

"Arabella, why do you think I sent all the servants away when my mother brought them to your home to tend me?"

Bella looked up at him in confusion. His question seemed at odds with their conversation. "Because there really was very little for them to do?"

"Why do you believe that I made no protest to our marriage?" he asked, ignoring the answer she had given to his previous question.

"Because you are a man of honor," she replied, her expression confused.

"Why do you think I have squired you around town to museums, and to Almack's, and to the theater?"

"Because you are a gentleman and very kind."

At that Westlake threw back his head and laughed. His laugh was rich and deep, and when it faded he looked at Bella with an expression of tenderness she had never seen before. "Arabella, I thought I was being quite transparent in my attentions toward you. I must have lost my touch," he said with a slight smile.

Bella was so astonished by this comment, she could say nothing.

"The day I fully regained consciousness in your bedroom, Tommy told me how the two of you found me and how you removed the slug from my shoulder. Right then I knew you were the bravest, most quick-thinking and intelligent woman I had ever encountered."

The breath caught in Bella's throat at his words, and the way he was looking at her made her pulse race.

"I sent the servants home because they would have interfered with our getting to know each other. I made no protest to our marriage because I did not want to. I have been showing you how enjoyable London can be in hopes that you would see what our life together could be. Now do you understand?"

Not fully, she thought, biting her bottom lip. Looking into his eyes, she felt the intensity of his gaze make her weak.

"Why did you arrange for there to be flowers at our wedding?" she asked.

She saw one dark brow go up in mild surprise at her question.

"I wanted something about the ceremony to be beautiful for you, because you were so beautiful to me. Being forced to marry certainly interrupted all my plans to court your love," he said with a wry smile.

Bella closed her eyes against the joy that seemed to burst within her. She could not speak. Courtship! He had been courting her and she had been too blinded by her fear to realize it!

Bella struggled to find the words that could express what was in her heart.

"So now you know my feelings," he continued. "I would ask you to take some time to consider what we have discussed."

Her lashes flew open and she looked with shining eyes into his. The expression in his gaze told her the truth of everything he had left unsaid.

"I do not have to think about it," she whispered. "I would like to begin again."

After looking at her searchingly, he reached over, took her hand, and raised it to his lips.

The feel of his warm lips on her flesh broke through her restraint. No longer did she shrink from the passion she now recognized in his gaze. She met his eyes with the dawning desire in her own.

"While I was still in a fever, your voice was the only thing that soothed me," he began, the deep timbre of his voice sending chills down her body. "It still haunts me. When I am away from you I think of little else. I don't expect you to love me yet, but in time . . ." His deep voice trilled to a stop.

She smiled, and her heart seemed to leap from her body. "I did not realize it until this evening, but I have loved you from the moment I found you struggling to stand in my bedroom. I never thought such things as love even mattered before I met you. But now everything is different, Alex."

Very slowly, still holding her hand in his, he leaned forward and kissed her.

It was the most beautiful experience of her five and twenty years.

Pulling back a little, he looked deeply into her eyes. "When I saw you lying on the stair steps, all I could think of was that nothing mattered without you. Without you . . . Without you . . ." He could not complete his sentence, and kissed her lips gently once again.

Bella's heart soared at the wonder of his love. Nothing else in her life could compare to the feel of his lips and the sudden, indelible knowledge that he actually loved her.

He drew back again and inhaled deeply. "It is very late, my darling Arabella. I do not want to tire you after such an ordeal. Will you stay in this room with me and let me take care of you?" he asked, his voice husky.

Putting trembling fingers to his lean jaw, Bella met his gaze with a look of sheer joy.

"Yes, Alex," she said softly.

"Forever?"

"As long as you will have me," she said, just as his lips took hers with such compelling passion that her pain was barely noticeable.

"Forever," he murmured against her lips.

Epilogue

The Duke of Westlake was leading his good friend the Duchess of Severly around the impromptu dance floor to the steps of a lively reel. There were several other couples dancing in Autley's large sitting room on this late autumn eve. As the music ended, Westlake twirled the duchess around in a great flourish before escorting her back to her husband.

He stood with his old friends, watching the others as another dance began almost immediately. His eyes shone with pride and tenderness as he watched Arabella, his bride of almost six months, dancing with the Duke of Malverton. They were attempting a new dance. Both were obviously having a wonderful time, laughing and teasing each other over their missteps and mistakes.

At that moment Hollings approached him, bearing a silver salver with a sealed note resting upon it.

Westlake took it with a curious frown, excusing himself from his friends to read it by the fireplace.

> *My darling! I can resist what is between us no longer! I shall be waiting in the atrium for you at midnight! I am yours!*

He read the note again before folding it and putting it in the pocket of his waistcoat. Turning, he went back to join his houseguests.

*   *   *

At one minute to midnight, Westlake strolled into his candlelit atrium. Glancing around, he at first thought he was alone. But as he walked farther into the room, he saw a familiar figure at the other end, partially shielded by the lush greenery.

Slowly he approached the young beauty, enjoying her silhouette in repose. A moment before she turned to him, Westlake caught a dreamy, half-smiling expression on her face.

As he drew near, she greeted him with love and laughter in her gaze. He swept her into his arms in a passionate embrace that caused her body to melt familiarly against his.

"What were you thinking, minx, just before you saw me?"

Bella looked up at her husband with frankly adoring eyes. She raised herself on tiptoe and wrapped her arms around his neck.

"I was just thinking that Autley is the most wonderful place in the world. I do not know why I ever thought otherwise. And I was also thinking that an atrium is a perfect place to meet one's husband."

With a rich laugh, the duke pulled her closer. "I could not agree more, my love," Westlake said the instant before his lips met hers.